A HITCH AT THE FAIRMONT

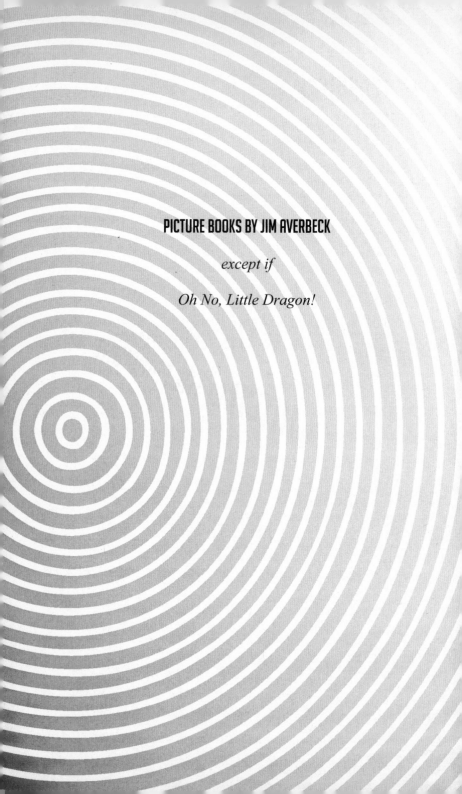

PICTURE BOOKS BY JIM AVERBECK

except if

Oh No, Little Dragon!

JIM AVERBECK
PRESENTS

A HITCH
AT THE FAIRMONT

Atheneum Books for Young Readers
New York London Toronto Sydney New Delhi

ATHENEUM BOOKS FOR YOUNG READERS

An imprint of Simon & Schuster Children's Publishing Division

1230 Avenue of the Americas, New York, New York 10020

Text copyright © 2014 by Jim Averbeck

Interior illustrations copyright © 2014 by Nick Bertozzi

Jacket illustrations copyright © 2014 by Laz Marquez

The verse on p. 55 is a variation of one written by Charles K. Field in response to the 1906 earthquake.

ATHENEUM BOOKS FOR YOUNG READERS is a registered trademark of Simon & Schuster, Inc. Atheneum logo is a trademark of Simon & Schuster, Inc.

For information about special discounts for bulk purchases, please contact Simon & Schuster Special Sales at 1-866-506-1949 or business@simonandschuster.com.

The Simon & Schuster Speakers Bureau can bring authors to your live event. For more information or to book an event, contact the Simon & Schuster Speakers Bureau at 1-866-248-3049 or visit our website at www.simonspeakers.com.

Book design by Debra Sfetsios-Conover

The text for this book is set in Times New Roman.

The illustrations for this book are rendered in ink and Adobe Photoshop CS5.5.

Manufactured in the United States of America

0514 FFG

First Edition

10 9 8 7 6 5 4 3 2 1

Library of Congress Cataloging-in-Publication Data

Averbeck, Jim.

A Hitch at the Fairmont / illustrated by Nick Bertozzi. — First edition.

p. cm

Summary: When his aunt is kidnapped, an eleven-year-old boy staying at San Francisco's Fairmont Hotel in 1956 tries to find her, with the help of Alfred Hitchcock.

ISBN 978-1-4424-9447-3 (hardcover)

ISBN 978-1-4424-9449-7 (eBook)

[1. Mystery and detective stories. 2. Adventure and adventurers—Fiction. 3. Hitchcock, Alfred, 1899-1980—Fiction. 4. Fairmont Hotel (San Francisco, Calif.)—Fiction. 5. San Francisco (Calif.)—History—20th century—Fiction.] I. Bertozzi, Nick, illustrator. II. Title. III. Title: Hitch at the Fairmont.

PZ7.A933816Ji 2014   JF
                        AVE
[Fic]—dc23

2013028921

The author is donating a portion of his proceeds from the sale of this book to the Cystic Fibrosis Foundation, for research into cystic fibrosis.

FOR ED

—J. A.

ACKNOWLEDGMENTS

FEW THINGS ARE MORE FRIGHTNING than a Hitchcock film. Writing acknowledgments is one of them. I am quite sure that I will forget someone, or several someones, whose help was indispensable to me, insulting them and sending them to their Hitchcockian bag of tricks for a means of revenge. But being an author requires a fool's bravery, so here goes:

First and foremost, thank you to the Hitchcock family for sharing their delightfully macabre relative with us. He stuffed us in a dark room to shock us and thrill us, which somehow made it easier to cope with the scary things in life. I was honored to use his name and character in this book.

Many thanks to the staff of the Fairmont Hotel, especially Thomas Wolfe, chief concierge; Ann Mayo, bell attendant; Mark Broydo, security officer; and Melissa Farrar, public relations manager. The enthusiastic access they gave me to the hotel—from secret passages leading to the roof to the deepest, creepiest underground corridor of the "back of the house"—was invaluable and inspiring. Thanks to Liz Schoff for exploring the dark corners with me.

There are whole languages we now consider dead. Thank you Joe Bosch, Betsy Turner, and Bobby Oliver, for helping me resurrect the corpse of Latin long enough to find a couple of words that worked.

Much of what I know about writing a novel I owe to two Masters-in-Writing programs I never attended. Thanks to Kristin Howell, Shirley Klock, Sharry Wright, Amy Laughlin, and Lynn Hazen for letting me spy on them as they honed their skills. A secret agent sneaking Cold War intelligence out of the country couldn't have been more delighted than I was with all the stolen information. Thanks also to Ed Porter and Rob Averbeck. Though the revision process was sometimes torturous, I thank you all for wearing velvet gloves as you tightened the screws.

Like a knife requires a final sharpening to do its business, so too does a book. Thanks to Linda Sue Park and Karen Cushman for whetting these pages to a fine edge, and to Deborah Warren and Namrata Tripathi for plunging them into the heart of the world.

Hitchcock's most famous character owed a lot to his mother. She tirelessly kept him on the straight and narrow. I had three moms who kept me going—Kristin Elizabeth Clark, Ellen Hopkins, and Susan Hart Lindquist. A boy should love his mothers. And I do.

And to those I have forgotten, please keep your butcher knives far from my shower. I'll remember you in the second edition.

CHAPTER 1

YOUNG AND INNOCENT

NO BODY MEANT NO CASKET, so they used her headshot instead. This was a Hollywood funeral, after all.

Jack Fair sat perfectly still in a cold metal folding chair in the first row. The dark blue suit he wore was two years old and two inches short in every direction. The cuffs of his dress shirt dug into his skin like manacles, and the starchy collar chafed and itched. But Jack didn't make a move to scratch. He stayed completely motionless, willing time to freeze with him. Because if time could stop between one heartbeat and the next, then it could roll backward too, like a movie in reverse. And Jack could find out what he did (or didn't do) or said (or didn't say) that made Mom do it.

Jack's hands rested, immobile, in his lap. He stared at the picture perched in its silver frame on a white pedestal up front. A wreath of silk gardenias surrounded it. The display, even the frame, was made of props lent to Jack by his mother's acting troupe. The funeral home had placed a gold-lettered card with Mom's name and the years of her life in the corner of the frame: Helen Fair, 1927–1956. The publicity picture was the only part of the display Jack owned. He'd drawn it himself, with the art supplies he'd gotten for his eleventh birthday. A photographer had given his mother a "free" photo shoot, then tried to charge her a dollar apiece for prints—"minimum five hundred"—a sum she couldn't afford. Jack had glimpsed the best of the proofs, then drawn it from memory in colored pencil—8 x 10, like the real headshots actors used.

Mom loved it. Jack planned to draw copies any time she had an audition. But she never had another.

The clock on the funeral home wall kept ticking away. (Was it slowing a little?)

Staring at Mom's picture without moving took a great effort of will. Jack's eyes longed to track the curves of her face. His hand itched to follow, as it would when he drew. Eyes and hand wanted to slide in concert down the wave of blond hair, swooping past her green eyes to the gardenia pinned behind her ear. Her features were so different from Jack's. Mom once told him he had his father's deep brown eyes and crow-black hair, but Jack had no way of knowing. Over the years, he'd tried to sketch his father from Mom's descriptions. But when he'd show her his work, she'd always say it looked just like "the butcher at the market" or one of his teachers, or a neighbor or President Eisenhower.

All Jack had from his father were the dog tags and the silver charm the size of his thumb from knuckle to tip, which he wore around his neck. He resisted an urge to hold them, to ask his father's spirit what to do now. He knew his father wouldn't answer. He never did. And from now on, it seemed, his mother wouldn't either.

Now Jack's eyes burned. Tears pooled above his lower eyelids. He willed them to stop, but they brimmed over his lashes and streaked salty trails down his cheeks. Did that count as moving? Were his tears a part of him? He didn't brush them away, in case they didn't count. *Time might be slowing a bit.*

But when the picture of Mom blurred and Jack saw only bright stars of reflected light, he blinked. He took out his handkerchief and wiped his eyes. Now he would have to start all over again.

"After life's fitful fever, she sleeps well," said a voice behind him. It was George Barrister, the financier and lead actor from his mother's troupe, Subsurface Shakespeare. That was his way of offering condolences.

Jack couldn't answer. He knew his eardrum vibrated with every plummy word George uttered—and with each metallic creak of a chair or each whispered "How could she?" from somewhere in back. It was no use trying to stop time, with all the noise.

George made a sweeping gesture around the crowded room. Other actors from Mom's troupe milled about with friends of the company. The guy who owned the diner in whose basement they performed sat with his pregnant wife, his head down. The landlady from the rooming house where Jack and his mother stayed was surrounded by the other boarders. Jack's best friend, Schultzie—Bernard Schultz—and Schultzie's father sat quietly in the second row.

"Your mother always could draw an audience," George said. "We shall miss her dearly."

"Me too," Jack said, his voice full of piccolos. Even though he no longer stared without blinking, his eyes began to sting. He sniffed. *It must be the fumes of the Ajax cleanser the funeral home uses.*

"Perhaps the boy would like a bit of fresh air," Schultzie's dad said. He was pretty good at figuring out what boys wanted to do. For years Jack had joined Schultzie and Mr. Schultz once or twice a month to do stuff with a local Scout troop. Jack's mom had arranged it, saying he needed a masculine influence in his life. She panicked a bit last year when they started spelunking—climbing up, down, and around in caves and old gold and silver mines. She said it sounded dangerous. Still, her tuna–potato-chip casserole always warmed them up when they got back from their expeditions. For Jack, caving with Mr. Schultz was almost like having a real dad.

Some caves had what was called a bottomless pit, a

narrow hole that went down hundreds of feet. You could throw a stone into it and wait forever, but you would never hear it hit bottom. That's how Jack felt now—like a bottomless pit. People at the funeral were speaking to him, and he heard their remarks and let them fall deep, deep down inside him. But not a sound would come back out.

"Bernard, why don't you and Jack go sit on the front steps for a little bit," Mr. Schultz said. Schultzie guided Jack outside. They settled on the crumbling cement stairs. The steps radiated warmth gathered from the Southern California sun, but Jack still shivered.

Some people collected trading stamps. Others collected salt shakers or spoons. Jack collected images. Like memory, they became a part of him. They calmed him. He could draw anything he had ever seen. He took the small sketchbook he always kept with him from his jacket pocket. Gazing at Mom's picture for so long had given him an idea. On the first page of every sketchbook, he transcribed Mom's description of Dad. This he read once again now. "You look just like him," she'd said. "Brown eyes. Black hair. He was handsome too, at least to me. And brave. Very brave."

Jack closed his eyes. Normally he needed to concentrate to call forth the subject he meant to draw, but Mom's face leapt to his mind with no effort. He dragged his stubby pencil across the paper. Two forms quickly appeared. Mother. Father. They were together now, after all, or so Jack hoped. Mom's image took shape rapidly, a replica of her living self, full of love and laughter. The other image was more difficult, despite the description of his father he'd just read. The pencil seemed directionless, the lines uncertain. In the end he had a shadowy figure that looked a bit like Mr. Schultz with black hair.

When Jack noticed Schultzie looking over his shoulder, he snapped shut the sketchbook, hoping embarrassment didn't color his face.

They sat silently for a long while, until Schultzie said, "It will be okay."

"How?" Jack asked.

"Huh?"

"How? How will it be okay?"

Schultzie knocked a piece of concrete from the stairs and threw it into the street. "You're right. It can't be."

"How could she do it?" Jack asked.

"Maybe there's been some kind of mistake."

"They found her car under twenty feet of water," Jack said.

"Maybe she had a heart attack or something."

"Right," Jack said. "Look, Schultzie, there were a dozen witnesses."

Mom always could draw an audience.

And for this performance she'd driven full speed off a cliff west of Malibu and into the ocean.

"Maybe . . ."

"They found a note." Jack rubbed his hands together but couldn't get them warm. Schultzie kicked another piece of concrete from the edge of the stairs.

"It stinks in there," he said.

"Ajax," Jack replied.

"No. Something else."

Schultzie sniffed the air. So did Jack. Mostly it smelled like California, but there was an undertone—too sweet and a little acrid.

"I know—," said Schultzie.

"That's formaldehyde," said Jack, "in the embalming fluid . . ."

Schultzie looked confused.

"From the bodies?" Jack pointed to the basement window.

"Oh," said Schultzie. "I was going to say 'pickles.'"

Jack knelt down by the window and pulled Schultzie after him. The odor wafted from the spot where a small triangle of glass had broken out from the top of the frame. The glass was grimy, but they could easily make out two tables where smooth white sheets covered two still figures.

"Pickled people," Jack said.

He was about to wipe away the grime with his jacket sleeve when Schultzie stopped him.

"Gotta keep yourself looking nice for when your Aunt Edith comes to get you," his friend said. He spit on the window and wiped it clean with his own sleeve. "Think you'll like San Francisco?"

"It's a million miles away," Jack said. "A zillion." They peered in through the clean spot in the window. Behind the tables was a row of cabinets, and a countertop loaded with bottles of colored fluid and strange chrome instruments. Tubing hung over the side of the counter like translucent tentacles, and, weirdly, lipsticks fanned out from a rack in the back. But all these things receded to obscurity behind the sheet-covered slabs.

"I think I can reach the window latch," Jack said. He snaked two fingers into the triangular hole.

"Maybe you'll like it," Schultzie said. "San Francisco."

Jack pushed his hand in as far as he dared. The edge of the glass pressed sharply against the first joint of his fingers. "What choice do I have? I'm a full orphan now."

"A full— Awww, come on," Schultzie said. "Don't tell me you believe all that junk McNeal spouts at school."

Mousie McNeal was the littlest guy in their class, but he had the biggest mouth. Last year he'd had the whole fifth grade calling Jack "Ward." Mousie said it was because Jack didn't have a dad, so he was a half-orphan and just one heartbeat away from being a ward of the state. Jack had pulled out the dog tags and the little coffin-shaped silver charm to prove he did have a father. But Mousie'd just said, "Dead dads don't count—Ward!" The nickname almost stuck, until Schultzie reminded everyone that he only had one parent too, and would they like to see how a half orphan threw a full nelson slam. Schultzie was the biggest guy at school, and he had the biggest heart.

"Mousie's a moron," Schultzie added. "They call him Mousie 'cause he squeaks too much. You're way smarter than he is, and he just wanted to make you feel left out—by poking your soft spots. Dirty squeaker."

Jack lifted the glasses from Schultzie's face. He stuck one of the J-shaped arms through the hole in the glass and slid it into the ring of the window latch. "Yeah, but look, he was right. I'm a full orphan now." He levered the glasses forward, and with a *thunk* the window fell inward. The hinges on the bottom squealed in protest before the frame caught on chains attached to its sides. A rush of the acrid odor made the boys cough. The window stuck out like a shelf from the basement wall. Jack hoped it would support his weight.

Even with the grimy window opened, little light made it into the room. The blood pounding in Jack's ears urged him to turn around. Dark windows and dead bodies? No, thanks!

But Jack had questions.

"C'mon," said Jack. He slid through the window, feetfirst.

Schultzie hesitated. "What are we doing?" he asked.

"Looking," Jack said. *For answers.*

When he'd been peering through the window, he hadn't been able to resist the call of the slabs. Now, with no glass separating him from them, Jack couldn't look past the hem of the sheets. These were two real people. Or had been. Two people who, a week ago, had been playing catch in the yard, or dancing to the Platters, or making tuna–potato-chip casserole.

"You're my best friend," Schultzie said from the window, "but you are just a little creepy."

"I'm curious," Jack said. The hem of the sheet on the left-side slab curved and undulated up to where a man's hand stuck out from beneath. A gold wedding band was on his finger.

"About what?" Schultzie asked. The figure on the right, though completely covered, was clearly female.

Had they been married?

"About . . . what happens after," Jack said. His sweaty shirt stuck to him beneath his jacket. The taste of fear in his mouth overcame the tangy formaldehyde flavor in the air.

A grunt and a scuffle came from behind Jack. Then Schultzie was whispering into his ear, "I'm here. Which one should we ask?"

"The left," Jack whispered back. "Uncovering the woman seems more . . ."

"Likely to scar you for life?" said Schultzie.

"Disrespectful," Jack replied.

He approached the table and gently folded the sheet to below the man's shoulders.

He was in his late thirties. Handsome. His hair was black. His eyes were closed. He looked quite natural, except the flesh-tone makeup ended in a stark border at the collarbone. Jack wanted to make a quick sketch, but first he had to ask his question. He held his hand above the man's for a moment, then gently cupped it. The man's hand was the same cool temperature as his wedding band. The fingers were slightly rough, like fine sandpaper. A father's hands. Jack leaned over, bringing his lips to the man's ear. He asked the question he so wanted answered.

"Where are you?" he whispered.

But the dead weren't talking.

Suddenly a light came from above.

"Hey! What are you boys doing here?" The funeral director stood in the doorway, thumb still on the light switch.

"Looking," said Jack.

"For the bathroom," Schultzie added.

The funeral director gave them a doubtful scowl. "It's upstairs. And please hurry. We need to wrap up your service. The Veronica Sanders wake is this afternoon. She was a big star. Her and her bodyguard's tragic demise is already a media sensation. We're expecting a mob of autograph seekers to arrive any moment."

"Autograph seekers?" Jack looked at the female figure still under her sheet, then at his friend.

Schultzie shrugged. "Optimists."

In the lobby upstairs the funeral director jangled his keys, glaring at Jack. He locked the door to the basement with two dead bolts and sniffed as he walked away. Schultzie gave a little whistle.

"Guess he doesn't want any of his customers to escape," Jack said.

He pulled the sketchbook from his pocket. He closed his eyes and ran his thumb along the pencil. The ridges on the eraser's metal collar sent shivers up his arm that vibrated and formed points of light in the darkness of his mind. Points that shifted and drew themselves out into lines that curved and crossed, forming shapes. Shapes rotated and connected, becoming objects—a hand, a sheet, a twisted rubber tube. Objects took on mass, cast shadows, until Jack envisioned the entire tableau from the room below. Now he opened his eyes, and the vision had anchored itself to the paper. Already the pencil followed the pattern, separating light from darkness, and shading the areas between. He drew the tables, the bodies, the undulating sheets and the weird equipment, then drew them again from several angles.

"Not bad," said Schultzie, looking over his shoulder. "I have no idea how you do that."

Jack shrugged. The drawing gave him something to remember, but it didn't answer his question.

"Time we went back in," Schultzie said. He held the door to the viewing room open.

Jack walked to the display to retrieve the picture of Mom from the pedestal. He began to remove the frame. George's big hands covered Jack's. They felt warm and rough. "Please, Jack, keep it," he said. "My good will is great, though the gift small."

George removed his hands. Jack's own still felt cold.

"Shouldn't your aunt be here by now?" George asked.

What followed was a procession of Mom's friends,

the ladies in gloves and the men in dark hats. They filed past Jack sporting careful smiles and grim eyes, with many a squeeze on his shoulder and promises to help. Jack felt bottomless again, so it was Mr. Schultz who said thanks on his behalf, while Jack gave a small nod of his head.

Soon everyone was gone, except Jack, George, and the Schultzes. The four stood by the door of the funeral home, in the light of its stained-glass window. A single dust mote floated through the multihued beams, looking for a place to land.

"I thought my aunt would be here for the funeral," Jack said.

"Better she were three hours too soon than a minute too late," George said.

"Maybe he could stay with us," Schultzie said to his father.

Mr. Schultz put his hand on Jack's shoulder. "Maybe . . ."

The door flew open, slamming against the wall. The stained glass shook in its frame. A shadow fell across all four of them. Jack swallowed hard and clutched at the silver charm beneath his shirt. Standing on the threshold was Aunt Edith, waving around some legal-looking papers. Her hips pressed against the doorjamb on either side. Dressed in a black silk suit with fur trim too hot for the weather, she blocked out the sun— an eclipse in a feathered hat. Her eyes fell on Jack's shoulder, where Mr. Schultz's hand still rested.

"Unhand him," she said. "That child is mine."

CHAPTER 2

SPELLBOUND

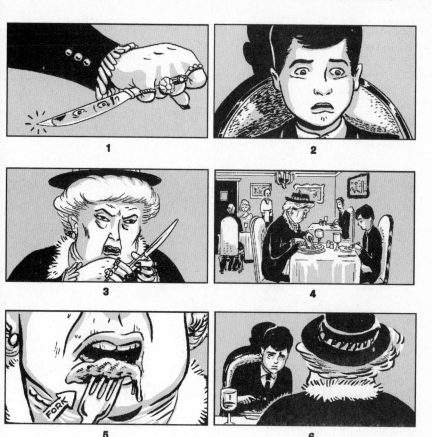

AUNT EDITH'S 1953 PACKARD CONVERTIBLE was deep green with pink leather interior. Two wooden crates occupied the rear seat. One had a strip of beige packing tape stuck to the top with the word "boy's" written on it. The other, "hers."

"Get in," said Aunt Edith.

When Jack opened the front passenger door, she held up her palm to him.

"Tsh," she said, then waved her hand toward the rear seat. "In back."

Jack squeezed into the sliver of space between the crates, twisting sideways to avoid a nail that stuck out from "boy's." He clutched the framed picture of Mom and leaned his head against the top edge of the "hers" crate. It bit into his scalp, but that was fine.

Aunt Edith unpinned her hat and set it carefully on the front seat next to her. A curl of white fur was perched right on top of her head. This she removed and held up to her face, making little kissy noises. She placed it tenderly next to her hat. Jack wasn't sure, but he thought the fur thing blinked at him as she set it down.

Aunt Edith scratched the back of her neck. Her finger slipped under her blond wig. A tiny lock of gray stuck to her neck when she returned her hands to the steering wheel. She turned north when they pulled out of the funeral home drive.

"Our boardinghouse is the other way," Jack said.

In the rearview mirror Aunt Edith's pale blue eyes

shifted to regard him. "Do you know my name?" she said.

"Yes," said Jack.

"Then use it when addressing me," she said. "I'm Aunt Edith, dear."

"Yes, Aunt Edith," said Jack.

"I'm Aunt Edith, *dear*," she barked.

Jack was confused. Had he said something wrong? Oh.

"Yes, Aunt Edith, dear," he said. He slid his mother's photograph beneath his jacket.

"That's better," his aunt replied. "And we aren't going to your former home."

"But all my stuff is there," Jack said. "And Mom's."

"What's important is in those boxes," she said. "The rest will be sold to cover my expenses for this little pickup trip."

"Oh. I see."

Her eyes shifted again to him, the brows slanting sharply down toward her nose. Jack corrected himself. "I mean, I see, Aunt Edith, dear." But he didn't see. How could his life with Mom fit into two wooden crates? Laughter was big. Love was bigger.

They sped north along the Pacific Coast Highway. Aunt Edith wanted to "make San Francisco by midnight," so Jack was alternately squished between the crates as she careened around one bend after the next, or thrown against the back of the front seat when she braked at the small villages dotting the route. There was an inertia to the drive that Jack couldn't defy.

The ocean glittered on their left most of the way. Jack stared over the top of "hers" at the water's vast, never-ending movement. He'd tried to draw it many times. His renderings were accurate in every detail but could never capture the ceaseless change of its surface. The afternoon sunlight sparkled and danced on it, like flashes from a hypnotist's watch, trance inducing. Jack found his mind slowly drifting and shifting, then diving deep below the ocean's skin. Through the murk around him enormous shadows swam, singing of a slow life of falling and rising and finding and losing. Jack let himself be swept along in their wake, protected somehow from the pressure and depth. He knew that a person lost down here would be nothing, so small and unprotected. Doomed. Down they went, until the murk became gloom, and the gloom became pitch. And the only things darker than the water around him were the shadows that sang and pulled him farther down, to a black mountain at the bottom of the sea. There Jack, swirling in the shadows' wake, plunged into the mouth of the mountain and came up inside, in a mer-cave similar to the land caves he had often explored. But this one had a floor of glass holding back the ocean, and different, ominous shapes swam below, their shrill voices not quite penetrating the glass. At the cave's center an island glowed orange and yellow. Seated on the island was a woman, her long legs stretched out before her, her wavy hair obscuring her face. Mermen had built her a driftwood fire, and mermaids had given her shells filled with food and drink. Jack crawled carefully across the glass floor to the island. The woman heard and turned toward him. Her eyes were green.

"Mom?" Jack said. "You're alive?"

But the only answer was a rising scream from the creatures below, their cries like the screech of tires on pavement. The woman's eyes turned pale blue, and the glass floor exploded upward in ten thousand shards. One pierced Jack's shoulder. Then the screamers rushed all around him, wrapped him, squeezed him, the intense pressure crushing his sides.

He awoke, smashed again between the crates, the protruding nail pressed into his shoulder, drawing blood. He pushed hard against the crate and managed to move it across the back seat.

"Don't scratch the upholstery, boy," Aunt Edith said, staring at him in the mirror.

They stopped for dinner at a surf-n-turf restaurant north of San Luis Obispo. Aunt Edith ordered. She had the turf. She gave Jack the surf, though after his dream he had no desire to eat anything from the cruel ocean. Each time he picked at the flakey fried fish, he heard the shriek of tires and the shattering of windshields and felt lonelier than ever before.

Aunt Edith sawed into a rare porterhouse, trailing bloody red streaks on the plate as she speared each chunk of meat.

"I suppose we'll need to enroll you in school," she said. "Public, of course."

Jack nodded. He liked school, but wished he could go back and finish the year at his old one, living with Schultzie and his dad.

"They'll need your birth certificate," his aunt said. "Do you know where that is?"

Jack shrugged. "Mom always had those kind of things. I don't know where . . . um . . . ma'am."

"Well, they'll be in her crate, then," Aunt Edith said. She looked at Jack quite intently. She even put down her fork. She pointed her knife right at him. "Sometimes they want other identification as well. Like they might call for a special ID number. Did your mother ever mention a special ID number for you?"

"Like Social Security or something?" Jack asked.

"Sort of," Aunt Edith said. "But not exactly. But a string of numbers, yes. Maybe your mother made you memorize a special set of numbers once?"

"I know the addresses of the last three places we lived, and the phone numbers too. She always made me memorize those," Jack said.

Aunt Edith looked cross, so Jack added, "Aunt Edith, dear."

"Never mind that," she said. "Maybe she told you it was a code, just for you."

Jack was at a loss. If he said the wrong thing, would she turn him over to the state? He'd been with her only a few hours, but already he knew she required specific answers he didn't seem to have.

"No codes," he said.

Aunt Edith looked at him for a moment longer. She picked up her fork. "Eat your fish," she said. "The waitress won't ask what I want for dessert until you're finished."

Aunt Edith ordered two pieces of chocolate cake for dessert. She told Jack she would give him some if he could remember a time when his mother gave him a paper with numbers on it or if he ever saw such a thing. Jack pulled forth every numbered paper he could recall, but none seemed to satisfy her. In the end she asked for a doggie bag for the half slice of cake that remained.

In the car she opened the bag. Jack thought she was going to give him the leftover dessert, but instead she set it down next to her on the front seat. "Dinner, Poopsie-Muffin," she said. A series of satisfied chirps came from in front.

As they traveled north, the warm sunny coast of beaches and sand disappeared, replaced by rocky cliffs and patches of tall trees, where night fell before it came to the rest of the world. Wisps of fog became fingers of fog, and eventually the gray clouds sat like a funeral pall over the land. The change didn't bother Jack. It suited his mood. What right did the world have to warmth? What right the sun to shine? The gray was as it should be.

Still, when they finally pulled off the highway late at night and topped a hill overlooking downtown San Francisco, Jack couldn't help being moved by its beauty. The sparkling lights of the city were like the Milky Way, come down to play on the hills. Maybe a city where the fog could block out the real stars needed to make its own galaxy of light.

"Beautiful," Jack said.

Aunt Edith crossed her arms. "Don't be fooled by the bright lights," she said. "You can hide a lot of darkness in the folds of those hills."

CHAPTER 3

THE LODGER

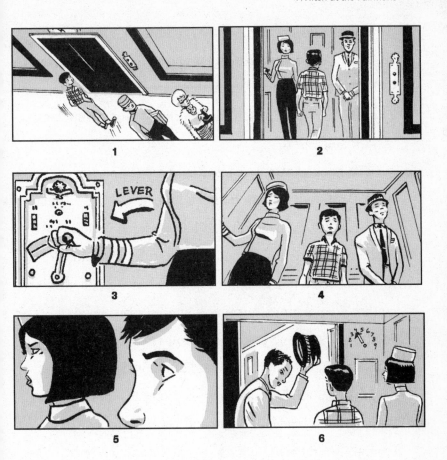

JACK PERCHED ON A SEAT at the Merry-Go-Round Bar, rotating slowly but going nowhere. As his little booth turned, he imagined all the territories represented on the first floor of the Fairmont Hotel: the African beasts that roamed the murals of the Cirque Room's walls, the South

American flowers at Podesta Baldocchi Florists, the Garden Room entrance with the flags of all the countries who had signed the UN charter here a decade before. The whole world came to the Fairmont Hotel. But Jack was all alone in it.

The pocketknife he carried in his back pocket made an uncomfortable lump beneath him. It was an artifact of an old life. Aunt Edith had let him keep it, and most of the things from his wooden crate, after she had carefully inspected it. She ran the same inspection on all his mother's belongings, turning them up, over, inside out, and back. Then one day all his mother's things and both crates vanished. Aunt Edith said nothing about it.

Jack pulled his sketchbook from his pocket. He flipped to the image of Mom and Dad he'd drawn at the funeral. Mom was laughing. He missed that. He hadn't laughed much this past month. But seeing the laughter in the image of his mother, he knew it was still inside him. He'd captured her laugh in his art. And his art was a part of him. So her laughter was a part of him.

He'd long since erased the head of his father, the one that had looked like Mr. Schultz. But a ghost image remained, featureless and tantalizingly out of reach.

Jack turned to the first page of the book and reread Mom's description of Dad. "Brave. Very brave." Jack tried again to draw his father. He could use some bravery now. Otherwise why was he sitting here, afraid to return to Aunt Edith's suite? If he could capture his father's image, he could capture his courage, make it part of him. But when he closed his eyes, nothing came to guide his pencil. And when he looked at the paper, only that ghost image stared back at him.

Jack sighed. He could put off his return no longer. He grabbed the peanuts he'd been sent to get, and crossed to the elevator. The lobby was vast and intimidating. Its marble columns frowned down from the heights as he navigated his way. The ornate ceiling was white and gold, the carpet and furniture red and black, as if all the room's blood had pooled at its feet. Charcoal-colored walls absorbed what light the chandelier threw on the scene. Groups of ladies, businessmen, even a few late-night families bustled about him, coming for a stay or going home. Jack's home *was* the hotel now—unless Schultzie could get his dad to let Jack move in with them. And a lonely home it was.

His letters to Schultzie had gone unanswered in the

month since he'd moved to the Fairmont. His aunt was one of those few permanent residents, whom the head bellman described as "a bunch of rich old dames who moved in as children when their families lost their mansions to the Great Quake, and won't leave until another one shakes them loose." Jack himself had heard old Maud Flood say the only way she would leave was "horizontally in a box, feetfirst." As Jack stepped onto the elevator, he thought Maud was old enough that she might go soon, but not exactly as she planned. The elevator was so small, they'd surely need to stand her on end.

A Chinese man in a beige porkpie hat stood in the corner. That was strange. because usually the elevator emptied at the lobby.

"Going up," said Shen, the elevator operator. She was a young Asian woman like all the other operators. With her dark hair bobbed six inches below her cap, and her crisp red uniform jacket, she matched the hotel décor. Jack wondered if that's why they'd hired her.

The Chinese man got off on the second floor, tipping his hat twice to Shen.

On the third floor a bellboy got onto the elevator. His luggage cart was stacked high with flat boxes wrapped in gold paper that was intricately folded and held by an embossed seal that read "Blum's." A thin pink string snaked out from each seal, tied at the other end to a card with a hole in the corner. The card on the top box read "Mrs. Edith Smith, Room 562." Jack pointed to it.

"That's for my room," he said.

"Really?" the bellboy replied. "Wanna do me a favor and take it? I got a bunch to deliver and every little bit helps." He handed the box to Jack.

"What is it?" Jack asked.

"Chocolates. From Blum's. Part of the Festival of Progress in honor of the earthquake anniversary. Compliments of the hotel," the bellboy replied. He pulled a cream-colored envelope from inside his jacket. "And, hey, take this, too. I was bringing it up to your room. That's why I put your box on top. To remind me."

The bellboy exited, pulling his cart after him. As the wheels hit the little gap between the elevator and the fourth floor, the gold boxes bounced up and down like Jack's own heart. He pressed the envelope to his chest. Was this finally word from Schultzie? He wanted to open it right away, but not in front of Shen, who stood frowning next to him.

When he got off the elevator, Jack examined the envelope more closely. It was addressed to Aunt Edith, but it could still be for him. It was unsealed. Odd. He pulled out the sheet of paper from inside. It was a rich creamy color and felt like stubbly linen as he ran his finger along the fold. It was the kind of paper that marked its texture in the charcoal or lead as much as it was marked when the pencil was drawn across it. Schultzie would never use this. He was strictly a blue-lined-paper kind of guy. This was stationery. Hotel stuff. Jack drew in a breath and held it. He unfolded the letter.

"Just a hotel bill," he muttered. His stomach felt gourd-hollow. He let his breath out slowly. It tasted bitter, like he'd eaten raw onions for lunch.

Aunt Edith lay on her bed. Her white dressing gown draped out around her. The bedspread was blue, so she looked like a map of Antarctica. She glanced at the hotel bill while Jack poured peanuts into the food bowl of her pet chinchilla, Muffin.

"Hmph. I'll just put this with the others." She refolded the bill. "Everything in its place, I always say." From somewhere she produced a small pile of envelopes held together by a blue steel paper clip. She slid the new bill in with the others, then read the card that accompanied the gold box. "'In celebration of the fifty-year anniversary of the Great Quake and Fire of 1906. *From the ashes a phoenix shall be born.*' Ha! That's not all that was born that day. A survivor was born too. That's me. A survivor."

Jack had already heard, several times, about the infant Edith, just one hour old, lying in the crib when the Great Quake struck. He secretly wondered if she had somehow caused it. He wouldn't have put it past her.

"Chocolates!" Aunt Edith said. "And not cheap either." She took a napkin from her nightstand and popped two treats into her mouth. Muffin's buckshot eyes greedily followed every move of her hand. A delicious raspberry scent filled the room when she bit into a third chocolate. Jack remembered the day he and his mother had eaten tart raspberries right off the bush at a little farm north of Simi Valley. Mom had gotten the red juice on her white blouse and pretended to be Juliet, dying from her dagger blade. Jack had laughed and applauded.

"Can I have a chocolate?" he asked his aunt.

Aunt Edith placed a protective hand on the chocolates.

"May I," she said. "It's 'May I please have a chocolate.'"

"May I please have a chocolate?" Jack asked.

"May I please have a chocolate . . . what?" she prompted.

"May I please have a chocolate, Aunt Edith, dear?"

"That's better," she said, "more polite. And orphans have no business being anything but." Muffin glared at Jack from her shoulder. Aunt Edith gave a curt smile. Flakes of face powder fell onto her imposing bosom and caked up in her wrinkles like the pattern on a frosted windowpane. She plucked a spiky confection from the box. It looked like a small chocolate hedgehog in her hand. Jack knew the flavor. It was the most recognizable treat in the box. Nevertheless Aunt Edith speared it with her pink lacquered thumbnail and squeezed until the guts oozed out. This she offered to Jack.

"A coconut cream," he said. His shoulders sagged a little. When she sent him to Blum's, Jack bought her the variety boxes that didn't contain them. Aunt Edith detested coconut creams, so naturally that's the choco-late she chose for him. But when Muffin flowed down her arm and drooled all over the chocolate, it was unfit for anyone.

"No, thanks," Jack said. He pressed his hands to his stomach. He didn't want to give Aunt Edith the satisfaction of hearing it growl.

"Suit yourself," she said. She dropped the coconut cream onto the pile of chocolates in the designated crystal bowl on her nightstand. When she had a taste for a specific flavor, Aunt Edith would bite into chocolate after chocolate, spitting them out if they weren't what she wanted. Now the bowl was nearly full with yesterday's rejects, covered in spit and pink lipstick that matched Aunt Edith's nails.

"You'll need to clean that out soon," she said. It was Jack's job to empty it, along with any other cleaning in his aunt's bedroom. She wouldn't let the hotel maids in. "They'll steal from me," she said.

The coconut cream disposed of, Aunt Edith wiped her fingers on the elegant white napkin she had tucked beneath her chins. But the napkin came away clean. Chocolate never melted in Aunt Edith's hands. Whether it was bad circulation or a lack of human warmth, Jack wasn't sure.

"You know, boy, an orphan like you should be more grateful for the things he is offered. Right now you could be in an orphanage, eating gruel and stale bread. The matrons would thump you awake in the morning and thrash you to sleep at night. And if you lived long enough, they'd sell you to a steamer ship. You'd be swabbing decks all the way to Shanghai. An orphanage is no place for an orphan. Believe me—I used to run one."

She popped two more chocolates into her mouth. "And if any nice couples came looking for a child to adopt, no one would want you. Not after they found out what your mother did. Insanity runs in the family."

Jack's head shot up, and his fierce gaze met Aunt Edith's. "My mother wasn't insane."

"She purposely drove off a cliff, didn't she?"

"No!" said Jack. "Yes . . . I . . . I don't know."

Aunt Edith pointed a sharp pink fingernail in his direction. "Does a sane person drive off a cliff just because she's a failure?"

"She wasn't a failure," Jack said. "She was a great actress!"

"Ha! What role did she ever have?"

"She was Lady Macbeth last year."

"For that Bard in the Basement group?" Aunt Edith laughed. "Pfah!"

"And her agent said he had just landed her a big gig," Jack said. "Hollywood big!"

"Then she was crazy to leave, wasn't she?"

"Look, she wasn't—"

"Enough!" Aunt Edith said. "Just because your mother asked that I be your guardian doesn't mean I have to do it, do I?" Muffin groomed the fur between his back toes but kept his eyes on Jack.

"No," Jack said. He unclenched his fists. He wished he had his father's courage and could stand up to Aunt Edith. But in his stomach a hollowness not from hunger kept him bowed—a knowledge in his heart that he was all alone.

"No, what?" Aunt Edith said.

The words stuck in his mouth like barbed wire. "No, Aunt Edith, dear."

Aunt Edith stifled a little yawn. "Now. It's ten p.m.! Time for my show." She pointed to the television. "Channel five."

Aunt Edith was the only person Jack knew with two televisions, this one an RCA color model. Jack turned the TV's knob slowly. His hand was shaking, but with each satisfying *thunk* the knob made, he steadied a bit.

The *shush* of static between the four available channels lulled his anger, a little. When he arrived at the correct station, a creepy but comical waltz came from the speaker. On the screen a simple line drawing outlined a fat man's silhouette. Jack loved this show. The host, Alfred Hitchcock, talked about things that grown-ups usually wouldn't discuss: mysteries, murders, and death. Like the story of the man all the doctors thought was dead, until they saw tears in his eyes. Jack stroked the silver charm beneath his shirt. Maybe tonight the host would say what really happened after you die.

It was past his bedtime, but Aunt Edith made Jack sit on the floor, awaiting her orders to adjust the antennae, the volume, or any of the other half dozen knobs that controlled the reception. Right now there was a slight ghost image and a little warp in the picture at the top. But Aunt Edith didn't seem to notice.

"Good eee-vening, ladies," the host began. "Has your husband recently acquired a faraway look in his eyes? In the event something unforeseen happens to you, do all of your worldly goods go to him? Is he at this moment nervously excusing himself from the room? If you answered yes . . ."

Aunt Edith was calm at last. Calmer than usual, in fact. As the show progressed, her head nodded until she woke with a sudden snort.

"I'm almost out of chocolates," she said, though there were several still in the box. "Run down to Blum's before it closes and get me another box." Her eyes drooped as she counted out change from the handbag she kept looped over her bedpost.

Jack stared at the television. The commercial in the middle of the show was just starting. He would miss the rest of the show and not be able to see it until it reran over the summer. The coins rested coldly in his hand.

"Get moving," Aunt Edith said. She closed her eyes and sank back into the mattress.

Since Aunt Edith had claimed him, Jack lived under thick ice. He could see the world above but couldn't break through. As he walked out the door, he wondered if he had the guts to run past the sweets store and on and on, as fast and as far as he could.

But, really, where would he go?

CHAPTER 4

THE LADY VANISHES

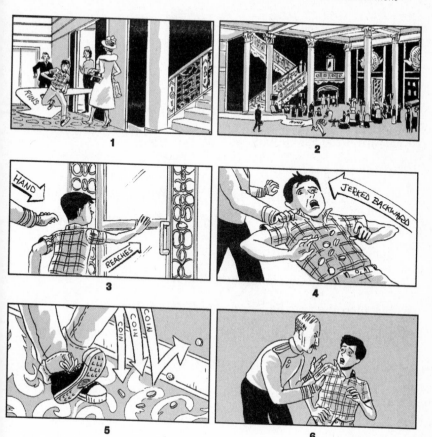

THE ELEVATOR TOOK FOREVER to arrive. Jack punched the call button over and over, until he finally leaned on it to make the elevator hurry. It was just like Aunt Edith to send him away when he wanted to stay. At least she'd stopped talking about his mother. Jack touched his head against the cool elevator door and remembered the last time he'd seen Mom, back in LA.

Before Jack had drawn the picture of her, when she'd been looking at the proofs for the photos she couldn't afford, he'd asked why they didn't have any photographs of his father around.

"Jack, love," she'd said, "I really didn't have very long with your father. I only just met him a few weeks before we married. But I was sure in love with him, and he wanted to get married before shipping out. Seems kind of crazy now, but then the war had been dragging on for years and the whole world seemed crazy. We thought we'd have plenty of time to get to know each other after his service."

Jack wondered if that was why Mom did what she did: to finally get acquainted with Dad. He could sympathize with that. A little. Jack clung tightly to the father of his imagination, because he never knew the real thing. How do you let go of something you've never really held? Maybe if he'd known his father, letting him go would be easier. . . . But then again, accepting that Mom was gone was a million times harder, so that theory was shot.

The elevator bell rang. The door slid open. Jack

tried to push his way in but was stopped dead by a sea of navy-blue wool. A large, balding man in a dark suit stood in the elevator. He held his wristwatch at eye level, scowling at it, then at Jack.

"Good eee-vening," the man said, his voice a low, slow monotone.

"Hello," Jack squeaked in reply. But he forgot to move. He was rooted to the spot, awestruck, because the man was impressive in both size and fame.

"Alfred Hitchcock!" Jack said.

"The same," said the man. He raised his chin a bit, and a smile played over his plump lips. Then he noticed his watch, still held high, and the scowl returned.

Jack stood in the doorway, unmoving.

"My dear boy," Hitchcock said, "it is customary for the ocean liner to set sail before the dinghy puts up at her dock."

It took Jack a moment or two to work out what that meant, but when he did, he took three giant steps backward. The big man glided past him, the air from the elevator swirling in his wake. He opened the door to his suite, next to Aunt Edith's. Before stepping in, he turned to Jack.

"Carry on. No need to hold the elevator." His voice was slow and six feet deep. He gave Jack a little salute.

Jack raised his hand to his forehead in reply.

"Going down!" called Shen. Jack jumped in, and the doors slid shut.

The whole thing had happened so fast, Jack barely had time to react before it was over. Alfred Hitchcock! The famous movie director was staying right next door! Jack was missing his TV show, but seeing him in person was better anyway. Jack had so much to ask him. He hoped he would see him again. Maybe next time he'd be able to do more than just blurt out the director's name and get in the way, like some overanxious fan.

"Floor, please," Shen said. She was all business. Jack guessed she was used to having important people in her elevator.

"Lobby. Thank you." Jack counted the money his aunt had given him, each piece clinking coldly in his hand. He found it was the exact amount needed for her chocolates—$2.95—and not a penny to spare for him to get a little something for himself. Oh, well. Full orphans had to take what they were given, even when it was nothing.

Shen regarded the money with a disapproving frown. "More chocolates for your aunt?"

"As usual," Jack said. The elevator vibrated and jerked as it descended. No wonder Shen ran it so slowly. Jack wondered how he might arrange to see Mr. Hitchcock again.

"Too many chocolates make you fat," Shen said.

Jack raised an eyebrow. Shen never said anything more than was required to deliver people to the proper floor. Was she trying to be friendly?

"Was she thinner once?" Shen asked.

A little brass plaque with the elevator's weight limit was affixed to the wall. Maybe Shen's interest in Aunt Edith's size was purely professional. Jack shrugged. "How should I know?" he said.

"Maybe she has photographs of herself when she was younger. Does she have photos? Maybe in your room somewhere?"

As a matter of fact, Aunt Edith had taken the picture of Mom in the silver frame and disassembled it, searching for something. After she put the frame back together, she slid a photo of her wedding to Uncle Tim into it, over the picture of Jack's mother. "He's the only person I ever loved," she'd told Jack. "Don't touch it!" That hadn't stopped him from slipping Aunt Edith's photo out every night before bed to look at his mother. Aunt Edith was, in fact, slimmer in her wedding photo, but Jack didn't see that it was any of Shen's business.

The elevator dinged.

"Lobby," Jack said before Shen could. He shot out the opening door, heading for the concourse of shops and restaurants across the way. He would miss the end of the Hitchcock show, but if he hurried, he might be able to hang out in the hall, in case the director went for ice or something. The red-and-black carpet blurred beneath Jack's feet. He was about to push through the pink-lettered door of Blum's—San Francisco's Sweetest Confectaurant—when a man grabbed his collar. The abrupt stop nearly knocked Jack off his feet. He felt his silver chain pull noose-tight around his neck, his dad's dog tags and the little charm digging into his collarbone. The coins he held scattered everywhere.

"Boy," said Mr. Sinclair, "we do not run through the Fairmont Hotel like a jackrabbit with its tail on fire. We walk. We make way for adults, and we do not throw coins about as if the lobby were a wishing well."

Mr. Sinclair, the head bellman, was a tall, dour man with great bags under his eyes. He grew his hair long on the right side and combed it over his bare head to the left, holding it in place with heavy wax. His mustache hung down below his lower lip, so it flapped in and out when he spoke, like a curtain in the breeze. Jack had had run-ins with him before, and each time the list of rules grew. Besides no running, there was no spinning in the revolving door, no sliding down the mezzanine banister, and no riding the luggage carts. Jack didn't have time for a long discussion on hotel etiquette.

"Aunt Edith sent me for chocolates," he said. "She's almost finished with the complimentary ones." Mr. Sinclair was a bully, but he wouldn't cross Jack's aunt. There was a pecking order to these things.

Mr. Sinclair looked confused. "Complimentary?"

"For the earthquake anniversary," Jack said. The man's grip on his collar loosened but didn't release.

"But the anniversary isn't for several days," the bell-man said.

Jack's shoulders popped up and down. "Look, the chocolates came today. And sweets don't take root around Aunt Edith."

Mr. Sinclair pushed Jack through the door to Blum's, his patent leather shoes sweeping two of Jack's quarters under a heavy planter. Inside, Blum's décor was like the frosting on a fancy wedding cake, all pink swirls and white curlicues. A glass case with expensive chocolates and pastries in it wrapped around a corner leading to a dining area. Ornate white stools stood around a marble counter for ice cream and sodas. Small tables dotted the store's white fretwork perimeter. Stacks of gold boxes were piled everywhere. The scent of caramel and chocolate played in Jack's watering mouth.

Three sisters—Opal, Ruby, and Beryl—usually served the customers Coffee Crunch Cake and sold them tins of Almondettes with a sweet smile and a shake of their ample hips. Now Opal walked up to Jack and the bellman. If Jack ever drew her, he'd need the softest pencil lead to depict her cushiony figure. She tucked a stray lock of hair into her hairnet.

"Hi, sugar," she said to Jack. Then she nodded to the bellman. "Mr. Sinclair."

"The boy says his aunt received her anniversary chocolates early," the bellman said.

"Could be." Opal crossed her arms.

"And yet the anniversary isn't until Wednesday," the bellman said, "which is when the chocolates were to be delivered."

Opal nodded to the stacks of gold boxes. "With the hotel full I got nearly four hundred specialty boxes to make and label, all alone. And the space! It can't be done in one day. Would you rather folks got 'em after the anniversary?"

Opal gently pried the bellman's hands from Jack and straightened his shirt. Her index finger pointed little circles around the store. "Blum's only rents this space," she said. "The day you sign my paycheck is the day you can complain to me."

"Well!" Mr. Sinclair turned on his heel and left.

"You okay, sugar?" Opal asked.

"Fine," Jack said, "but I dropped my money."

Opal held the door while Jack collected his coins. He had to stretch to get the ones beneath the planter. Their ridged edges kept tickling his fingers, but he couldn't get a grip. It was a while before he handed the money to Opal. "The usual," he said. He looked around while Opal stepped up on a stool to reach the tins of chocolates. "Where are Ruby and Beryl?"

"Honeymooning." Opal sighed. "We used to be together 'in the fog and filthy air,' but now they both have husbands, so it's just me. Alone. At least for another week." She handed Jack the tin. "I've been working on those darn anniversary boxes all day. I don't care if I never see another chocolate."

Opal threw the coins into the register without counting them. She placed a fleshy knuckle under Jack's chin. "You sure you're okay, hon?"

Jack shrugged. "I guess I'm not used to living in a hotel," he said. "The staff is always mad at me."

"That's why I don't mix with 'em much. They got their back-of-the-house intrigue and political squabbles, and I'd sooner kiss a chicken butt than get involved. But don't worry about old flaptop," she said. "He's mad at the world."

"Shen, too?"

"Shen? Well, she's okay. Just give her a break." Opal's curled finger beckoned Jack closer, and she whispered to him, "I think her daddy's going a little crazy."

"Crazy?"

"Shen and her daddy were having tea right over in that booth when all of the sudden he up and starts screaming in Chinese, then calling out 'The eyes, the eyes' in English. It was all Shen could do to calm him down. Ask your aunt about it. She saw the whole thing."

"I better not. See, Aunt Edith isn't much for friendly conversation," said Jack. "She mostly just orders me around."

"Oh," said Opal, "I'm sorry."

She pulled two candies out of the glass case. "We have a couple of new flavors here," she said. She pushed one toward Jack. "This here's a Mean Ol' Aunt Meringue. It guarantees that living with sour relatives will soon be sweeter."

Jack smiled. "What's the other one?" he asked.

"This? This one's a Need a Man Nougat." She picked it up. "This one's for me."

"I thought you never wanted to see another chocolate."

"So? I'll close my eyes!" Opal held out her chocolate. "Just don't tell Ruby."

Jack knocked his candy against Opal's like they were toasting with champagne.

"I bet your mom named you Opal 'cause you're such a gem." The white confection was a wave of sugary almond in his mouth.

"Well, ain't you sweet," Opal said. "Why couldn't you be ten years older?"

"I will be," Jack said, "in about a decade."

Opal crumpled up the pleated foil cups and tossed them into the trash. "I guess until then I'll just be a single gal in the city. Of course, in the meantime I can always enjoy the company of Mr. Wall."

"Mr. Wall?

"Uh-huh," said Opal, pulling two more chocolates from the display case. "Mr. *Wall*-nut Toffee Chew." She winked. "One for the road."

The elevator was as slow as usual. Jack tucked the chocolate tin under his arm and pushed the call button again and again. Was Shen on a break?

While he waited, Jack looked at the earthquake celebration display opposite the elevator. The centerpiece was a newspaper article from a Midwestern town with the headline WAS GOD'S WRATH DESERVED? It said the earthquake was a punishment for a city where "good Christian men may be tempted by harlotry and drunkenness or fall prey along the Barbary Coast to robbery, battery, or the deplorable practice of shanghaiing." The rebuttal in a local paper mentioned how the A. P. Hotaling ware-house, which supplied booze to San Francisco's bar owners, had gone untouched. Included was a poem:

> *If, as some say, God spanked the town*
> *For being overfrisky,*
> *Why did He burn the churches down*
> *And save Hotaling's whiskey?*

The article made Jack uncomfortable. Did God send such destruction for sin? What about the good people who suffered in the quake? What about the kids who lost their parents? What sin could a kid commit that would deserve that kind of punishment?

The elevator bell rang, and the door slid back.

"Floor, please," Shen said, a bit out of breath. As they were going up, she pushed the lift button with her right hand while adjusting her jacket with the left. She turned to Jack like she had something important to say, but when the elevator arrived at Jack's floor, all she said was, "Watch your step, please."

A strange quiet covered Aunt Edith's suite. Approaching her room, Jack spied a chocolate in the middle of the floor, next to a brass button. He picked them up. The button was polished and cold. The chocolate was praline pecan. How odd. Aunt Edith would *never* let a praline pecan escape her grasp. Jack wrapped the chocolate in its little foil cup and put it and the button in his pocket.

"Aunt Edith?" he called. The silver frame had fallen off the end table. A thin crack marred one corner of the glass. His aunt's wedding photo wasn't scratched, so Jack figured his mother was safe underneath. Had they had an earthquake while Jack had been gone? He hadn't felt anything. More likely Muffin was to blame.

In front of his aunt's bedroom door Jack found the carcass of the gold box of chocolates. Pleated foil cups lay scattered about. Jack picked up the box. A few chocolates remained. He looked into the room. The crystal bowl was overturned and mostly empty. The rumpled bedspread sprawled on the floor. Half-eaten, spit-covered chocolates smeared a lumpy message on the bedsheets. It read:

wE hAvE hER

No PoLicE

And the coconut cream dotted the *i*.

CHAPTER 5

TORN CURTAIN

JACK STACKED THE BATTERED BOX of earthquake chocolates on top of the unopened tin and set them on the dresser, next to Muffin's empty cage. He circled the bed, staring at the lumpy chunks of nuts and fillings in the letters. The front of his brain screamed *this is a sick*

joke. But tendrils of doubt were twisting up his spine.

"Aunt Edith," he called, "this isn't funny."

Was she trying to teach him some sort of lesson? Show him just how alone he was, as if he didn't know? That would be just like her. And he'd be the one who would have to clean up this mess.

"Aunt Edith?"

He looked in the closet, behind the curtains, beside the dresser. There were only so many places a woman of Aunt Edith's size could hide. Under the bed wasn't one of them, but he looked there, too.

"Aunt Edith!" he called loudly, rushing to the sitting room.

She wasn't behind the sofa, where Jack slept, nor crouched behind the hi-fi stereo.

Of course! The bathroom!

He ran to the bathroom door. This was Aunt Edith's inner sanctum, where she engaged in what she called her beauty regimen, though Jack thought of it as an act of pure faith. He hesitated at the door. Just a few days ago Jack had accidentally opened it as Aunt Edith was stepping out of the shower. Jack knew boys at his old school who longed for a glimpse of a lady in the shower, but he was pretty sure the whole experience had put him off girls for good (and he'd only seen her from behind). Aunt Edith had bellowed like a foghorn on San Francisco Bay.

"You'd better knock from now on," she'd called as he backed away and shut the door. Well, you didn't have to tell him twice!

He knocked. No answer. No light coming from beneath the door. He turned the knob. He entered and switched on the light.

"Arrr!" he cried, and sprang back.

Aunt Edith crouched on the toilet.

But no. It was only the wooden wig form she kept atop the toilet tank with her auburn wig pulled over it. Two more wigs perched on the counter, along with a vast array of ointments, powders, and makeup. Otherwise the room was empty. Jack stared into the pedestal mirror on the vanity.

"Where is she?" he asked his reflection.

A *scritch, scritch* sounded behind him. In the mirror, the shower curtain swayed. Jack turned. The cold of the marble floor penetrated the soles of his shoes. He reached out. The nubbly texture of the shower curtain sent shivers up his arm. He inched the curtain back.

"Aunt Edith?"

A white blur lunged at him from the tub. He fell backward, tearing the curtain from its rod. He grabbed a towel rack. It ripped off the wall and swept across the vanity. The mirror fell and shattered, nearly on top of him.

"Muffin!" Jack yelled. Aunt Edith's pet sat on his chest and glared at him. With a scolding chatter it darted out of the bathroom.

There was a knock from the front door. Jack stood up, flapping his shirtfront to shed the slivers of glass. The knock came again.

Jack couldn't imagine who was knocking or what they could want, but maybe it had to do with Aunt Edith. He opened the front door. A familiar figure stood there, in profile, as if ready to return to his own suite. Jack half expected the creepy theme music from the man's television show to start playing. This time Jack remembered to step out of the way.

Alfred Hitchcock sailed into the room. He wore the same blue wool suit, and a look of concern.

"Are you quite all right, young man?" he asked. "I heard shouting and then a crash."

"All right?" Jack echoed. He backed into the sitting room, where he stumbled against a chair and sat down with a *plunk*. He wasn't hurt, but when was the last time he'd been *all* right?

"Are you?"

"Ummm . . ." Jack didn't know where to begin.

"Young man, it's quite late." The director ticked off items on his fingers. "I have a very important novel to review for screenplay potential, an actress to replace for my TV show with nothing but dreadful robots applying for the position, and a call to make to Mrs. Hitchcock. Now, since you seem fine, I shall get back to work."

"Don't leave," Jack said. "I'm not all right."

The director leaned over Jack, his attention focused, his lively eyes now keen and cutting, the eyes of a man who knew things. "Well, what seems to be the problem, then? Is someone here hurt?"

"No."

"Where are you parents?" The director spread a fleshy hand on the chair back and looked around the room.

"They're . . . they're dead." The words were a punch in the gut.

"Dead!" Hitchcock's eyes popped wide with surprise,

and maybe a little bit of . . . curiosity? "Good heavens! Young man, dead is usually considered to fall under the heading of 'hurt.' Very much so, in fact."

"Huh? Oh . . . No, look, my parents aren't here. I live with my aunt." Jack pointed to the bedroom. "Just go look."

Jack followed Hitchcock down the hall, but the director stopped short in the bedroom doorway.

"There's a weasel on the bed," he said.

Jack pushed into the room. Muffin sat on the bed, licking and eating the chocolate words. He'd polished off the *c* and most of the *i*. He was just finishing the coconut cream.

"That's just Muffin," Jack said, "my aunt's pet chinchilla." He picked Muffin up by the scruff of his neck, holding him at arm's length. The rodent glared at him but curled up in a still ball while being carried. Jack locked him in his cage. Muffin circled his cedar shavings twice, then settled down to sleep.

Jack turned to the director and told him all that had happened from the time he'd switched on the TV until now.

"Well, young man, we had best ring up the police."

"But what about the message?" Jack cried.

"'We have her. No pole'?" Hitchcock read. His brows crinkled in obvious confusion. "What pole?"

"It used to say 'police,'" Jack said. "What if they find out and hurt her? What if they kill her?"

"Stay calm, young man," Hitchcock said, "though I know that can be difficult when someone you love is in danger."

"Someone I love?" Jack's head was spinning. How quickly things can be taken from you. Friends. Family. Orphans in books were always full of pluck. Or clever. Or courageous. Jack just felt queasy.

He looked at the director, this man who had the world in hand instead of on his shoulders, this man who knew all about the dark things in life, who had tamed them by throwing a light on them and projecting them onto a screen. You couldn't lie to a man like that.

"Honestly, I don't even like my aunt very much," Jack said. "But look, she's family. Since my mother died, she's the only relative I have. If something happened to her, I'd have nowhere . . . no one . . ."

"All the more reason to involve the police." Hitchcock took Jack by the arm. "Let's go to my suite and call the hotel. They'll send someone to take you to the station."

The director's grip was firm, gently urging Jack out of the room. But soon enough he would pass him off to someone else. There was darkness ahead. Jack tasted it yawning in front of him, vast and unknown.

"No!" Jack pulled away. "You. I want you to take me." The first time you explored a cave, you took a guide who knew the place.

"As I said, I am quite busy. I've a movie to plan and stories to choose for next year's show."

"Please," Jack said. "You know things. I see it every week on your show. You know about stuff like this. Kidnappers and murderers and thugs."

The director's eyes crinkled impishly. "So you've had a look at my résumé?" He seemed pleased, but still hesitant.

Jack pressed on. "Don't you want to see how the story ends?"

Hitchcock's eyebrow arched. "Perhaps."

"It could be interesting," Jack said.

"But . . ."

"It could be challenging," Jack added.

"True . . ."

"It could be . . . It could be . . . grisly."

A smile erupted on Hitchcock's face. "Grisly?"

"Very," Jack said, though he hoped it wouldn't be. "Please, Mr. Hitchcock. If I go to the police, I need someone who can help me."

The director's brow furrowed. His gaze seemed to lose focus. "When I was just a boy, my father sent me to the constable with a note. The man locked me in a cell and told me that's what they do to naughty boys. I've feared the police ever since." He bit his chubby lower lip.

Jack put his hand on the director's. "I'm afraid too."

Hitchcock blinked. "Nonsense," he said. "Let's be quick. I have work to do."

CHAPTER 6

THE TROUBLE WITH HARRY

CENTRAL STATION ON WASHINGTON STREET wore an aggrieved look, as if it had indigestion from so many years of swallowing murderers, swindlers, and thieves. The large oak door opened inward but grated against the floor on the last half of its swing. The linoleum tiles sported a stark black-and-white checker pattern, except where the shuffling feet of decades of perpetrators had worn a gray path, its edges soft and rounded, from the door to the front counter.

A pudgy, balding police sergeant perched behind the counter, his arms stretched as wide as the newspaper in front of him. Another policeman, bamboo-thin, with a pointy nose and eyebrows that met above it, sipped coffee and read over the sergeant's shoulder. A bright overhead light reflected off their silver badges, making Jack blink and squint as he approached.

"I'd like to report a kidnapping," Hitchcock said.

"Kidnapping?" the sergeant turned his head slightly toward them, but his eyes stayed locked on the paper.

"Yes. This boy's aunt has disappeared."

The sergeant's eyes caught up with his face. He looked directly at them. "Hey! You're Alfred Hitchcock. Look, Larry. It's Alfred Hitchcock."

"Really," said the thin policeman, still reading. He blew a tiny whirlwind of steam from his coffee.

"Yes. Yes, I am." The director smiled.

The sergeant did not. He pressed his lips together and squinted at Hitchcock. Then he leaned to the side to look around the director at Jack.

"What makes you think his aunt was kidnapped? Maybe she went for a walk or something?"

"The kidnappers left a note," Hitchcock said.

One of the sergeant's eyebrows arched up at this. He unfolded his arms just enough to extend his right hand, palm up. After Hitchcock and Jack had stared at his calluses for several seconds, he snapped his fingers, twice, then laid his palm up again.

"The note?" said the sergeant. "May I see it?"

"I'm sorry. No," said Hitchcock.

"No?" The sergeant recrossed his arms. The gesture made his badge flash again.

"No. I'm afraid it was rather too large to bring," said Hitchcock.

"I see."

"It was written on a bedsheet."

"A bedsheet?" The sergeant's voice curled up at the end, like a damp piece of paper.

"Yes. In chocolates."

"Chocolate." Now his voice was flat.

"Chocolates," Hitchcock corrected. "The note was written in little chocolate bonbons, on a bed, room five sixty-two, the Fairmont." The overhead lamp cast little pinpricks of light where perspiration had beaded up on his forehead.

"Hear that, Larry? He says the note was written in chocolate."

"Maybe it was the Easter Bunny who kidnapped her, Harry," Larry offered.

"The Easter Bunny!" Sergeant Harry said. "Hey, Larry, that's good!"

"Gentlemen," Hitchcock said, "I assure you this is no laughing matter." Hitchcock took a handkerchief from his pocket and wiped his brow. He could do nothing about the flowers of dampness blooming around his collar.

"No. Kidnapping is quite serious," Harry said. "Anything that involves the police is serious. Or it should be."

"Quite."

"You know, I used to live in LA," Harry said.

That seemed like a random, unrelated statement to Jack. Still, he piped in with a squeaky "Me too," hoping that might help smooth over the tension he sensed in the room. But the sergeant ignored him.

"Used to read the *Hollywood Scoop* all the time," he said, staring at Hitchcock.

"Oh?" Hitchcock sounded curious.

"Even appeared in it once. Right after I removed a horse from a dressing room."

"Oh." And now contrite.

Jack found it hard to follow this conversation. But the sergeant was looking at Hitchcock like the director had something to do with this story. Jack tugged Hitchcock's sleeve. "Wait," he said. "Did you put a horse in a dressing room?"

Hitchcock twisted the handkerchief in his hands. "It was merely a pony."

Bam! The sergeant slammed his palm down on the desk. "It was a Belgian draft horse, and the room was narrow. Horses get nervous backing up, you know. Took two officers to get the job done. One in front. One in back. Guess which I was."

"Hey," Larry said, "is that why they call you Harry Horsepi—"

"The studio wouldn't even pay the dry cleaning bill," Harry interrupted.

Hitchcock stood straighter. He balled the handkerchief into his fist. "That was meant to be a private joke," he said. "The police were not intended to be involved."

Jim Averbeck

"But we were, weren't we?" said Harry. "Just like when you released your jewel heist movie and the police were called to arrest a gang of 'cat burglars' in Beverly Hills, only to find it was a room full of kittens in prison uniforms."

"I admit the studio publicity departments get carried away at times. But I think it unfair that I be held responsible."

"You have a couple of films coming out this year, don't you?" Harry asked. "See, I still keep up with the *Scoop*."

"The Man Who Knew Too Much," said Hitchcock, "and *The Wrong Man*."

"That first one is a remake," the sergeant stated. It wasn't a question.

"Yes." The director's collar was stained with sweat. *He really is afraid of the police,* Jack thought. It must have taken a lot for him even to walk through that big oak door. But now Jack just wished they would walk back out.

Harry laid his hands flat on the counter and hoisted himself up to tower over Hitchcock. "I saw the original. It's about a kidnapping. Kidnapping! In Switzerland."

He pointed an accusing finger at Hitchcock. "Where they make all that chocolate!"

This wasn't going at all the way Jack wanted. He planted himself in front of Hitchcock. "You said they'd help."

The sergeant looked at Jack and sighed. "How old are you, kid?"

"Eleven."

"I'm not gonna waste any police time on this, but I'll send the kiddie patrol around, just to be safe."

"Kiddie patrol?" Jack asked.

"Youth services," the sergeant said.

Now Jack's shirt collar felt damp. And cold, like an iron noose.

"Alice Trapp from YS is in the back," Larry said. "Want me to get her?"

"That'd be great," said Harry.

Larry disappeared down a dim hallway behind the desk. Jack caught Hitchcock's eye and nodded toward the exit, but the director shook his head no.

The *clop, clop* of footsteps echoed from the hallway, along with a murmur of voices. The only words Jack could make out were "Chocolate note!" The director

Jim Averbeck

stared at the ceiling. As the footsteps got closer, he took Jack's arm.

Thank goodness. We're leaving, thought Jack.

But when he turned to go, his arm didn't go with him. Hitchcock held it, anchoring Jack to the spot. The director continued to stare at the ceiling, a pained but resolute look on his face. Jack tried to peel Hitchcock's hand off his sleeve, but he couldn't budge the pudgy fingers.

Alice Trapp rounded the desk. "This him?"

She wore a plain beige overcoat atop a beige tweed suit. The sensible hat pinned to her head had a narrow brim, from under which tufts of brown hair were peeking, like wary mice from their holes. She was of medium height, medium build, and, Jack eventually thought, medium-rare intellect. This he decided by the way she held strictly to the rules, in this case spelled out to her by the clipboard clutched in her hands. She dug in a few pages.

"Parents?" she said.

Jack didn't answer.

"Parents?" she repeated.

"Deceased," Hitchcock said.

She glanced at the director and made a small check mark on the page. "Legal guardian?"

Hitchcock again answered. "Kidnapped."

"Allegedly," added Harry with a frown.

"Allegations are your department, not mine," said Alice, making another check mark. She turned more pages forward and back on the clipboard, and read, "'If no parent or legal guardian is available, the minor shall be conducted to the Youth Guidance Center.'" She turned to Sergeant Harry. "You want me to take him there?"

"Youth Guidance Center?" Jack said. "Is that an orphanage?"

"Don't be a silly willy," Alice said, like he was a baby. "It's more like a waiting room. Somewhere for you to stay tonight while we process you."

"Process me?"

"Until we find a placement for you," Alice said. She looked again at her clipboard, licking the tip of her finger, swiping through the pages one by one. "Oh, look. You're in luck. A bed just opened up at the Fogbottom Home for Boys."

Jack pulled against Hitchcock's grip, but his shoes got no traction on the smooth gray path to the door.

The director cleared his throat. He fidgeted a bit. After a moment he pushed Jack toward Alice. "That might be for the best," he said.

"What? No!" Jack cried. He stared at Hitchcock, but the director wouldn't meet his eyes.

Alice held the clipboard against her side with her elbow, leaned forward, and took Jack's free hand in both of hers. "Don't worry, little boy," she said. "I'm here to help."

Just looking, you would think she was gently cupping Jack's hand in hers, a gesture of caring and support. But pulling against her grip was like trying to pull your foot out of deep mud without losing your shoe.

Hitchcock said again, "It's for the best."

The sergeant grunted and turned back to his paper.

Alice reeled Jack in a little closer, murmuring, "There, there."

The director shuffled for the door.

"Wait!" Jack cried.

Every eye in the room curved toward Jack. He had their attention, but what should he do with it? The seconds stretched out. Jack looked from one face to another. What were the magic words that would get him out of here?

Sergeant Harry's badge flashed again in Jack's face. *Harry Horsepie,* he thought. He smiled and looked Hitchcock right in the eye. "I haven't said my lines yet."

"Lines?" the policeman said.

Jack turned to the sergeant. He rocked his right foot back and forth, on the outside edge of his shoe, and stared at the floor. "Yes. Um. How did they go? Oh, yeah." He opened his eyes wide and put on a little pout. "Please come to our hotel, or the bad guys will kill my aunt and I will be . . . I will be . . . Oh, yeah. I will be alone in the cruel world at the mercy of . . . of . . . things." Jack turned to Hitchcock. "Did I do that right? I couldn't remember all the words we rehearsed. Can we go to the hotel and get pancakes now? Aunt Edith and the reporter will be waiting."

Hitchcock stood, openmouthed, his twisted handkerchief dangling uselessly at his side.

"I knew it!" The sergeant set down his newspaper and clapped his hands together. It sounded like a freedom bell to Jack. "Another stunt. Out of here, both of you. Now."

"But . . . ," Hitchcock said.

The sergeant picked up the handset of the phone and

shook it at them. "And I'll be calling the other precincts. If you or this kid pull this anywhere else, we'll be coming straight to your door. Falsifying a police report is a crime."

"And you were going to abandon that child here," Alice added. "That's . . . That's . . ."—she released Jack's hand and paged through her clipboard—"child abandonment!"

Hitchcock turned on his heel and rushed from the room. He pulled the door open so hard it stuck at the far end of its swing.

Jack followed, but when he turned to pull the door shut, he saw Alice making notes on her clipboard.

"Child labor. Child endangerment. Attempted abandonment. I'll need the big book to see what else. That man is a menace and shouldn't be let near that little boy. The Fairmont Hotel, you said? I better check it out tomorrow." She slid her pen beneath the clip. "Besides, it would be a shame to waste that opening at Fogbottom."

CHAPTER 7

THE WHITE SHADOW

HITCHCOCK HAILED A CAB. He got in and slammed the door. The car tilted to the side where he sat. Jack had to scramble to the other door to get in before the taxi left.

Hitchcock was still shaken but seemed to calm down as he mopped his sodden brow. He folded his damp handkerchief precisely in half four times. When he stuffed it into his pocket he was fully composed.

"I suppose you thought that was clever," he said. "That woman wanted to help you."

"Into an orphanage," said Jack. "Who would find Aunt Edith then?"

Hitchcock shrugged. "The police—"

"Didn't believe us. They wouldn't do anything. They didn't believe *you*." The taxi turned off Stockton and up the steep incline of California Street, full of silence. Jack tried to make himself calm, but it wasn't easy. He wondered how the director regained control so easily. "You were going to leave me," Jack said. *Before I had answers. Before I could even ask the questions.*

Hitchcock moved his right wrist next to Jack's left and made a little jerking motion like he was trying to pull away but couldn't. "Young man, I am not sure I like the handcuffs you've clapped on me."

"Handcuffs?"

"Metaphoric ones, with links forged of guilt."

Jack imitated the same jerky motion with his hand. "They look more like Belgian draft horses and convict kittens to me. Look, the police would be helping if you hadn't messed with them so often before."

An uncomfortable silence rode between them the rest of the way to the hotel.

The whole scene had shaken Jack badly. He took out his sketchbook, hoping the soft *shish* of pencil on paper would calm him. He put a few marks on the erased image of his father but quickly gave up. He didn't need the frustration right now. Capturing bravery when he felt so afraid seemed a futile undertaking.

His mother smiled up at him from the opposite page. He wanted to crawl into the picture and scratch it out in equal measure. Could you feel fury and love for someone at the same time? Could you be at once hurt by their external absence and comforted by their presence inside you? But the portrait of Mom's laughter inspired him. He drew a cartoon of five cats in handcuffs in the margin. It helped some.

The taxi dropped them at the corner of California and Mason Streets. Opal was coming out of the hotel entrance next to Blum's. As Hitchcock entered, she glanced at the director's back. She caught Jack's eye, tapped her ring finger, and mouthed the question, "Married?" Jack shrugged. Opal gave an exasperated sigh as she stepped out into the fog.

Jack usually took Shen's elevator on the north side of the hotel. It let out closest to his room. But Mr. Sinclair glared at him from the bell desk, standing between the door and the north elevators. Jack didn't want another confrontation with him tonight.

"Let's take the south elevators," Jack said.

"You may go however you wish, young man. I shall be taking the one that is closest to my rooms. I have no desire to walk the length of the hotel hallways, stepping over room service trays and shoes put out for a shining," the director replied.

Jack looked toward Mr. Sinclair again. Now he was glaring with his arms crossed and his mustache quivering slightly. That was never good. Jack headed south, his shoes making raspy noises on the carpet. He'd see Hitchcock upstairs again anyway. Shen's elevator was usually so slow, Jack might even arrive first.

In the elevator on the way up, Jack thought about what to do. Mr. Hitchcock would know. Maybe it was best to give him a little space so he would see how he just had to help Jack now.

The elevator dinged. "Fifth floor," the operator called. "Watch your step."

Jack walked down the hall toward Aunt Edith's room. There weren't many room service trays in the hall, and no shoes at all. He passed a tray with a steak chopped up into pieces and small silverware, the remnants of some child's meal. A waste, really. He wondered how many residents at the Fogbottom Home for Boys would love to have those scraps, or even the meat still on the bone. He needed to find his aunt right away. He needed Mr. Hitchcock to help.

The corridor at the Fairmont formed a giant square. You could walk around and around if you wanted to, passing the same rooms and features over and over. When Jack turned the corner of the square where his aunt's room was located, he noticed the hall lights had burned out. He picked up his pace. He wanted to be at his aunt's door when Shen's elevator opened. He didn't want Hitchcock to slip into his own room and lock the door. Would he even answer if Jack knocked? Maybe he should have stayed with the director after all. What if Mr. Hitchcock abandoned him? What if he called the lady from Youth Services and convinced her to come get Jack? Jack jogged faster down the hall.

He was relieved to see a figure squatting by his aunt's door in the shadowy hallway.

"Mr. Hitchcock, thank goodness," he called.

At Jack's call the figure sprang up. But something was wrong. He wore white coveralls and was far too short to be Hitchcock. And too thin. He turned to look at Jack. A white ski mask covered his face. He pulled something out of the door lock and ran.

"Hey!" Jack cried. "Stop!" He ran after the man.

Jack pursued him into the stairwell. The stairs wound round and round, like switchbacks in a cave. If Jack had had a rope, he could have rappelled down the four-foot space between the flights. The man ran down the flight below Jack. Jack leapt over the railing from one flight to the other, hoping to cut him off. But the space between the flights was greater than he'd thought. His foot caught on the railing below and he landed badly. By the time he got up, the man was dashing through the door at the next landing.

"Stop!" Jack called, and followed.

A door slammed.

Did he go into a guest room? They'd all be locked. He couldn't have gotten in unless he was a guest. Was he? Had he had time to find his key, insert it into the lock, and turn it before Jack had rounded the corner? Jack began trying doorknobs. As he tried the third one, the door flew open. A woman stood there, wide-eyed. She was young, and pretty, like Marilyn Monroe. She wore a pale pink robe and had a towel wrapped around her head.

"You're not Walter," she said.

"Um, no," said Jack.

"Where's Walter?" she said. "And what were you doing breaking into my room? Are you some kind of Peeping Tom? Walter? Walter?" The pitch of her voice rose to a screech.

The door across the hall opened. A man in a business suit with his tie undone and two drinks in his hand stepped into the hall. "For crying out loud, Ethel," he said, "keep it down. I'm right here. . . . Who's this?"

"A peeper, that's who," said Ethel.

Walter made a grab for Jack, but he didn't want to spill his drinks, so Jack easily evaded him. But more people were coming into the hall.

"Catch that peeper!" cried Ethel.

Doors up and down the corridor opened. Jack

retreated from the growing crowd of hotel guests, until his back came up against an unopened door. A sign on it said EMPLOYEES ONLY. Jack turned the knob. It was unlocked. He jumped in and fumbled for the lights.

It was a utility closet. Mops dripped grayish water into a sink in one corner. A maid's cart rested in another. Pipes of varying sizes, some thicker than Jack's waist, crowded vertically in a third. No one was in here, and there was no way out. The man in white had escaped some other way. Jack turned, cracked the door open, and steeled himself to play a game of dodge the tourists when a muffled grunt and a metallic *clang* sounded from the pipe corner.

Jack pushed the door shut and tiptoed toward the pipes. Closer, he saw that they extended up and down through the ceiling and floor via a large hole. The pipes formed a barrier that would keep anyone from falling into the hole accidentally, but a small person could squeeze between them and find himself in a sort of shaft. Jack pressed his eye to the space between the pipes. He saw a shadowy figure two floors below squeezing back out, presumably into a closet on that floor.

Jack flattened against the wall, snaking his collarbone,

then his chest, then his whole body into the ersatz shaft. This was no different from doing the chimney at Mystic's Cave. Technically, he should have had a rope. He had just thought that, when he began to slide down the slick pipes. He pushed his back up against them and pressed one foot against each wall, a few feet in either direction from the corner. His legs were extended too far for him to get any leverage to climb, but he could work with gravity, controlling his downward movement. This was a one-way trip. The cold pipes jammed into his back, the occasional bell end, where one pipe met another digging against his vertebrae. He wall-walked down two floors.

It was awkward work getting out of the shaft. Fortunately, on this floor there were horizontal braces that held the pipes to the wall. Grabbing one, Jack kept from sliding farther while he monkeyed out of the shaft and onto solid floor.

Just as he touched down, the lights went out and the door slammed. Jack dove for the door.

And nearly knocked himself out with the force of his impact. The door was locked.

Jack was trapped.

CHAPTER 8

VERTIGO

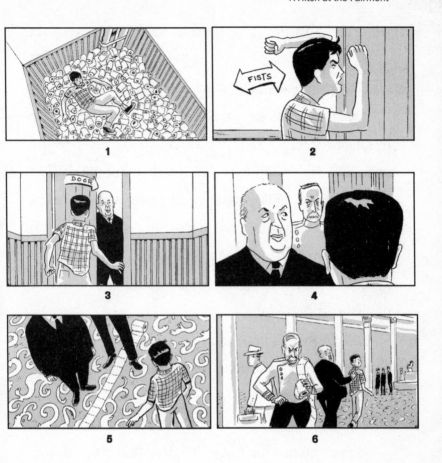

"HELP!" JACK BANGED ON THE DOOR, rattling the knob
to no avail.

No one heard him. This was just another closet on
another floor. Despite the commotion Ethel had caused
upstairs, guests usually kept to their rooms, and the

walls at the Fairmont were thick. Maybe if he were out in the hall someone could hear him. But he wasn't. He was stuck until someone wandered past the door.

Jack had felt alone since Mom's death, but never like this, isolated with no one else around. No one who would miss him. No one to look for him. Even in the darkest cave, he had a buddy, usually Schultzie, who'd make a fuss if Jack strayed too far. Would they open this closet months from now and find a mummified boy, curled up in the corner? Now the heat of the chase turned cold, a perfect nest for fear.

Jack flicked on the light. As he suspected, this closet mirrored the one two floors above. A similar sink stood in the same corner. But against the other wall, from floor to ceiling, rose a skyscraper of toilet paper rolls.

Jack examined the door. The dead bolt was thrown. It gleamed solidly in the crack between the door and the jamb. He traced the sharp zigzag of the keyhole with his finger. A maid with keys dangling at her waist could easily have escaped if she were somehow locked in. But Jack had no key. And he couldn't pick a lock. The only thing he could think of doing was to keep going down, in hopes of finding an unlocked door.

But when Jack peered down into the shaft to figure the best way to descend, he got a surprise. The light from his floor illuminated the shaft a few feet down, where the pipes veered off horizontally in different directions. The shaft they created didn't continue. Jack lay down on his side and again squeezed his body past the pipes, but only to the waist. Hanging partially into the room below, he could just make out a small sliver of light coming from under its door. The drop from ceiling to floor was much higher than typical. It was the lobby level, where the grand ceilings and high columns were meant to impress incoming guests. Jack judged that if he shimmied down the pipes as far as he could, then dangled from the horizontal leg of their L shape, he'd have a drop of six or eight feet from his toes to the floor below. The door there might be locked, but more people milled about the lobby, so someone was bound to hear his calls.

Jack hauled himself back up into the locked room. The drop wasn't too far, but the landing worried him. A marble or concrete floor would be bad enough, but who knew what might be stored, unseen, below? Jack searched the room, hoping to find a rope or electrical cord. But there was nothing. Two floors above, dirty sheets sat in the laundry bag of the maids' cart. If he had those, he could make a sort of rope. But there was no way up.

Here there was only a tower of toilet paper.

A huge tower.

Of soft toilet paper.

Jack kicked out the bottom rolls, and the tower toppled. Using his outstretched arms, he bulldozed the toilet paper toward the pipe shaft. Down they tumbled, a snowfall of soft white cylinders. Jack imagined them piling up in a drift below. He scurried after the last roll, sliding down a pipe like a fireman down a pole.

He came to an abrupt halt at the *L*. He lost his balance, if ever he had it, and hurled over the side. He was falling headfirst. Suddenly he saw his mother saying "Don't break your neck" the first time he went spelunking with the Schultzes. He had just enough time to cover his head and wonder if he'd have to apologize to her in death—before he landed in a mound of soft. He did a sort of uncontrolled somersault onto the pile and slid down. His feet slammed against the door.

It was a jarring stop. Jack took stock. He was lying at an angle on his back on the mountain of toilet paper.

Nothing seemed broken. He pushed a few rolls to the side with his feet and found the floor. The door felt solid and thick when he banged on it.

"Help!"

A muffled voice called back from the other side, then went silent for a minute or two. The door swung outward. Jack blinked in the light of the lobby.

"Good evening," Hitchcock said. He peered into the closet. "Have you changed your room?"

"Very funny," said Jack.

He was about to tell the director about the shadowy figure, when Mr. Sinclair stepped up beside him. A roll of toilet paper tumbled down the pile and out the door, leaving a trail behind it. It unwound between the bell captain's feet and bumped the wall across the hallway with a soft *thump*.

"Boy," Mr. Sinclair said, "the lobby is not the proper place—nor, indeed, is anywhere in the hotel—for a game of hide-and-seek. Though I've no idea how you got into a locked closet in the middle of the night, let us add this to the list of amusements that are forbidden to you. I have responsibilities here, and they do not include opening rooms that should remain empty." With that, he pulled the key from the lock and stuck it into his pocket. "Furthermore—"

The ding of the elevator bell around the corner interrupted him. Hitchcock started toward it.

"Going up?" Shen asked.

"No, thanks," answered Jack, dragging the director away.

Several calls rang out from the elevator. Judging by their insistence and repetition, angry customers waited on higher floors. Shen shrugged, pushed the door closed, and went to answer the calls.

"I waited forever for that elevator to come," Hitchcock said. He frowned at Jack.

"Please, Mr. Hitchcock," Jack said. "I need your help. There is no one else."

Hitchcock's frown softened.

"Now see here," the bell captain began. He was holding the roll of toilet paper. It trailed like a tail behind him and around the corner. The director silenced him with a gesture. Hitchcock picked up the toilet paper trail and draped it around the bellman's shoulders. "Hadn't you better get this mess cleaned up? Your guests expect better organization at a hotel like this."

"But—"

"I'll take charge of the boy." Hitchcock led Jack away by the arm. Once they were out of earshot of Mr. Sinclair, Hitchcock asked Jack what had happened.

Jack told him as the director led him across the lobby and down a stairwell.

"So this person eluded you?" Hitchcock asked.

"Yes," said Jack.

"I wonder how," said the director.

"I just told you."

"Indeed."

Jack trailed Hitchcock to the Tonga Room, one of several restaurants in the hotel. A forbidding Polynesian tiki statue glowered from the other side of the door. Little flames burned in its eyes. The room felt humid, as if one really were vacationing in the tropical locale the décor mimicked. The restaurant was built around an indoor pool, with a boat docked on the far side for the band. The sarong-clad hostess guided them around the pool to a thatched bamboo hut. She set down two glasses of water. "Your waitress will be right with you," she said.

Hitchcock pushed Jack into the booth. "Wait here," he said. "I'll be back in a jiff."

A knobby lump squished into Jack's thigh. He took the lump from his pocket. The praline pecan chocolate stuck to the brass button he'd found in the suite. He separated the two and set them on the table.

Jack dipped his finger into the water and wiped the bits of chocolate from the button. He'd almost forgotten he'd found it, with all the excitement. His thumb glided across its cold smoothness. It wasn't from anything he owned. Maybe it was his aunt's. There were no marks or emblems on it. His reflection stared back at him, captive and alone in the inscrutable brass.

Jack wondered why the director was taking so long. What was he doing? He'd said he'd be right back. The waitress came and went twice. Jack was just about to go looking, when Hitchcock heaved himself down in a chair opposite, his back to the entrance.

"I've had a little talk with the lobby staff," said Hitchcock, his breath slightly labored.

"Oh," said Jack, looking past the director. As he did, a suavely dressed man and an older woman entered the place. The man was small, not much bigger than Jack. But the woman stood tall and sturdy, in a wide-hipped, broad-shouldered sort of way. Something about her reminded Jack of an ox. He had a brief impression that they were looking at him, the man from under his hat and the woman from behind her large round glasses. *They must recognize Mr. Hitchcock,* he thought. They were seated opposite Jack and Hitchcock, on the other side of the pool. They continued to stare. Then thunder crashed and an artificial rainstorm fell from the ceiling into the pool. The boat drifted to the middle of the water as the band began to play, obscuring the couple from view.

The waitress came again. "Ready to order now?"

"Brandy for me. Hot milk for the boy," Hitchcock said. When she had gone, he turned to Jack. "No one on staff saw your aunt leave the building. None of the elevator operators took her aboard after she went up earlier."

Jack bit into the praline. He smoothed out the pleated paper cup and set the half-eaten chocolate on top. "I don't see how anyone could have gotten her out without someone noticing. Aunt Edith is hard to overlook."

Hitchcock's pudgy finger tapped his chin. "Perhaps they took her out in a large suitcase or steamer trunk."

"I don't think so. She is a pretty big woman."

"Several large trunks, then."

"Sever—" Jack threw Hitchcock a horrified look. "No . . . ," he stumbled. "I don't see how they could have. . . . I . . ."

Hitchcock frowned. "See here, how long were you gone?"

"Maybe fifteen minutes," Jack said.

"No, of course you're right. Even an expert could hardly dismantle her in fifteen minutes. Let alone clean up the mess."

"In the movies they could," said Jack

"But there's no relationship between filmic time and real time," Hitchcock said. "In the cinema, time moves at the whim of the director."

Jack's stomach felt knotted and wrung. He thought he might be sick. "Then where is she?"

"My dear boy, if your aunt was too large to leave the hotel unnoticed, and no one did notice her leave, then there is only one possibility."

Jack understood. "She's still inside the hotel."

"Quite."

"So we should be able to find her pretty easily," Jack said as the artificial rainstorm diminished.

"It's a big hotel," Hitchcock pointed out. Their

drinks arrived. Hitchcock put the hot milk in front of Jack. "Drink that up. It's good for you. Just like medicine," he said.

Jack took a sip. It tasted bland and uninteresting, though the cup warmed his cold hands. He looked around the table for honey or sugar to add to it, but there was none. So Jack dipped the praline pecan into the hot milk, licked off the melted chocolate, and took a sip of milk. He alternated sips of milk and nibbles of chocolate. Soon he stifled a yawn.

"I suppose we could request a room by room search," Hitchcock said, "but I doubt the management will allow it, which means we'd need to involve the authorities to make them do it."

Jack stared through the director. "Belgian draft horses," he said. He put his head on the table.

"Yes," said Hitchcock, "it seems the authorities are not currently an option." His lips pursed in thought. "I suppose one could pull the fire alarm, and then go through the crowds to see if your aunt is there, but it is all too likely that she is restrained in some way. . . ."

"Mmmmm," Jack said. The tabletop cooled his cheek. The grain of the wood wavered and danced before his eyes. The world gently rocked. The movement was peaceful.

"There is really only one thing to do," said Hitchcock.

The sturdy woman and the well-dressed man stared at them from a table across the pool. The director's words seemed to be coming out of the man's mouth, but Jack couldn't make out what they meant. It seemed odd, but he was just too tired to think about it. He closed his eyes.

"Sleep on it?" Hitchcock said. The director sighed heavily. "Not quite what I had in mind. Wake up, young man. . . ."

But just like that, Jack was dead to the world.

CHAPTER 9

TO CATCH A THIEF

JACK STRUGGLED TO OPEN HIS EYES. They felt painted shut, like the windows of an old Victorian on Alamo Square. The intricate design of the brocaded sofa he slept on imprinted itself on his cheek. Mr. Hitchcock must have deposited him back in his aunt's suite, unloading an inconvenient problem before returning to his work.

The phone rang. Jack wanted to sit up, but the sound pinned him to the cushion like a moth on a corkboard—right through the center of his head.

The receiver clicked out of its cradle, and a sonorous voice said, "Good moooorning."

Jack squinted into the bright sunlight streaming through the curtains. It looked like Aunt Edith's sitting room but a bit larger, with different art on the walls. Stacks of books and files stood neatly arranged on the desk. Jack could make out the largest title, *D'entre les morts*.

"Yes, Alma. I prefer the French novel to the African.... We'll need the screenwriter quite soon. . . . Anderson, I should think, unless you've someone else in mind. . . ."

Jack's brain was swimming through wet cement. A bulletin board leaned drunkenly against the wall. Photographs covered its surface. In one the towers of the Golden Gate Bridge thrust up from a heavy fog bank like the rigging of a haunted schooner. In another the lonely finger of Coit Tower pointed accusingly skyward. But Jack did not recognize any of the Spanish missions or the odd little camera-shaped building at the edge of a cliff.

". . . checking a few potential locations later. It's a marvelous city for a murder."

Murder? Could Aunt Edith have been murdered? Jack hoped not. As many times as he'd wanted to do that job himself, he wouldn't wish murder on anyone.

"Is Joan there? I need to discuss *Alfred Hitchcock Presents* with her. . . . Yes. . . . As I do you. . . ."

Silverware clinked against a plate and brought a whiff of something that turned Jack's stomach.

"Joan," Hitchcock continued, "these stories you've sent. Not one of them will do for next season. . . . They simply aren't grisly enough. Our audience has come to have certain tastes. . . . Keep looking. Think Woolrich or Dahl . . ."

Jack's tongue felt like it had sprouted fur over night. Metallic fur. His arms were corpse-stiff, but he was finally able to move them. He rubbed the patterned ridges on his cheek.

". . . and these actresses—could we find someone who has traveled the road less pampered? Beautiful, yes, but someone who has seen the ugliness of life. . . . This lot aren't actresses, Joan. They're poodles. Pampered poodles!"

Jack wiped drool off his chin. Oh, gosh! He'd drooled on Alfred Hitchcock's sofa. He tried to erase the little puddle with the heel of his hand but succeeded only in pressing it into the fabric. He moved a pillow to hide the evidence.

". . . by this afternoon. Yes." Hitchcock hung up. "Good mooorning," he said.

A rolling room service table sat next to the director's desk. Hitchcock grabbed a covered plate from it and set it on the coffee table in front of Jack. The warped reflection of the room in the silver cover made Jack's stomach spin. He leaned over.

"Last evening's events have you overwrought," Hitchcock said. "Perhaps we can get one of the staff to call your school and say you are ill."

"I'm not enrolled. Aunt Edith said it was too late in the year so I'd have to go to summer school." Jack took a breath—half sigh, half groan.

"This will get you on your feet and make you feel better," Hitchcock said, removing the silver cover from the plate.

"Ugh! What is that?" Jack asked.

"A traditional English fry-up," Hitchcock replied.

"Had it specially made. Eggs, blood pudding, kippers, kidneys, and a special side of bubble and squeak."

Jack's legs finally began to work, though the effort cost him. He ran unsteadily for the bathroom. When he got there, he practically dove into the toilet. Just in time. He didn't have much in his stomach, but what was there spewed out in a stream of burning chunks from his nose and mouth.

Hitchcock came in. He rubbed Jack's back in a slow figure eight. "There, there," he said.

The gesture was the same his mother had used whenever he was sick. Just as he was thinking his mother would also hand him a moistened washcloth, a pudgy hand holding a wad of toilet paper dipped into view. Jack wiped his mouth, blew his nose, and dropped the tissue into the bowl. "Mom used to call this bobbing for porcelain." He laughed a little.

Hitchcock helped Jack stand and flushed the toilet. "You see. I told you some good English food would make you feel better."

Jack closed the toilet lid and sat down. With nothing in his stomach, he did feel better.

For a moment or two.

"Why did you let me fall asleep?" he asked, suddenly panicked.

"Let you? You were out cold. It was nearly one a.m. You must have been exhausted."

"We have to find Aunt Edith," Jack said. "They could have taken her anywhere by now."

"Do give me some credit," the director replied. "Once you were safe in my rooms, I tipped the staff handsomely to keep watch for your aunt. As you say, she is a hard woman to miss. And word of a generous tip spreads fast. With so many eyes watching, she won't have left the building—in whole or in parts."

"So what do we do now?" Jack asked. He stood and rinsed his mouth out at the sink.

"We?"

Jack pressed on. "I need your help."

"You need the police," the director said.

Jack looked him in the eye. "Belgian draft horses."

The director bit his upper lip. "I believe I shall be quite tired of those three words before too long." He tapped his fingers against his trousers. He sighed. "Did you notice if anything was missing?" he asked.

"Only Aunt Edith."

"We have the chocolate note, but I believe in these cases there is usually an indication of the kidnappers' demands. Did you find a ransom note?"

"I didn't look." Jack's mouth tasted like a movie-house floor. "I really didn't know what to do last night. I guess we should search my aunt's room. Besides, I need to brush my teeth."

In Aunt Edith's suite Jack tried to look at the rooms with fresh eyes. The décor was quite modern and dramatic—the spindle-legged couch where Jack slept, the hi-fi console with the built-in shelf neatly housing Caruso and Liberace albums.

"I don't see anything missing," Jack said. "There isn't really anything to steal out here anyway. Aunt Edith kept anything valuable in her bedroom. She didn't trust the maids."

Hitchcock cruised into the master bath while Jack surveyed the bedroom.

"The shower curtain has been pulled from the bar," the director called.

"That was me," Jack said, "when I fell last night."

The chocolate message still occupied Aunt Edith's

bed. The crystal bowl lay overturned, two half-eaten chocolates glued to its side.

Jack checked Muffin's cage. He had plenty of food and water, though he kept sniffing at the chocolates Jack had put on the dresser the night before. Jack opened Aunt Edith's jewelry box. Muffin chattered and ran back and forth in his cage, and kicked some of the cedar shavings at Jack with his hind legs. "It looks like her jewelry is all here," Jack called.

"Does your aunt have a handbag?" Hitchcock said from the bathroom.

"She has a few. She keeps her favorite slung over the bedpost. It's still there."

"I have it on good authority that her most important things will be in that handbag. Do check it and see."

Jack dumped the contents of the handbag onto the floor. "Ick! Used Kleenex . . . a coin purse."

Some ticket stubs from a place called Peter Pawn's Neverland. Wrinkle cream. Spot cream. Eye cream. Skin firmer. Skin smoother. Face powder. Lipstick. More face cream. A bunch of envelopes held together by a blue paper clip, including a bill from Ransohoff's department store and the hotel bill Jack had given his aunt the day before.

"Hey! Look at this!"

Hitchcock joined Jack as he pulled a fat envelope from the others in the clip. There was no address, but a slip of paper and a stack of cash were sticking out. The paper was plain and white, folded to the same size as the money. A note was written in a big, cursive hand. It read:

We'll agree to $200,000.

Bring it to the noon service at Mission Dolores on Monday.

And let's not play games, or I'll be forced to end this job immediately.

She'll be dead and you'll be blamed.

Yours,

S.

"A classic ransom note," Hitchcock said. He took out the money and handed it to Jack, checking the envelope for anything more. "A rather peculiar place for it, though. Monday. That's today!"

Jack counted the money. "There's ten thousand dollars here."

"As I said, most absurd," Hitchcock said. "If you were a kidnapper asking for two hundred thousand dollars, would you ignore ten thousand dollars right in front of your face?"

"Maybe he didn't see it."

"It's green and crisp. A criminal would smell it before opening the bag. Besides, it was in the envelope with the ransom note. But why they left it remains, by all accounts, mysterious."

"More than mysterious," Jack said. "It makes no sense at all. Still, the ransom note is clear enough and shows a way to solve that mystery."

"Yes? How?"

"Ask them at noon when we drop off the ransom." The idea filled Jack with dread. He had none of his father's courage. He'd rather just stay in his room and draw, but it was clear the only way to go, and to stay out of the Fogbottom orphanage, was forward.

"We?" the director said again.

"If we can find Mission Dolores," Jack replied.

"It's an old church here in the city," Hitchcock said. "As a matter of fact, I intend to view it later today for a potential location shoot."

"So we can go together," Jack said.

Hitchcock's fleshy lips pressed together. "I suppose if the kidnapper planned to do something truly dastardly or dangerous, he'd choose a place where less divine attention might swing his way. But where would this ransom come from?" Hitchcock added.

"You're rich," said Jack.

"Young man, even the wealthy don't keep that kind of money in their pockets. It would take days to get it together, at least."

"We've already got ten thousand," Jack said. He waved the stack of cash in front of his face.

"That would be stealing," the director said.

"Well, you know what they say. 'It takes a thief...'"

"Indeed."

"Now, do you know where I can get the other hundred and ninety thousand in just three hours?"

Hitchcock drifted toward the dresser. "We'll probably both end behind bars, but as long as we are being naughty boys..."

He opened the jewelry box. When he turned back to Jack, he had a large ring on each finger.

"Perhaps these would help us? They must be worth a few quid."

CHAPTER 10

THE RING

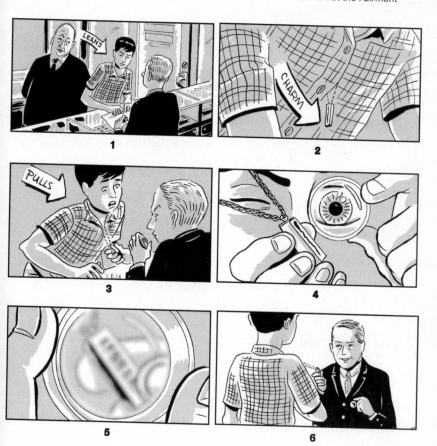

"WORTHLESS, JUST LIKE THE OTHERS," the jeweler said.
"Worthless!" He was a lean, shriveled man. His tongue
darted in and out when he wasn't speaking, as if he
were taking little tastes of the air. With his loupe held
stationary in one eye and the other eye flitting from face

to face between Hitchcock and Jack, he looked positively reptilian.

"But diamonds that big must be worth something," Jack said.

"Diamonds this big are worth a fortune, sonny. A fortune," the jeweler replied. "Even crystal this big is worth something. But this? Paste. Just paste! Don't take a bath in them or they will melt away. Ha!"

"But—"

"You would get better from a box of Cracker Jacks. And have something sweet to munch. Heh!" The jeweler threw the rings onto the counter with a careless toss of his hand.

Behind him, on a round table, blue flames flickered from a one-ring burner. A little pot with an intricately engraved copper bowl the size of a billiard ball sat on top. A long silver handle extended from the bowl. The handle vibrated and the pot rattled as the water inside it boiled over and splashed on the burner with a hiss.

Jack leaned forward to pick up the rings. As he did so, something slipped out between the second and third buttons of his shirt. The jeweler's hand shot forward and formed a fist above Jack's heart. He yanked Jack toward him a little before loosening his grip to reveal the dog tags and silver coffin. The tip of his tongue peeked out through his lips, unmoving for the moment, as he peered at the little silver charm. His loupe swung up and down like some mad optical metronome.

"This may be worth something, boy," the jeweler said. *Hiss*.

"The coffin?" Jack asked. "It's not for sale." He pulled gently on the chain. The silver charm adhered for a moment to the jeweler's palm, then slipped away and disappeared into Jack's shirt.

The pot hissed a third time. The jeweler grabbed the far end of the handle and poured the steaming water into a tiny cup in front of Jack. A caramel-colored froth bubbled up in the cup and spilled a little over the side, leaving a trail of black grounds.

"Coffin? Heh!" said the jeweler. "Still I will give you something for it. You came to sell jewelry, no? You need money, yes? Money?"

"Look, it's not for sale," Jack repeated.

"Bet you don't even know what it is. Do you? Coffin! Huh! Why do you want to hang on to something, when you don't even know what it is?"

"I know what it is."

"Yes? Yes? Well, what then? What?"

Jack held the pendant beneath his shirt. He bit his lower lip and mumbled, "Amum . . . ento mrrr . . ."

"What? A memento? Did you say 'memento'? Of what?"

"A *memento mori*," Jack said. "All right? Have you heard of that? A token of mortality. A reminder of death. Jeez."

"Death. Death? Whose death?"

"My father's, all right?"

"Father's? Heh!" The jeweler peered at Hitchcock through his loupe. Up and down the eyepiece swung, taking in the dark suit, the sunglasses and hat. "Not sure I give him long, but he is not dead yet."

"Good heavens! I'm not the boy's father," Hitchcock said. "I am a director in the cinema."

"Movie pictures?" the man said. "Pfff. Never watch them. Foolish food for fools."

Hitchcock's placid, round-eyed face broke out in lines and squints. "Well!"

"My father died a long time ago," Jack said, "in the Second World War. And the Marine Corps must have made this as a memorial." He fished out the charm. He turned it over to show the words written in capital letters on it. "See. It has a phrase in Latin, like the armed forces use for mottos and stuff. *IPSE DIS*."

"And what does the phrase mean, sonny? Hmm? Tell me." The jeweler removed the top from a little ceramic dish and pinched up the gray-brown powder inside. This he sprinkled from a height above the tiny cup. A dusting of it blew through the air. It smelled a little like cinnamon, but with a lemony tang that bit at Jack's nose.

"I don't know for sure," Jack said. "I looked up the words, though. *'Ipse'* means 'himself.' *'Dis'* is from 'dives.' It means 'having value or worth.' I guess it means, 'He was a worthy man.' He must have been a hero."

"Heh! So you think the marines gave out little silver coffins to heroes? Stars, yes. Crosses. Eagles. Even ladies with flaming swords. But coffins? Hah! No."

Jack's bottomless pit engulfed him. He said nothing.

But Hitchcock did. "You know," he said, "there isn't much to be said in favor of grown men who pick on young boys. Dreadful habit. Perhaps, instead, if you know something about the little charm, you would be so kind as to tell us."

The jeweler looked toward Jack, whose bowed head hid his eyes. The jeweler's eyepiece sagged a little. "No harm meant," he said. "It is just funny to know what little boys think. Hmm? Hmmm? A little coffin! Memento! Ha! Little know-it-all."

"Well, then," Hitchcock said. "What is it?"

"It . . . Hm! Well, it is sort of . . . You could say . . . Heh!"

"Yes?"

"A memento," the jeweler finished.

Jack looked the jeweler square in the eyepiece. "Oh, really."

"Yes. But not a *memento mori*. No! More of a . . . *memento fortuna*. Yes. *Fortuna!*"

"What's that?" Jack said. "You're making it up."

"*Memento fortuna?* Maybe. But perhaps you have heard of the Gold Rush? Hmm? When men of bold heart dug up the West to look for precious minerals? Heh? But do you think gold and silver come out of ground in the shapes of coins and bars?"

"I guess not," Jack said.

"No. Of course not. So! Before the federal government set up a mint here, they gave the authority to assayers to strike coins and bars. Ingots really—gold and silver bars. *Coffin*-shaped bars, yes. Reputable assayers stamped ingots with an alphanumeric"—he said the word slowly, like he was unaccustomed to its shape in his mouth—"a string of letters or numbers—the name of company to assure quality. Maybe numbers to show purity, say, or a serial number, or a dollar value. Most coins and bars they sent east to Philadelphia, to make into federal money. But some circulated here. It was the only time a state legally made its own money." He scooped the air in front of him, as if running his fingers through a pile of coins. Then his hands swung to the side and he shrugged. "Maybe some miner forty-niner kept a bar to remember his lucky strike."

Jack took out the silver ingot and looked at it. "Kind of small for a silver bar, isn't it?"

"Maybe." The jeweler waved his hand vaguely in front of him. "Many sizes were made. Maybe a miner had a little one made, like a souvenir. Heh! Or maybe he had only a little strike. Ha!" He looked closer. "*IPSE DIS*. Maybe this is the name of assayer's company?"

Jack rubbed the little silver bar between his thumb

and forefinger. "*Memento fortuna*. And it's worth a lot?"

"A lot? Who knows? Eventually the U.S. mint came here and made federal money. So assayer coins and ingots are rare. Museums and collectors may pay big for a 'memento' like this, if it is a verified ingot from those days. It must have a proper, authentic stamp though. Heh! Wait here." He ducked around a curtain behind the counter.

Jack stared at the silver coffin—no, *ingot*—for maybe the millionth time. For so long it had been the only connection he had to his father, besides his mother's sparse knowledge. He'd gone to the library in LA. The librarian was helpful, but couldn't identify it. She suggested that it was from the Marines, since it was on the same chain as the dog tags, and that seemed plausible. She had shown him a Latin-English dictionary, so he could translate the words. Would he now finally find out something that would tell him who his father was? Had he been a coin collector? No. Something more adventurous.

"Maybe he was a treasure hunter," Jack said out loud.

"Who?" asked Hitchcock.

"My father. He died before I was born. I don't know

much about him. I don't even know what he looked like. Except Mom said I look just like him." *Never knew him, but miss him just the same. Sort of. Does the paper miss the erased line?* Jack wondered what scores and smears of his father's life would impress themselves upon him.

"I see," said the director, "and you think perhaps he was a treasure hunter because this man believes this charm is some sort of historic artifact?"

Jack looked again at the string of letters on the charm. "Maybe if he had lived, we would have gone caving in an old gold mine together and found a new vein that everyone had overlooked and we'd be rich." A wistful look played across Jack's face. "I wish all the time I could speak to him." He looked at Hitchcock. "Have you ever been caving?"

"I haven't the proper shape," Hitchcock replied.

"We should go. You'd like it, I think," Jack said.

Hitchcock stood a little straighter and buttoned his jacket. "If my schedule allowed such frivolity, it is possible I would."

"Oh," Jack said, looking down, "right."

The jeweler came back, leafing through a little book. "All assayer marks are here. I . . . IP . . . IPE . . . IS—No.

Nothing. Not here. No assayer left this mark." He bent over and looked at the silver ingot again through the loupe. "A few dollars for the silver. Otherwise—worthless."

Jack closed his hand around it. "No, it isn't."

"Worthless," the jeweler repeated. "Like the rings. Leave now. Take this worthless junk with you. Passing off ragweed as roses. Heh!" He took a sip of his coffee. "Hurp." He burned his tongue.

"Pity," Hitchcock said. "Come, Jack, let's leave this man to his work. I'm sure he has many brass rings to gold-plate."

Hitchcock collected Aunt Edith's rings. As they exited the shop, a limousine pulled up. The chauffeur got out and opened the car door for a well-dressed elderly gentleman with a pretty young woman on his arm. Hitchcock glanced back at the jeweler. Then he flipped the sign on the glass door to CLOSED. He pulled the handkerchief from his pocket and began coughing into it. When the old man reached the door, Hitchcock held out his hands, pointing to the sign.

"So early? But it isn't closing time yet," the rich man said.

"Sorry—aherm ahrharharharh," Hitchcock sputtered.

"Touch of the flu. Ah—Ahchooo!" He sneezed on the old man, who covered his face with his hat and pushed the young woman back into the limo.

Hitchcock smiled and peered in at the unwitting jeweler. "Poor bloke," he said. "Looks as if he just lost a major sale."

CHAPTER 11

REBECCA

"LOOK. WE HAVEN'T GOT TIME FOR GOOFING," Jack said. The limousine squeezed up the narrow alley of Maiden Lane. Jack followed on foot, searching for another jeweler.

"On the contrary," Hitchcock replied, striding to

keep up. "There's always time for a practical joke."

"We have a deadline," Jack said. The shadows of small trees sprouting from the sidewalk crowded up to their trunks. Noon was fast approaching.

"Actually, I have several deadlines, ones that I am currently postponing to be here." The director's voice was diamond hard, much as Aunt Edith's rings were not.

"But this is important," Jack said. He crossed over Grant Avenue, a main thoroughfare. Cars coughed out exhaust as they dodged delivery vans. Truck drivers unloaded boxes large and small.

"As is my work." They continued down the relatively quiet alleyway, past the many small shops of luxury goods.

"Adults always talk about work. But this is my life. My life is more important than your work. My life isn't supposed to be an orphan." Anger scrambled Jack's words. "Adults aren't supposed to leave," he ended miserably.

"Yes. Well . . ." Hitchcock trailed off. He looked down at the sidewalk. So did Jack. The concrete was fractured and pitted. From habit, Jack avoided stepping on the cracks. He'd never wanted to break his mother's back. It seemed pointless now, but he noticed Hitchcock did the same thing. The silence stretched as the pair trooped past the storefronts. Then Hitchcock said, "I don't think another jeweler will help. That's the third one who said these rings are worthless."

"I don't understand how that could be," Jack said. "I mean, what's a lady who carries around ten thousand dollars in her purse doing with fake jewelry?"

"Perhaps the money is fake too? I myself had a distant aunt who liked to run off ten-shilling notes on a little press in the potting shed. Strictly butter and egg money, of course."

Jack stopped, tilted his head, and closed one eye. "Is that true?" he asked.

"True enough for the movies," Hitchcock answered.

Jack shrugged. He pulled a hundred-dollar bill from his pocket. If he had ever seen one before, he might have pulled up its image in his mind for comparison. But he hadn't. His artist eyes, however, found nothing suspicious in the etched loops and whorls of the greenback he held. "It looks real enough."

"Young man, I hope you aren't carrying around the whole wad. Not in this neighborhood."

Jack looked around. They had come to the end of

Maiden Lane, where its trickle of commerce flowed from the headwaters of a vast public space surrounded by department stores, hotels, and specialty boutiques.

"Union Square?" Jack said. "But this place is perfectly safe. It's full of rich people."

"Well, yes. And how do you think they got that way? Thieves, murderers, and Mafia dons are likely nesting nearby."

"Actually I think the police commissioner and some city politicians live around here."

"Criminals of a worse kind!" said Hitchcock, taking the bill from Jack. He held it up to the sun. He rubbed it between his fingers. "Yes. Authentic beyond question. Now put this away safe."

Women in hats and gloves with shopping bags slung over their arms bustled past. Across the square a display of old-time firefighting equipment was being assembled, part of the Festival of Progress earthquake celebration.

Jack stuffed the bill back into his pocket. He was now extra conscious of the lump the money made there. "I hope we don't get robbed."

"Despite my warning, young man, the square is full of good people at this time of day." Hitchcock sat down on a bench to rest. "But I wouldn't walk it in the wee hours of the night. Imagine how that would be." Jack did. He would like to draw it that way, just the solid reliable stones and monuments, empty of the flowing, unstable crowds of people. Hitchcock stretched his arms out in front of him, making a rectangle with his hands, and panned across the square. People glanced in his direction but kept walking in a sophisticated urban sort of way, until his arms lined up with a school group on a field trip—a pack of young girls in plaid skirts who giggled and pointed.

"You have a fan club," said Jack, joining the director on the bench.

"One of the dangers of being a public figure," Hitchcock said, still panning with his hands. "A single man walks across the abandoned square. A lonely image, made more so because one doesn't expect such a place to be empty."

"Mr. Hitchcock, please. We need to find a way to get the ransom money."

"Do we?"

"What? Yes!" Had he said "we" with just a little too much emphasis? As if only Jack needed the money?

"Look, didn't you read the ransom note?"

"Young man, there are certain principles of film-making that I have found translate acceptably well to life. One of them is best summed up by saying 'If the audience wants what it sees, it will see what it wants.'"

"Huh?" Jack stared at the director. Behind him the fan club girls were coming closer. They'd circled around for a rear attack.

"In the cinema an audience can be manipulated, through camera angles, through story sequencing, through counterpoint and the creation of suspense. And once you have manipulated the audience's emotion, you can make them see what you wish them to. And we do have an audience—an audience of one."

"The kidnapper!"

"Yes. And we have something that he wants, and wants badly." Hitchcock leaned back on the bench, turning his face to the sun overhead.

"The money. But we don't actually have it."

"No, but he wants it. He is expecting it. When an audience is expecting something you needn't give it all to them. Just show them a little, and their imagination will do the rest."

Jack considered this. "So we can make ten thousand dollars look like two hundred thousand?"

"With a little planning and a little luck. And we have a lucky charm, after all."

"I don't think the jeweler was right about that," Jack said.

"Why?"

Jack unbuttoned the top of his shirt and pulled out the silver charm. Behind him he heard the girls.

"You talk to him."

"No, you."

Jack traced the blocky letters of the Latin phrase with his finger. *"Ipse Dis,"* he said. "My father may have been a worthy man, but he certainly wasn't lucky."

"Oh?" Hitchcock glanced behind him at the girls. They were closer now.

"If it wasn't awarded after he died, he must have been wearing this on his last mission," Jack said. "He was in the Pacific, on a little island where the fighting was fierce. The War Department told my mother he saved seven of his fellow soldiers by disguising himself as Japanese and releasing them from a makeshift prison behind enemy lines."

"Well, that sounds very lucky indeed," Hitchcock remarked.

"They got back to the part of the island held by Allied forces sooner than they expected," Jack continued. "They were challenged, but before his fellow soldiers could speak up for him, he was shot by a guard at the Allied camp. A charm with even a little luck would have helped that guard see through his disguise, don't you think?"

Hitchcock was silent for a moment. "I'm sorry," he said. "Your father was very brave."

"I wish I were," Jack said.

"You don't think you are?" asked the director.

"I'm scared a lot," said Jack

"It's a scary world," said Hitchcock. "If it weren't, I'd be out of a job."

They both started when someone behind them squealed "Go!" Two of the girls were pushing a third forward.

"Perhaps we should follow that advice before she arrives," Hitchcock said. He waved down a taxi across the street. "Fans can cause quite a delay."

The girl ran up to the bench and stood before Hitchcock. But she faced Jack. "Hi," she said.

"Hi," Jack replied.

"My friend Becky thinks you're cute."

"Uh . . ." Jack froze. He didn't know what to say or do.

"What school do you go to?" the girl asked.

"Our Lady of the Clean Escape," Hitchcock answered for Jack, "and we really must get him back." He dragged Jack into the waiting cab. "Well, that was a close thing."

Jack looked back through the cab window. He wondered which one was Becky.

"Mission Dolores," Hitchcock said to the cabbie. He smiled at Jack. "We must check out the scene of the crime, before we commit it."

CHAPTER 12

SECRET AGENT

THE STOP AT MISSION DOLORES was quick. It was nearly noon, and they had preparations to make. Back at the hotel Hitchcock picked up a stack of phone messages at the desk.

"From the studio," he said, "asking if I have finished

reviewing the location sites for the movie I will soon be filming here. I suppose I shall be able to tell them I have seen the mission, if only briefly."

"You'll see it again at noon," Jack said. "Right?"

Hitchcock walked his fingers through the pile of messages and sighed. "Yes. I suppose." He stuffed them into his pocket.

Once in the director's suite, preparations began immediately. The director asked Jack to fetch a duffel bag or small satchel. Jack went to his aunt's room and returned with a pink makeup case. "It's all I could find."

Hitchcock sat at the desk and produced a large pad of paper and a pencil. "In the cinema," he said, "we have a most important tool, known as the storyboard."

He began by drawing large rectangles, one after the other, on the blank page. "The storyboard is a series of pictures meant to show the action as it will appear on-screen in the finished movie. It indicates the objects seen on-screen as well as the camera angles and movement."

"It looks like a comic strip," Jack said, coming to stand behind the director.

"Yes. It does resemble one. Both tell a story by using

pictures in a sequence. But the storyboard is more utilitarian, the art less developed. And the frame is always the same size, and in direct proportion to the frame of the film. Now we must see as the camera sees." Hitchcock sketched quickly, casting lines on the paper with efficient ease. Soon a view of the Mission Basilica pews, as seen from the main entrance, took shape beneath the master's hand. "We will sit in the last pew but one, so he will see us right away. He will sit behind you to hide his face and be in control." In the first picture a closed makeup bag rested on the seat between a boyish figure and a heavyset man. In the next panel the bag was partially opened, with stacks of money showing.

"Hmmm," the director muttered. "There's a problem if he enters the pew from the right while standing. He might see more than we'd like."

"You forgot a column," Jack said. He didn't like to correct the director, but Jack could see every detail of the church in his mind. Hitchcock had forgotten things.

Hitchcock regarded Jack with arched eyebrows. He stood and held out the pencil.

Jack took it. It felt smooth and cool in his hand. He closed his eyes and ran a thumb along the debossed letters on the pencil. He pressed the spot where the smooth yellow paint had been sharpened away and the rough, exposed wood angled toward the lead. As always, the intersections of arcs and cords appeared in his mind, and grew into the scene he was remembering.

Jack opened his eyes. He sat down and drew. There was that thrilling moment when pencil caught paper and dragging it across was like striking a match. And like fire the pencil burned the paper with black lines and curves. Small bits of lead popped and leapt behind as it tracked along with a satisfying *scritch*.

"There was a column outside the row of pews," Jack said. "He can't enter from the right. The column won't give him enough room to pass." If Hitchcock's lines were quick and efficient, Jack's were draftsman-like, fast and detailed. Soon the entire image in his mind was transferred to the paper.

Hitchcock stood, openmouthed, behind him. He retrieved a magnifying glass and a stiff paper from a stack on the desk. He held it up to the drawing.

"This is a photographic contact sheet from the advance location scout," he said. There were several small photos on the paper. He handed the glass to Jack and guided it to the sheet so a particular image filled the circular lens. The angle was slightly different, but Jack's picture and the photo were otherwise an exact match, down to the martyred saints on the wall.

"Remarkable," said Hitchcock. "Draw a view from the confessionals, looking toward the main altar."

Jack closed his eyes again. He rolled the pencil between his fingers and inhaled the oily scent of the pencil lead. He drew the view the director asked for, and another of Hitchcock's photos mirrored his drawing.

"And you drew this from memory?" the director asked. "But we were only there a brief time."

Jack shrugged his shoulders. "I can draw anything I see."

"But we never looked at the altar from the confessionals," Hitchcock said.

"But we looked at the confessionals from the altar," Jack said. "You just rotate things around in space."

"Remarkable," Hitchcock said again. He thumbed the edge of the pad and tilted his head this way and that in appraisal. "To be able to draw anything you see is quite a skill."

"Mr. Hitchcock, if we try this, what happens when

the kidnapper counts the money? Won't that be the end of Aunt Edith?"

"The kidnapper must not lay his hands on the money until we have your aunt by our side," said Hitchcock. "Once we have her, he can have the money. By then your aunt will be safe and we can go to the police. But until then he mustn't touch it. That's why you must be very brave and strong, young man."

"Then maybe it would be better if I could draw things I haven't ever seen," said Jack.

The director gave Jack a perplexed look. "I don't understand."

Jack sighed. He pulled his sketchbook out of his pocket and folded it to the first page, Mom's description of Dad. "'Black hair. Brown eyes,'" Hitchcock read.

"See, I've been trying for years to draw a picture of my father. But I can't."

"Because you've never seen him?" Hitchcock asked.

"Right."

"What's that got to do with—"

"If I can't capture an image of my father, how can I ever hope to capture some of his courage?"

A little series of hills and valleys popped up in the

flesh between the director's brows. "You've got that backward," he said. "Spirit, emotion, character—these things flow from the artist into his work. Not the other way around. Our work is a manifestation of things found inside us."

"Then if I can't draw my brave father," said Jack, "it must mean I have no courage inside."

"That's not what I said."

"Shouldn't we keep planning?" Jack asked. He didn't want to talk about this anymore.

"Yes. Yes, of course," Hitchcock said. "Now, we cannot control the movement of our kidnapper, but we can assume he will come through one of the doors. . . ." Hitchcock went over what he felt were the most likely scenarios, always emphasizing, "We must control what our audience of one sees."

"But what about when he sees you?" Jack asked. "You aren't exactly inconspicuous. A famous director at the service might cause a stir."

Hitchcock rubbed his chin. "Yes, so we shall take such precautions as we deem necessary to prevent that." He went into his bedroom. When he came out he was wearing a beret, a false goatee, and sunglasses. He'd traded his navy-blue suit for a black turtleneck and slacks. With the point of black made by the beret above the dark expanse of his roundish body, he looked more than anything else like a walking, well-padded semicolon.

"Mr. Hitchcock?"

"Young man, you'll give away my disguise. Which would be a pity after all the work the costumer put into it for the introductory spot I'm to film for my television show."

"Then what should I call you?" Jack asked.

"Please call me Mr. Green—Shamley Green."

"Ummm . . . are you a Frenchman?"

"My dear boy"—Hitchcock peered at Jack from above his sunglasses—"don't you recognize a poet when you see one?"

"You don't look much like a poet," Jack said.

The director struck a pose, his hands extended dramatically before him, pushing as if against an invisible wall. He began to recite, "'I saw the best mimes of my generation destroyed by madness,' hysterical . . . um . . . hysterical and mad . . . Well . . . you get the idea. I shan't be reciting poetry at the mission, in any case."

"You still sort of look like you, though," Jack said.

"Nonsense," said the director. "I have transformed myself completely."

"Maybe we should test it out," Jack suggested, "in the lobby on the way."

Hitchcock lowered his hand. "Very well."

In the elevator on the way down, Shen was unfazed by Hitchcock's getup.

"Going out, Mr. Hitchcock?" Shen asked.

"Going down," the director growled.

As they walked across the lobby, Jack said, "Shen knew who you were."

"Well, she knows my room number. She must have seen me come out of the door," Hitchcock said. "No one else will recognize me."

"We better make sure," Jack said. He pulled Hitchcock through the door to Blum's.

"Hey there, sugar," Opal called from behind the counter. "More chocolates for your aunt? Care to share a sample?"

"No thanks, Opal," Jack said. "I just stopped by on my way out to say hi."

Opal took a chocolate from the little pile on a pink plate in the case. "You don't mind if I . . ."

"Oh, no. Go ahead," Jack said.

Opal looked past Jack at Hitchcock. "Who's your friend?" she said, straightening her uniform.

"This is Mr. Shamley Green," Jack said. "Mr. Green—Opal."

"How do you do," said Opal. She held out her hand.

"I'm cookin', baby," Hitchcock replied. He kissed her hand. "You?"

"Oh . . . uh . . . charmed, I'm sure," said Opal. She looked closely at the director, up and down. Jack felt sure she was about to recognize him. Opal reached up to adjust her glasses, then realized she still had the chocolate in her hand.

"Oh . . . silly me," she said. She held out the little confection to Hitchcock. "Do you know what these are called, Mr. Green?"

"I'm afraid I don't— I mean, 'fraid not, baby," answered Hitchcock.

"This here is a Cowgirl Kiss," she said. "Can I interest you in one?"

"No thanks, Dolly . . ."

"You can call me Opal." She took a bite of the chocolate. "It's very sweet. Are you sure you wouldn't like one?"

"Sorry, Dolly. Gotta cut out. Got a poetry bit to do," said Hitchcock.

"You're a poet?" said Opal. "I love poetry. It's a sort of candy with words. And as they say, lovers are given to poetry." She looked down and ran her finger along the edge of the countertop.

"I dig," said Hitchcock, "but poems can be bitter-sweet, see? Now we gotta make the scene. My public's chompin' to hear my latest work."

"Oh," said Opal. "Well, good luck with your reading."

As they walked out the door, Hitchcock turned to Jack.

"You see. She had no idea who I was."

"Or what," Jack said. "Let's go."

CHAPTER 13

THE WRONG MAN

ON A BROAD AVENUE BENEATH THE HILLS of the city, the twin towers of Mission Dolores Basilica, like the arms of a felon at the end of a policeman's gun, reached for the sky. The Old Mission squatted like an accomplice beside it. The white buildings were bookends of the city's history. The Old Mission, built before the city itself, was simple, handmade, and sparsely adorned. The Basilica, built after the city's decades of treasure and tragedy, was as soaring and opulent as a wedding cake.

Jack and Hitchcock passed under the scant shade of a palm tree that grew in the grassy divider of the boulevard. They were early, as Hitchcock had insisted that they needed to set the scene before the kidnapper arrived. Jack nervously wrung the handle of the makeup bag, his grip alternating between tight and stranglehold.

A line of cars pulled up, led by a grim black hearse. The noon service was apparently a funeral. Six linebacker-size men approached the rear of the hearse and opened the back door. Their necks were as thick as Jack's waist. They pulled out a coffin of burnished mahogany and balanced it on the shelf of their shoulders, three men on each side. They proceeded up the white steps, followed by the mourners in black, heads bobbing over their rosaries—like a murder of crows pecking their way up a corn trail.

"Quickly!" Hitchcock whispered. "We must get the proper pew."

They mounted the stairs, rushing past the mourners.

The pallbearers tossed them a vicious look when they overtook the casket.

"Maybe we should fall back a bit," Jack said.

They did but remained at the front of the line. They claimed their chosen pew at the rear of the church as mourners filed past and settled up front. The bereaved nearly filled the church.

"The deceased must have been quite popular," Jack said.

"He is now, in any case," Hitchcock answered. "A corpse is an easygoing friend."

"How will we know which one is the kidnapper?" Jack whispered to Hitchcock.

"I believe he will find us," was Hitchcock's reply.

"Perhaps he already has," a cultured voice behind Jack said. "Please open the bag."

A hand grasped Jack's shoulder. It felt small, like a child's, but the strength in the grip was all adult. A sharp leathery smell told Jack the man was wearing gloves. The casual familiarity and creepy warmth of the touch made Jack shiver.

He glanced over his shoulder. The man behind him dressed well. He was small and looked vaguely familiar.

Except for his size, he was what Jack's mom used to call a "suave operator." His face offered a friendly, warm smile. His hair was a warm auburn, graying at the temples. He sported an impeccably trimmed pencil-thin mustache. Where had Jack seen him before?

"Please don't make me repeat myself," The Suave Man said, "as I should find that tiresome in the extreme and think you rather dull. You don't look like a dull boy. Eyes ahead. Do as I said." He was very calm and cool.

Hitchcock seemed on the verge of saying something, but Jack beat him to it. "Is she safe?" he asked, pulling the bag closer to his side.

"She's under wraps as agreed, and safe enough. But I can't finish the job until you give me the money. I have expenses, you know."

Expenses? Jack didn't understand.

"Show the man what's in the bag, Jack," Hitchcock said. "He seems rather eager."

Jack set the bag down in the exact spot indicated by the storyboard. The brass clasps clacked against the side of the case when sprung. The sound echoed off the vaulted ceiling. The priest missed a word, and a few mourners turned annoyed faces toward Jack. There was a sudden spike of tension in the church, but then the priest resumed speaking, and the natural reluctance of people to cause a scene in a sacred space smoothed everything back to normal.

Jack carefully opened the case lid. He knew The Suave Man was seeing exactly what he wanted—a case full of money.

"Very well," the man said. "I'll go ahead and take that now."

The Suave Man reached out for the bag with gloved hands, but Jack pressed his palms against the money inside and slid the bag over next to his hip. He feared the money would stick to his sweaty hands, revealing the stacks of newspaper underneath, but he swallowed and plunged forward with the plan.

"Look, I need to see my aunt first," Jack said.

Just then the great pipe organ began to play the opening bars of "Amazing Grace." The people in the pews up front reached for their hymnbooks.

"Surely she's authorized payment, or you two wouldn't be here," The Suave Man said.

This wasn't going at all how Jack had hoped. Remembering the director's admonition that the money mustn't change hands until they had his aunt, Jack took the only step he could think of. He closed the case and quietly snapped shut the clasps.

For the first time anger wove through The Suave Man's voice. "If you don't give me what's coming to me, I'm afraid things may get rough. I could just take that case from you. I am bigger than you, you know."

"Barely," Hitchcock said, "and as you can see, I am bigger than you."

The cool returned to The Suave Man's voice. "And if you'll be so kind as to look toward the confessional on your left, you'll see something small that is bigger than all three of us."

Jack hadn't noticed in the gloom of the church that the confessional door was open. A little light above it glowed, indicating that a penitent sat inside. Now, at a signal from the man, a thin steel cylinder crept forward from the shadows inside.

"That cylinder is a silencer and is attached at the other end to a high-powered pistol, which in turn is attached to the hand of a very dear friend, who is, I assure you, a crack shot. In just a moment she'll aim the pistol directly at your heart. Please believe me when I say that she will be able to shoot, and no one will hear a thing, especially with that lovely hymn playing."

"Now see here," Hitchcock began loudly. People in front turned and scowled.

"Quiet," the man hissed, "or this boy won't live to taste his first kiss."

Hitchcock gave a little wave to those who turned to look. "Sorry," he mouthed.

"Now," The Suave Man whispered, regaining his composure, "let's all behave normally. Sing along to the lovely hymn. It's my friend's favorite. But if you don't hand over the bag by the last note, her trigger finger might just slip."

Am I already dead? Jack thought. Why didn't he feel his heart pounding? He knew it was, but all he felt was a wet clay of fear molding onto his bones.

The Suave Man had trumped them. Their audience of one was an audience of two. Jack tried to think, but the man had said to sing. Already Hitchcock had taken up the verse. But singing wouldn't help them escape. Jack listened to the song. "Amazing Grace." Jack's mother loved this hymn too. But he and Schultzie had made up another version during a caving trip. Mom had laughed but told him never to sing it in public. But maybe she wouldn't mind in this case. Jack sang the hymn, just as The Suave Man demanded, but with a slight change:

> *"When I eat beans*
>
> *It always seems*
>
> *An odor fills the room.*
>
> *The gasps of those*
>
> *Who hold their nose*
>
> *Tells me it ain't perfume."*

Immediately the people in front of Jack twisted around to stare at him. Those closest said "Shhhh" or "Quiet!" The pallbearers turned back to see what the trouble was. One pointed at Jack. *Good,* Jack thought. *Let's see if I can get the whole church staring at me.* The Suave Man touched the bag at Jack's side. Jack pulled it up close to his chest and wrapped his arms around it. He clung to it like a life jacket, though its paper filling seemed insubstantial when he thought about the pistol in the confessional now taking aim. *At least if I get shot,* he thought, *people will see this man trying to pull a makeup case from a dead boy's arms. There will be witnesses.*

The man wouldn't want that. Jack's mouth was dry. He was trying to work up some spit so he could sing a second verse, when a booming English baritone beside him sang out:

> *"My teacher's face*
> *Is a disgrace,*
> *As wide as a rugby ball.*
> *But that's ho-hum*
> *Compared to her bum,*
> *Which spreads from wall to wall."*

Jack owl-eyed Hitchcock. He had never heard that version before, but he liked it a lot, particularly because of the stir it was causing in the pews near the front. The pistol was level now and emerged inch by inch from the darkness. Jack gripped the bag more tightly with his right hand, while his left crept over to clutch Hitchcock's wrist. The feel of the rough wool turtleneck calmed him a bit. He breathed deeply.

"My teacher's face is a disgrace . . . ," Jack sang with Hitchcock, as loud as he could.

The reflection of votive candles flickered off thick

round glasses in the confessional as the pistol sight lined up with them. Jack squeezed Hitchcock's arm, singing all the while. The makeup case slipped as he shifted his grip. A hot sizzle started in his stomach and threatened to push past his chest and erupt from his mouth. He wondered if he'd see his mom, or meet his dad—a family together at last.

Jacked gazed into the round, black hole of the pistol's barrel, perfectly circular, perfectly aligned.

And then he couldn't see anything at all, except for the chests of the six pallbearers who surrounded him.

"I'm afraid we'll need to ask you two gentlemen to leave," the biggest pallbearer said.

"Why?" Jack asked. He never thought he'd be glad to have six huge men getting ready to toss him out of a church.

"Your singing. Show some respect."

"But I thought singing was allowed in church. My mom always said, 'He who sings prays twice.' I figure with as loud as I was singing, I was praying enough for ten people."

The pallbearer looked at Hitchcock and said, "You just going to let your son mouth off like that? What kind of father are you?"

"I am a poet, sir," said Hitchcock, "and I would never discourage my son from expressing himself!"

Son? Jack thought. No man had ever claimed him as such. Jack pressed the charm around his neck through the shirt fabric. He smiled at the director.

"You two creeps are interrupting the service. Now go before I throw you out." The man looked big enough to carry out the threat, which was exactly what Jack wanted him to do. But an escort was what they needed, not a semipolite request to leave.

"But don't you want to hear the verse about my teacher's underpants?" Jack said.

"That's it!" The pallbearer grabbed Jack like he was a football and stomped toward the door. Two more of them took Hitchcock by his arms, and the others surrounded them. The Suave Man was pushed out of the huddle of men, who blocked his every attempt to reach Jack.

Curbside, muscled arms hailed a cab, tossed Jack and his bag into the backseat, and then piled Hitchcock on top of him.

"Here's two bits. Take these clowns as far away as you can on that," one of the pallbearers told the cabbie. He slammed the door and watched the cab with crossed arms, his five buddies beside him. The Suave Man's fancy shoes peeped out from behind the wall of pallbearers, but not a hair of his head was visible.

"Okay. Where to?" the cabbie asked Hitchcock.

The line of pallbearers formed a wall beside the cab. The Suave Man tried to push his way between them.

"In the cinema," Hitchcock said, "our primary function is to create an emotion, and our second job is to sustain that emotion. We've awakened his greed. Now we must nail it in place."

Hitchcock caught The Suave Man's eye and called loudly out the open window, "Wells Fargo Bank. We have something we urgently need to deposit in their safe. And step on it."

The cabbie eyed them suspiciously in the rearview mirror. "You got enough money? It's ten cents a mile. Two bits won't cover it."

Jack opened the case he still clung to and pulled out a bill. "Will a hundred dollars do?" he called as loudly as Hitchcock.

The cab tore forward as The Suave Man pushed past the pallbearers and reached for the door.

"Wells Fargo," the cabbie said. "Steppin' on it!"

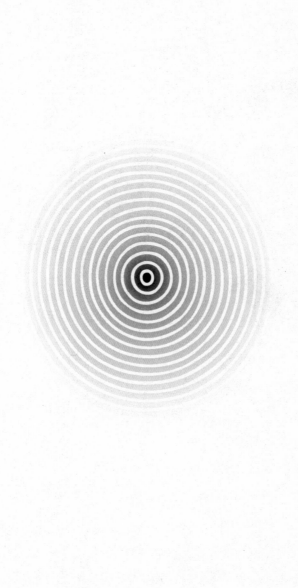

CHAPTER 14

THE MAN WHO KNEW TOO MUCH

"WELL, OUR ESCAPE WAS BRILLIANTLY PLAYED,"
Hitchcock said.

Jack bounded through the door and into the lobby of the Fairmont. He wanted to jump over the furniture and kiss the red-and-black carpet. He wanted to hug the marbled columns. Instead he hugged Hitchcock. There's nothing like a brush with death to sharpen up the colors of life, and Jack had just had a gun pointed at his heart. A heart he could now feel pounding in his chest, and he was grateful for every beat. He plopped into a chair, tossing the empty makeup case beside him.

"I liked your version of the song. Maybe you can teach me more someday," Jack said.

"I made it up on the spot," Hitchcock replied. He too took a chair, though in contrast to Jack, he seemed momentarily calm—like a Buddha in a bubble bath—his hands linked upon his belly. But a ghost of worry danced around his brow.

Jack bounced in his chair. "Did you see his expression when the cab drove away? And the way he was completely fooled by the money?"

Hitchcock frowned. "My dear boy, the scene was brilliant but not flawlessly executed."

"Huh?"

"Our flight was completely ad-libbed. Thank goodness you were so clever when things escaped our control. It was touch and go . . ." Hitchcock closed his eyes, though his brow remained furrowed. For the first time

Jack noticed the little beads of sweat that had gathered on his bald head.

"Touch and go . . . ," Hitchcock repeated.

"Well . . . I'm glad we got away from that creep," Jack said, "but we still don't have my aunt."

Hitchcock opened his eyes. "True. But the kidnapper now believes that you have the money. He'll be more eager than ever to get his hands on it. When he contacts you again, and it is without question that he will, you will be in a better bargaining position to get your aunt back."

"What did he mean about expenses?" Jack asked. "He said he had expenses to pay."

Hitchcock's plump lips pressed into a line. "I suppose kidnapping is a business, and the conscientious kidnapper must spend some time on his balance sheets."

"But he said Aunt Edith had authorized payment of the ransom," Jack added.

"Well, she would do, wouldn't she?"

"He just wasn't what I expected," said Jack. He linked his hands on his stomach in imitation of the director and leaned back in the chair. "He didn't look desperate for money. His clothes were nice."

"He must be the guilty party. Don't forget that he showed up with an armed accomplice and threatened to have you shot if he didn't get the ransom! An innocent man doesn't generally come to church to threaten or extort the congregants," Hitchcock said. He gave Jack a little wink. "Except, of course, if he's the minister."

At the mention of the accomplice, Jack recalled the shadowy figure in the confessional. Those round glasses with the fiery reflections, like demon eyes. And that suave little man so gleeful in the pew behind him. Jack suddenly remembered where he'd seen him before.

"They were here!" His eyes darted around the busy lobby. "I remember seeing the kidnapper and his accomplice yesterday, when we were in the Tonga Room."

"I don't recall seeing the little man." Hitchcock didn't move.

"No. They came in after us. They sat down behind you." Jack jumped from his seat. "They might be here now." The columns, so lately the objects of possible embrace, now felt menacing, a potential hiding place for assassins in unholy horn-rims. The shadows around him grew, until the entire lobby seemed cave-dark.

Hitchcock looked around the vast lobby, the alarm

clear on his face. "We need to talk," he said. "Perhaps we should return to the privacy of my suite."

When they reached their floor, Hitchcock headed for his rooms, but Jack pulled him toward Aunt Edith's suite. "We better go in here, in case the kidnapper calls."

Hitchcock hesitated. "Yes . . . perhaps it is best." He pulled uncomfortably at his turtleneck collar. "I'll just change out of this costume and nip over."

"Can you bring back that big pad of paper?" Jack asked.

When Hitchcock was comfortably encased in his usual dark blue suit and they had settled in his aunt's room, Jack took the pad. He closed his eyes, pressed his thumb into the pencil, and let a picture flow into his mind. Then he opened his eyes and drew. Unlike the simple lines for the storyboard, this would be a fully fleshed-out portrait.

While he sketched, he asked the director, "So, what do we do now?"

Hitchcock turned away from Jack. Behind his back his left hand cradled his right, which nervously fidgeted until Hitchcock curled it into a fist. "After our close call at the mission, there is really only one course of action left. I must insist that—" He stopped. His hand began its fidgeting again.

"Mr. Hitchcock," Jack whispered. Then his stomach let out an enormous growl.

"There is only one thing to do." Hitchcock turned to Jack with a relieved smile on his face. "Order room service."

As Hitchcock ate his meal of steak and salad, Jack rolled a sauce-covered meatball back and forth on his plate. Despite his growling stomach, he didn't feel like eating. Something was wrong with Mr. Hitchcock. He was pre-occupied. He'd ordered a double brandy with lunch (and a malted milk for Jack). Every time Jack had asked what their next move was, he had merely replied, "lunch" or "dessert" or something equally evasive. Jack figured it was time to try again. He picked up the sketchpad and showed Hitchcock the drawing.

It was two mug shots, with profiles, of the kidnapper and his accomplice.

"I think we should go back to the mission and see if anyone recognizes these two," he said.

Hitchcock sighed. He rested the blunt ends of his knife and fork on the table. "I, too, have been thinking about what must be done."

"Great!" said Jack.

"My dear boy," Hitchcock began, "I think it is time that we revisit the police."

"What? No!"

"Jack, I thought we could fool the kidnapper."

"We did."

"But as you noted, we didn't get your aunt back," Hitchcock said.

"We will."

"But we don't know that. In the cinema the director is God. He knows all. But this is a script that hasn't been written, the cast of kidnappers not fully revealed. . . ."

"We can figure it out together," Jack replied.

"The police are better equipped."

"Mr. Hitchcock, if the police come, that's it for me. The kidnappers will know. They'll kill her. And I'll be . . . sent to an orphanage."

"Would you rather end up dead?"

"Dead?"

"Barely an hour ago there was a silenced pistol

pointed at your chest," Hitchcock said. He put his knife and fork down. "It was not a prop. And this is not a movie. I now know there are things here beyond the control of even the greatest director."

The bottomless pit reared up inside Jack. He heard what Hitchcock was saying, but it dropped down inside him, and no sound came back out. Who was he trying to kid? He was a full orphan now. He had been for weeks. Maybe he was even already a ward of the state. Maybe he became one the moment his mother drove off that cliff. He should just accept it. But that wasn't what he wanted to do.

"Don't leave me," he said.

"My dear boy, it's what's best for you. You'll be safe." He picked up the phone and dialed the hotel operator. "Please connect me to—"

A knock at the door startled them both.

"Mrs. Smith?" a voice called.

Jack approached the door and stood on tiptoe to peer out the peephole. "Oh my gosh! It's the social worker from the police station."

Hitchcock quietly put the phone back in its cradle. "Perhaps, as I said, it is for the best," he said.

"No!" Jack's eyes fell on the door to Aunt Edith's bedroom. "Quick. Hide!" He shoved the mug shots of the kidnappers into the director's hands.

"Mrs. Smith? Please don't make me come back with the police."

Jack pulled Hitchcock toward his aunt's room. "She said you're a menace. If she sees you, she'll take me away. Hide!"

"Jack. We mustn't."

"Please! She can't see you, and she can't know that Aunt Edith is missing. Please just wait until she's gone and we can talk more. Please." He shut the bedroom door and hurried to the suite's entrance.

CHAPTER 15

WOMAN TO WOMAN

ALICE TRAPP PUSHED INTO THE ROOM with a bureaucrat's ease. She cradled her clipboard in her arms. The pen on its chain swung now before her like the pendulum of doom. She wore the same suit she had the previous day, or perhaps an identical one.

"Oh, hello, little boy," she said to Jack. She waved the clipboard. "I'm afraid I was unable to fill out the report on your visit to the police station last night, since I never spoke to your parent or legal guardian."

"My aunt Edith is unavailable at the moment," Jack said.

"This is the aunt who was kidnapped?" Alice asked. She didn't look at Jack as she spoke, instead surveying the room, making marks on her clipboard.

"That was just a story. For publicity." Jack widened his eyes to make them as large and innocent as he could. "I got pancakes."

"I see," said Alice, "and did your aunt know you were working for the director? Had she signed a consent form?"

"Ummm . . ."

Alice walked around the room as she spoke, checking things off on her clipboard.

She opened the window. Check.

She ruffled the sheets folded at the base of the sofa. Check.

"Shouldn't you be in school?" she asked.

Jack had a ready answer to that. "I arrived too late to

enroll. I'm to go to summer school to make up the work I missed."

Check.

Then she came to the room service cart.

And the brandy glass.

She dipped her pen into the remaining liquid, then tapped it on the rim. The sound rang through the suite like an out-of-tune piano. She held the pen up and stared at it, as if reading a thermometer. She sniffed the tip.

"Hmph." She flipped through her papers to a bright pink page and made a check. Then another. Then she began to write a long sentence. With a final look at the brandy glass, she added the period like she was crushing a bug.

"This meal is half finished," she said. "Where exactly is your aunt?"

Jack couldn't help it. His eyes flipped toward Aunt Edith's bedroom before he could stop himself.

"Is that her room?" Alice asked. "Let's just see if she's in." She started down the hall.

"No!" Jack called. What if she saw the wrecked bathroom? What if she saw Hitchcock? Or worse! What if she saw the chocolate message on the bed? He'd be orphanaged, and that would be that. He rushed past her and blocked the door. "My aunt doesn't like people in her room," he said, "not even the maids."

The woman took another sniff of her pen, then tapped it against her clipboard. "If there is something wrong with your aunt, I'll need to make a note," she said.

Jack shrugged.

"The rules say I must make positive contact with the parent or legal guardian." She read directly from her clipboard now, "'If no positive contact can be made, the minor is to be removed into temporary custody pending investigation of parental or guardian status.' Do I need to remove you?"

Jack stepped aside and watched helplessly as she reached for the doorknob. Soon it would all be over. She pushed past Jack and into the room. Jack followed.

The spread had been draped over the bed, covering all evidence of the chocolate message. The crystal bowl sat clean on the dresser. The bathroom door was closed. Water was running.

"I told you she was unavailable," Jack said.

The woman walked around the room. Making checks. Jack maneuvered between her and the bed. She knocked on the top of Muffin's cage. She leaned in close and sniffed it. When Muffin hissed at her, she shook the head in her sensible hat and made a note on her clipboard.

"Did you know rodents can be filthy and carry disease?" she asked.

"So can some people," Jack said.

"What's this?" she asked. She pulled the sketchpad from behind the television. She flipped through the storyboards of Mission Dolores and stopped at the mug shots.

"Did you do these?"

"Mostly."

She scribbled a word or two on her form. "We have another boy in the system who thinks he wants to draw pictures for the funny papers."

"Really?"

"Don't worry. He'll outgrow it. We've enrolled him in mechanics' school."

"What's wrong with drawing?" Jack asked.

"It isn't practical," the woman replied. "Orphans can't be artists."

A muffled gasp came from the bathroom. The woman's head snapped toward the door. "Mrs. Smith?"

There was a cough. Then . . . "Jack darling," a

falsetto voice called from the bathroom. "To whom are you speaking?"

"I'm Alice Trapp," Alice called into the bathroom, "I'm from social services. I have to make positive contact with you before I can leave."

"Oh—I didn't hear you come in. I had the water running just a moment ago."

Alice opened the bathroom door.

"Hey!" cried Jack, grabbing for the knob. But Alice had already crossed the threshold.

Inside, the shower curtain had been rehung and the bathroom straightened. Hitchcock was nowhere to be seen.

"Mrs. Smith?" Alice said.

"Yes, dear," came from behind the shower curtain.

"Mrs. Smith, I need to ask you about that brandy glass in the living room. Do you often drink with lunch?"

"Oh, my dear, that is strictly medicinal."

"It looked like a double," Alice said.

There was a moment when only the quiet lapping of water could be heard. "Are you saying I'm a lush, dear?"

"No . . . no . . . ," Alice said, "but . . ."

A pasty bare leg snaked its way from beneath the

shower curtain, covered in a mash of hair and foam, followed by a hand with an open straight razor.

"Just between us girls," the voice said, "today is my beauty day. Could a lush do this?"

The hand swished across the leg in three quick even strokes, leaving a bare expanse of smooth, clean flesh.

"Oh," said Alice Trapp.

The hairy toes wiggled. "Well?"

"I suppose not. Still, I must make positive contact. . . ."

"Surely speaking to me, even through the shower curtain, is contact enough. I'm too negatively dressed for anything more positive."

Jack could see the slow rotisserie of Miss Trapp's brain trying to decide if talking to a hairy leg could be considered "positive contact." Her no-nonsense hat seemed to vibrate with the effort. She consulted her clipboard, but apparently found no answer there, for she backed out of the bathroom and left the suite, calling, "I'll be back."

CHAPTER 16

THE BIRDS

JACK QUIETLY CLOSED THE BATHROOM DOOR, then pulled back the shower curtain. Hitchcock hunkered down in the tub with his sleeves and right pants leg rolled up. His brightly polished right shoe was floating in an inch of water, little fluffs of shaving cream stuck to its sides. The closed razor sat in the tub tray.

Jack offered his hand to help Hitchcock up but didn't let go once he was standing.

"That was great," Jack said. "I—"

"A gifted artist like you turned into an auto mechanic. Rubbish!" Hitchcock said.

"You heard?" Jack asked.

Hitchcock held up one of the hotel glasses and pressed its bottom to his ear. "I listened at the door," he said. "A good director never misses a chance for observation."

"Look, I don't know what to . . ." Jack paused. He felt a little dizzy. He released a deep breath that took with it a tightness that had infected his body since the knock on the door. "Thank you. Thank you so much."

"Well. I couldn't let my brandy be your downfall. I'd never get over the guilt of it."

Jack's shoulders slumped. "Oh . . . is that all?"

Hitchcock placed his free hand over their joined ones. "My dear child," he said, "no, that is not all." He squeezed Jack's hand more tightly, then let go. Jack stuck his hand in his pocket hoping to trap the warmth of Hitchcock's grip.

"Now, let's see what we can do about finding your

aunt," Hitchcock said. He stepped out of the tub, dripping onto the marble floor.

"But you said it was dangerous . . . maybe deadly, even."

Hitchcock nodded to the door. "Our Miss Trapp convinced me there are worse things than a bit of danger."

"But worse than death?" Jack asked.

"I intend to see it doesn't come to that," Hitchcock said. "Today I was distressed when a scene got out of my control. But any good director gets right back in the chair. Any good director"—he grabbed the closed razor and waved it before Jack—"can ad-lib as well as any actor."

"So you aren't leaving me?" Jack whispered.

"And not see how it ends?" Hitchcock asked. "Besides, I have a song to teach you."

Jack's eyes stung a little. A small sense of certainty flowed back into his limbs. Bits of sudsy foam merged together in the puddle at Hitchcock's feet. The bits came to rest on the sole of his left shoe. Jack handed the director a towel from the shelf above the tub. "Better stay here for a minute, while I check that Miss Trapp is gone."

In the sitting room he found the social worker gone,

but Shen was there, bent over the desk, with her back to him.

"Shen?" Jack said.

Shen sprang upright and faced him. She held a little pink box. "Blum's Coffee Crunch Cake," she said. "Opal sent it up. For your beatnik friend, she said. The door was open. Who's your beatnik friend?"

"I think she meant Mr. Hitchcock, next door."

"Oh," said Shen. "He's a beatnik?"

"Sometimes." Jack said. "You can leave it here. I'll see he gets it."

Shen left the cake, then left the room. "All clear," Jack called to Hitchcock. He closed the door behind Shen. The puff of air made something flutter down from the silver tray near the door.

It was an envelope. Letters cut from a newspaper were glued to the front. The blood rushed from Jack's head, and at first he couldn't read them. They seemed to be disjointed lines and circles, dancing around in no particular order. He closed his eyes tightly for a moment, and when he looked again, he read, "Open Immediately."

Hitchcock came in, blotting himself with the fluffy

hotel towel. "I'm afraid my suit is ruined. I'll need to go to my room for a fresh pair of trousers."

"But you'll be back—right?" Jack said. "I mean . . . Look, I think we've been contacted." He held out the envelope to the director.

"I see . . . ," Hitchcock said. He brushed his bulbous lower lip with a fleshy finger. "Well, then. We no longer need to keep vigil in your suite. Let's go to my rooms, where I can change out of these wet things, and we'll consider what this latest note says."

As they opened the door to the director's suite, the phone was ringing.

"Hello," Hitchcock said. "Oh, Joan . . . Yes. . . ." He combined the photos and papers on his desk into fewer stacks. Some of the stacks went to the side, some to a drawer, clearing a small space. "The actresses? Later. . . . Scripts? Later. . . . Joan, you'll just have to handle it yourself. I've something else on my plate at the moment." He looked at Jack. "Just a commitment that suddenly came up. I'll call when I can." He hung up, then pointed to the letter and tapped the space on his desk. "I'll change while we see about that letter."

Jack carefully opened the envelope. Inside was an

irregular-size piece of newspaper, folded in half. Visible was an ad for Colgate Dental Cream (with Gardol!) and another for hair tonic (with V-7). What Jack found when he unfolded the paper was more interesting.

"It's a newspaper article," Jack said. It was from a couple of years ago. A yellow brittleness marred its face, but the edge was white, as if it had been torn out recently from an older paper. It gave off a musty smell. "I wonder where they got this. It's old."

Hitchcock came into the sitting room, tying a black tie over a fresh white shirt. He looked over Jack's shoulder. "From the library?" he said. "What does it say?"

Jack read the article:

Birds Terrorize Coastal Town

Capitola—Sheriff's deputies don't know how to explain the arrival of an enormous flock of Sooty Shearwaters in this small seaside town, and, although the flock has departed, residents worry that the strange event could be repeated. No injuries were reported, though a signifi-cant number of plate glass windows were broken by the flock, estimated to number 5 to 10 thousand individual birds.

Local resident and ornithologist 'Sweet Betsy' Turner says she's concerned. "I have never seen such a mess. I live here for the fresh air. Now what a stench," she said. "Shearwaters, or more precisely *Puffinus griseus*, aren't dangerous, but neither are they housebroken. I doubt the garden will recover. They've covered my *Calycanthus floridus* in guano."

The local fire department used high-pressure hoses to disperse the flock. Most of the birds have only retreated to the cliffs east of town, causing those owning or renting houses near the ocean to remain fearful of their return.

Firemen say they will 'toil at' the hoses' until sunset today then check the situation each day following.

"We may need to bring in some men from neighboring departments, what with the size of the flock," Fire Chief John Saint-Robert said. "But I want to assure the good people of Capitola and Santa Cruz that the birds' numbers will soon be back to normal."

"They better be" was the reply of Jackson Small of the Santa Cruz tourist board. "Right now, if not sooner." When asked how this event might affect the tourist season, his reply: "Either you'll recognize this for the freak accident it was or you won't. We'll probably never, ever see the like of it again, but who knows? Either way, this is a great place to come for vacation. Again and again."

Here's hoping those Sooty Shearwaters don't agree.

"Jeez," Jack said, "that's weird. All those birds in that little town. It must have been pretty scary for the people there."

"No doubt it was much more frightening for the

birds," Hitchcock said. He leaned in toward the scrap of newspaper. "I believe we are meant to read the circled words."

Jack did. "'Don't worry. She's alive. the cliff house. men s toil at.' *Men s toil at*? Hmmm . . . 'Men's toilet,' I guess. 'The cliff house men's toilet sunset today. Bring what I want, and the numbers better be right. Or you won't ever see her . . . again.'"

"It appears we have a ransom note," Hitchcock said.

"To spare," said Jack, "but we only just left the kidnapper."

"It's as if he's trying to drive us, like cattle—or worse, actors. How dreadfully disrespectful. It's the director who directs!"

"There are a lot of houses on cliffs around here," Jack said.

In answer Hitchcock thumbed through a pile of photographs. He pulled out one that showed a building on the edge of a cliff. A sign above it read CLIFF HOUSE.

"What does he mean—'the numbers better be right'?" Jack asked. "Do you think he saw that we only had some of the money?" What would happen if he found out they had tricked him? Jack didn't need to close his eyes to call forth the image of the pistol's steel cylinder. It was well burned into his mind.

"Perhaps. Or he suspects we won't give him all of it until we have your aunt secured,'" said Hitchcock.

"Weird." Jack turned the article over, then over again. He ran his finger along the roughly torn edge. He held it up to the light.

"How did he find this article, work out the words of the note, and deliver it in such a short time?" Jack asked. "We weren't at the bank that long."

"Most peculiar," Hitchcock said. "Well, we shall have to work it out when we have time. For now we must plan our next scene. Sunset is just a few hours away, and our kidnapper will be waiting."

"Does he think we're crazy?" Jack asked. "I mean, look, we might as well paint targets on our shirts if we're going to walk into another trap."

"Agreed," said Hitchcock. "Though we cannot control every scene, we do not want a replay of this afternoon. He got the better of us."

Grim resolve pressed Jack's lips together and crinkled the corners of his eyes. He felt different than he had this morning. Then he'd been alone, grasping with a full orphan's thin hope to the director. Now there was no need to grasp. He had a friend who stood by him.

"Mr. Hitchcock, does the director ever learn from the audience?"

"In some ways. We may recut a film based on audience reaction in test screenings, for example."

"Wait here." Jack left the room and returned with the pad he'd used to sketch the Mission Dolores storyboards. He flipped past the mug shot to a clean page. "Can you hand me that pencil?"

In large block letters, he wrote, "I MUST SEE OR HEAR FROM HER BEFORE I CAN AGREE TO ANYTHING FOR YOU." He tore the note from the pad and folded it into the empty makeup case.

"There," Jack said. "We have the message about our requirements. Now we just need a hiding place to watch the men's room at the Cliff House without being seen, to see what the kidnapper does."

Hitchcock strode over to the bulletin board marked "Possible Locations." He ruffled through the layers of photos and notes pinned there.

"In the cinema," he began, "locations of interest can be used for dramatic purpose—a drowning in a lake, an avalanche on a mountain. After all, what is the point of building a skyscraper in New York, if not to have someone fall off it . . . or be pushed? Aha!" He'd found the picture he wanted and tore it from the board. It was the odd camera-shaped building at the cliff's edge that Jack had noticed earlier. "And what is the point of a camera obscura if not to give us a place to see while remaining unseen?"

CHAPTER 17

REAR WINDOW

"HAHAHAHAHAHAHA!" MANIACAL LAUGHTER drifted to the heights at Point Lobos, the cliffs at the northwestern point of the city, where the ocean tumbled through the Golden Gate to the bay of San Francisco. The cackle came from Laughing Sal, the ghastly automaton who guarded the entrance to the fun house at Playland at the Beach, as she doubled over in weird mirth. Jack had never seen her in person (Aunt Edith didn't approve of amusements for kids), but he'd heard children at the Fairmont trying to scare each other by imitating Sal's creepy laugh after a day at Playland.

Jack shouldn't have been able to hear it up on the cliffs, but some trick of the wind made the sound swirl in his ears, an undertone to the din of the amusement park below. Jack wondered if she were laughing at him for coming within striking distance of the ocean that had stolen his mother. That same wind made the waves peak and flash in the sunlight, like a semaphore mayday from a thousand drowned souls. Then it blew against Jack's chest with such a steady force, he could close his eyes and imagine he was plummeting off the cliff. The sea spray and fog gathered on his eyelashes and hair like dew, and dripped beneath his collar, leaving a chill trail down his spine.

"There it is," Hitchcock said, pointing to the building perched on a cliff buffeted by waves and blanketed by spindrift. A rectangle of redwood and glass, the Cliff House had a restaurant and was surrounded by terraces from which locals watched the gulls wheeling and crying above Seal Rocks. Like most of this corner of the city, the Cliff House had an air of shabbiness and neglect about it. The fog and sea spray coated wood and corroded metal.

The ruin of the Sutro Baths at the base of the cliff reinforced the forsaken feel of the area. A pretty façade had been maintained at the clifftop to lure in visitors to the ice rink and the museum of oddities. But the three-acre, multistory, glass-and-steel natatorium that hulked like an iceberg beside those small, maintained areas sported empty pools and danger signs. There wasn't an unbroken pane within a stone's hurl from the beach.

Or maybe it was that mad laughter, mingled with the cries of thrill-seekers trying to stop their hearts on the Playland roller coaster, that made things feel so desolate.

Or perhaps things built on the ocean always seemed a bit lost when facing its vastness and depth.

Another structure perched behind the Cliff House, at the very edge of the drop-off. It looked vaguely like a camera, with its lens pointed toward the sky. There was a little ticket-taker booth where the rewind crank would be.

"What's that?" Jack asked.

"The Camera Obscura," Hitchcock replied. Indeed, a sign above the door confirmed it—CAMERA OBSCURA. "It's the blind from which we shall observe our tiny quarry."

Hitchcock donned his hat and sunglasses, then turned away from the giant camera. He led Jack to the men's room off the terrace behind the Cliff House. Inside, a man with a red jacket was facing the urinal. Hitchcock went immediately into the stall, and Jack examined the towel holder until the man had zipped up and slipped out the door.

"That man didn't even bother to wash his hands," Jack said as Hitchcock emerged from the stall.

"Filthy chap. Let's hope he's not a waiter at the restaurant."

Jack slid past Hitchcock and placed the makeup case on the toilet tank. The note demanding to see Aunt Edith was inside. The money was not. As he positioned the case, another man came into the restroom. Jack slammed shut the stall door, and Hitchcock turned his face toward it. "Daddy's right outside, Son," he said. "We'll get an ice cream when you're done."

The man used the urinal and headed right out the door.

"Another waiter," Hitchcock said as Jack reappeared.

The pair were walking out the door when Jack cried, "Wait! How are we going to make sure no one takes the case to lost and found or something, before the kidnapper gets here?"

Jack went back into the stall and opened the bag. He tore a large piece of paper from a blank spot on the message to the kidnapper.

"Do you have a pen?" Jack asked.

Hitchcock took one from his pocket.

On the paper Jack wrote:

men's
toil at
_____

out of order

Jack hung the paper from the stall door latch.

"That should do it," he said.

When they emerged from the men's room, the sun had dipped below the fog and was closing in on the horizon. The tide was going out, leaving behind lifeless kelp and the reek of decay.

Jim Averbeck

Hitchcock drifted toward the Giant Camera's ticket booth, pulling Jack in his wake.

"Howdy, gents," said the man in the booth. He wore a cable-knit cardigan over his shirt and tie but would have been more appropriately dressed carnival-barker style, in a broad-striped red-and-white jacket with a cane and straw hat. He was mostly bald, with a tuft of red hair that sprang like a question mark from the crown of his head. "Care to witness the wonders of the camera obscura?" he asked. "Ancient instrument of Aristotle. Described in the writings of the great Islamic scholar Abu Ali al-Hasan ibn al-Hasan ibn al-Haytham. Aid to da Vinci and Vermeer. Only fifty cents, and the world can be yours in a bowl."

Hitchcock squinted toward the sun, raising his hand to his forehead as if in salute, and said with a casual air, "How much would it be for an exclusive rental from now until, say, just after sunset."

"Ah! Sunset!" the man said. "A blaze of glory projected for the pleasure of our patrons onto the camera's viewer. Why watch the real thing, exposed to the cold and wind, when you can see it from the comfort of the camera obscura?"

"How much to watch it exclusively?" Jack repeated.

"Exclusively? Well, sunset is our busiest time. And who can watch the magnificence and grandeur of the heavenly orb descending to the sea exclusively? A drama of light and water. Eternal forces in an endless dance. Why . . . the sunset belongs to the world!"

Jack slipped one of the hundred-dollar bills he had held onto out of his pocket and through the slot in the box office window.

"Sold!" cried the man. "One sunset. To the little boy with the big bills."

"We'll need you to stay on and be sure no one else comes in," said Hitchcock, "and we'll need you to rotate the lens about one hundred twenty degrees."

"To the rear? Away from the ocean? But you'll miss the sunset!"

"We prefer to see the glory and drama of the eternal dance of light played out against the door to the men's toilet."

"Suit yourself," said the ticket seller, and pulled a lever so the entrance door swung open.

Inside, the room was completely dark, except for the top of a round, waist-high white cylinder perhaps six feet in diameter, which sat in the middle of the room. It was concave, like a shallow bowl, and projected onto it was a scene of the ocean waves crashing against Seal Rocks.

The silence of dark spaces settled on Jack. He wondered where the image in the bowl was coming from. He couldn't hear the rhythmic *thwip, thwip* of a projector.

"You are standing in the bowels of history," Hitchcock said, his voice a reverent whisper. "'Camera obscura,' from the Latin for 'dark room.' And you can draw a straight line from these dark rooms to the cinemas of today. Somewhere in the depths of time, someone noticed a peculiar optical effect. A pinhole in the wall of an otherwise dark room projected an entire scene of the brightly lit world outside onto the wall opposite. Clever chaps have since added lenses and photosensitive paper, and shrunk these *cameras* until they could fit in your hand. And later they added cranks and motors and reels of film so you could capture movement. But these huge camerae obscurae—they were the beginning."

"Wow," said Jack. The image in the bowl reflected in Hitchcock's intense eyes.

"Many early exhibitors were denounced as sorcerers and burned alive for their trouble, an end some would find fitting for today's motion picture directors."

A mechanical cranking of metal on metal sounded, and the scene playing out on the pedestal before them began to turn, from the ocean to the broken glass ruins. Jack saw the man with the red jacket and the deplorable hygiene habits walking on the beach.

"Hey! This is showing what's going on outside right now."

"It wouldn't be much use to us if it didn't," said Hitchcock.

The scene continued to move as the lenses and apparatus above rotated away from the sea.

"But why do people pay to see this projected inside when they could see the same thing outside for free?" Light and shadow, reflected from the bowl, danced over Hitchcock's face. With him in his dark suit, his head seemed disembodied and ghostly.

"Indeed," he said. "You may as well ask why people pay to see my movies of blackmail, murder, and intrigue projected on a screen, when they could watch the same activities in their bedrooms, or boardrooms, or through their neighbor's window. Perhaps viewing life from the darkness, they can see things in a new light. All experiencing the same story, but each with his own reaction and thoughts."

The scene continued to rotate. It *was* different, watching what he could otherwise see outside, here in a darkened room. It felt safe. No one could see what he watched. No one could know what piqued his interest or made him angry—or made him sad. And more—here was this scene, projected for him in this shallow bowl, like someone had gathered the world and contained it, rendered it harmless, and then scooped it out for his uncomplicated consumption.

The scene came to rest on the men's room door.

"Now we wait," said Jack.

"And watch," said Hitchcock.

Wait they did. Men entered the restroom and men left, but all of them were taller, or fatter, or darker, or older, or younger than the kidnapper. Not one was as short as The Suave Man. None of them were women, like his accomplice. And no one walked out with the makeup case.

Life played out in the light of the bowl, surrounded by the shade of the tomb.

The darkness made Jack bold. He pulled the silver charm from his shirt.

"Mr. Hitchcock," he said, "I've been thinking about something a lot, and I need to know. What happens. What happens to people when they die?"

"I'm afraid my expertise on such matters ends when life does," Hitchcock said.

"But you must know something," Jack countered. "Your TV show deals with death every week."

"I've told stories describing dozens of ways to dispatch someone or to be dispatched, and read a thousand more, but none that can tell for certain what happens after. I was raised to believe all unblemished souls go to heaven. I have no reason to doubt that and every desire to believe it, though I worry sometimes about my own black marks. In any case, I feel certain that something goes on beyond death."

"But what if you become trapped," Jack said, rolling the charm between his thumb and finger, "like a phantom walking the earth or a soul in some limbo, or what if you disappear altogether?"

Hitchcock wrapped his hands around Jack's. "I think it is the memory and the emotions of the living that become trapped, not the souls of the dead," he said. "If we want to make sure they are free, perhaps we only need to let them go. Then we can honor them by living our lives as they would want us to."

The director gently pulled Jack's hands open, and the charm dropped and swung back on its chain. Jack felt the little tap it made as it struck his heart.

"Do you think I could someday be as brave as my father?" Jack asked.

"No," said the director.

"Hey!"

"I think you'll be just as brave as yourself," Hitchcock continued. "In the two days I've known you, you've faced down the police, a kidnapper, and an overzealous social worker, to say nothing of a very prominent director of films."

"But I was scared every time," Jack said.

"My dear boy, you are operating under the misconception that fear is the opposite of bravery, when in fact it is an essential component. Courage is taking action in spite of fear. The opposite of bravery is inaction."

Jack wasn't convinced.

"If your inability to draw your father is what's

stopping you from knowing this, then draw him. You have seen him, after all."

"Huh? When?" Jack asked.

"Your mother did say you look just like him."

Silence fell in time with the sun. A rose glow bathed the men's room door, and the image in the bowl had become nearly as dark as Jack's thoughts.

"Any sign of him?" Jack asked.

"None," said Hitchcock. "The last man left ten minutes ago, and sunset is nearly over."

As if to underscore his statement, the final light faded and the image winked out. Jack went to the exit and peeked out, then motioned for Hitchcock to follow. The director cast off from his observation post. With a wave to the ticket seller, they entered the men's room.

The sign still hung on the stall door but had been turned upside down. Jack pushed past Hitchcock and into the stall. The pink makeup case still sat on the toilet tank.

"I guess he didn't come," Jack said. Then he spied a piece of paper stuck to the side of the toilet bowl. It had writing on it. Jack turned his head to read it better.

"ROM HER." It was his own handwriting, torn from the note he'd left in the case.

Hitchcock was staring at the toilet bowl too. "Open the bag."

Jack did. The letter he had written was still inside, but when he unfolded it, he could see that words and letters had been carefully torn from it. They fluttered like dry leaves to the floor of the stall. The remaining letters now read: "OR F AN AG E FOR YOU."

"HAHAHAHAHA . . ." In his mind Jack could hear Laughing Sal crowing down by the beach, and he knew, this time, it was because the joke was on him.

CHAPTER 18

SHADOW OF A DOUBT

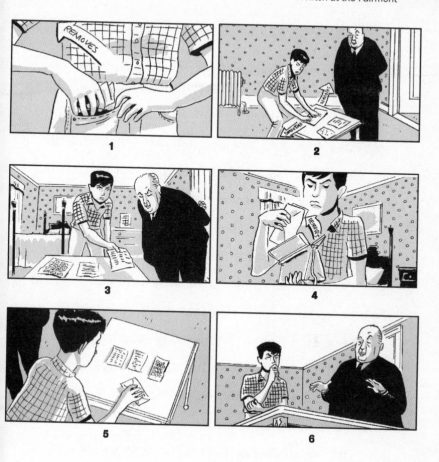

THE GLOOM IN JACK'S HEART remained for the rest of that evening as they returned to Hitchcock's suite and spoke long into the night about what to do next.

"I'm sure he didn't go in the restroom," Jack said. "I didn't see everyone's face, but the kidnapper is too short to miss."

"Perhaps he had another accomplice," Hitchcock said.

"And we're no closer to finding Aunt Edith," Jack said. He thought of the social worker's ominous "I'll be back" and wondered how long he had to find his aunt.

"One can't help noticing that things do not add up here," Hitchcock said. "Were I writing the events of the past few days as a screenplay, Alma— Mrs. Hitchcock— would have my head. 'Too many inconsistencies,' she'd say."

"It's more than 'how did we miss The Suave Man at the camera obscura?'" said Jack. "It's questions we've asked but didn't answer. Like why was my rich aunt wearing fake jewels? Why did she have ten thousand in cash? And why did the kidnapper overlook the cash when he left the first ransom note?"

"And the hidden location of the first note we found in your aunt's purse," Hitchcock added. "In the cinema, clarity is of paramount importance. It is indispensible that one's audience be perfectly aware of the facts. Without clarity the audience cannot be frightened, or anxious, or anything but confused."

"But what about the characters?" Jack asked. "They don't always know what's happening."

"Not at first. But eventually they must. Some final clue lets them know they're facing a murderer, or a foreign spy, and that they are in very real danger."

"So how do you get them there?"

The director waved his hand in the air. "With a revelatory scene. Something to move them from suspicion to certainty. A whispered conversation overheard. An overlooked clue discovered," Hitchcock said. "Flowers that grow down. A monogrammed hat that is too large. Bottles of uranium stocked in the wine cellar."

"Well, there aren't any whispered conversations to overhear right now. So how do we find an overlooked clue?" Jack asked. This was the director's area of expertise. Jack knew he'd have an answer.

Hitchcock made a little steeple of his fingers and pulled nervously at his bulbous lower lip. "Perhaps by reviewing what we already have, we'll see something in a new light," he said.

"Like we saw the ocean in a new way at the Giant Camera?" Jack asked.

"Precisely," Hitchcock said. "Though I think we should wait until tomorrow to take a fresh look. We are both tired now, and we would likely miss something important if we tried to give things a second look at this hour."

Jack reluctantly agreed. It was decided that he should again sleep on the sofa in the director's room. He went to his aunt's to grab his pajamas and toothbrush. He fed Muffin. Back in the director's suite he brushed his teeth. He stared into the mirror, making different faces to look like a brave man. But it was useless. He was an eleven-year-old boy in cowboy pajamas.

Hitchcock had folded Jack's clothes and set them on the coffee table. On top sat his sketchbook and pencil.

Jack turned to the ghost image of his dad and closed his eyes. His mother said he looked just like his father. Jack ran his thumb along the contours of the pencil. Up popped the face he'd seen every day in the mirror. He knew he could rotate it in space, but could he move it through time? He imagined the lines of his face stretching, the angle of his jaw sharpening, the chin growing more prominent. The eyes remained the same. When he looked at his sketchbook again, he saw this new face imprinted on the page. He let his pencil follow the lines.

In the end he had a very nice picture of what he might look like when he was older.

And no earthly idea if it looked anything like his father.

He threw the sketchpad onto the table.

The next morning they ate breakfast again in the director's suite. Jack found he was much more able to stomach the food this morning than he had been the previous day. He even found he liked the bubble and squeak.

Hitchcock had several different newspapers delivered with breakfast. "It's my habit. to review who bludgeoned whom while I sip my coffee," he said. GRACE'S BRIDESMAID ROBBED OF JEWELS the above-the-banner headline of one screamed. Others told the same story. "Life imitates art," the director said. He looked sad.

When they were finished, they went to Aunt Edith's suite. Jack dragged the coffee table from the sitting room into his aunt's bedroom. "I want to see everything all together," he said, "and we can't move all the chocolates from Aunt Edith's bed." He removed the bedspread that Hitchcock had used to cover the chocolate note. Then he retrieved Aunt Edith's handbag and the makeup case.

On the coffee table he laid out the note that had led them to Mission Dolores and the newspaper article with the circled words. Beside these he unfolded the note he had written, and which the kidnapper had torn and left in the men's room at the Cliff House.

"Three notes," Jack said. "Four, counting the chocolate one on the bed."

"'We have her. No Pole,'" Hitchcock read. "I mean 'police.'"

Below the newspaper article, Jack placed the envelope with "Open Immediately" in newsprint. Then he fished the blue envelope from the handbag and placed it below the handwritten note. Next he unloaded the rest of the contents of the handbag one by one onto the table. The used Kleenex he immediately tossed into the wastebasket.

He laid the pawn tickets beneath the blue envelope. The bill from Ransohoff's he examined closely. "All of her clothes were special ordered," Jack said. "Do you think that means anything?"

Hitchcock reviewed the invoice. "'Amount due: three hundred and seventy-five dollars,'" he read. "Your aunt had expensive tastes. And she was fond of using credit."

Likewise, another bill, for the television, showed an amount due. As did a bill from the hotel. Jack arranged all the bills on the table, as well as the coin purse, which contained three dollars and twelve cents in change. The last things he pulled from the handbag were the beauty potions, creams, and powders.

"I guess that's it," he said. He turned the handbag upside down and shook it. A small object dropped out, skittered across the table, and came to rest against a jar of wrinkle cream.

Hitchcock picked it up. "You overlooked this," he said.

"It's just a paper clip," Jack said.

"We shouldn't assume it's unimportant," Hitchcock said. "Clues don't have signs on them declaring what they are. And they come in all sizes."

"But if we examine every piece of lint in my aunt's handbag, we won't have time for the real clues." The frustration in his own voice shocked Jack. Would he see a new clue, or was he just wasting time?

Hitchcock turned the clip over and over on his hand. "I suppose you are correct," he said, and tossed it with the Kleenex.

They cracked open each bottle, jar, and tube of Aunt Edith's beauty supplies. One smelled of lavender. Jack sniffed another and got a sinus-clearing blast of eucalyptus. (No wonder Aunt Edith smelled like Ben-Gay, Jack thought.) Though most smelled cloyingly sweet, Jack decided that whatever was inside was just what it claimed to be. No hidden uranium here. He set them all on the floor.

He picked up the three tickets from Peter Pawn's Neverland. Printed on the left of each card were tags like "Item" and "Serial Number." Lines on the right had been filled in by hand.

"Look at this," Jack said. "This one says 'Item: diamond square-cut ring' and 'thirty-five hundred.' So does this second one: 'ring set with ruby and emerald, thirty-five hundred.' The final one says 'empire brooch, three thousand.'"

"Thirty-five hundred plus thirty-five hundred plus three thousand. That's ten thousand," Hitchcock said. "Dollars, one would imagine. Was that not the same amount you found in the envelope?"

"So she pawned her real rings?" Jack asked. "But she's rich. Look at her stuff. Nice clothes. *Two* television sets. Jewelry!"

"She *had* jewelry," Hitchcock replied. "The pawn-shop has it now. The rest bought on credit."

"I guess we are seeing her in a new light," Jack said.

"Yes."

"She lives at the Fairmont." Jack said. "Do they give credit here?"

"Her bill is unpaid."

Jack looked at the collection assembled on the coffee table. The four notes seemed the most informative. They were like a map with no compass. How strange they were, and ominous, each in its own way. The ravaged letter from the men's room seemed to say "Defy me, and I'll tear you up." The newspaper article. It said, "Beware of hidden dangers." And who writes a message with half-eaten chocolates? Only the handwritten note from the handbag, asking for two hundred thousand dollars, appeared normal. Jack felt impatient but forced himself to keep looking at the notes. There had to be something there. A missing piece to the puzzle. He looked and looked. Why couldn't he see it?

An inkling of understanding brushed against Jack's mind. Something he had just thought kept circling in his head. He picked up the note from the handbag. "This is the only one that looks like a normal note."

"Yes," said Hitchcock.

"But the others are abnormal—weird ways to write a note. Chocolate. Newspapers. Torn-up paper."

"So it would seem," said Hitchcock.

Jack closed his eyes. He saw two circles. One marked "normal," the other "weird." Into the "normal" circle he put the handwritten note. Into the "weird" circle he put the three others. Suddenly he saw it.

"But look at it in a different way," he said. He was speaking faster now, eager to work through his thinking. He held up the handwritten note. "If this is the only normal one in the bunch, then it is really the odd one out. Just a regular note, but odd in its normal-ness."

"Quite true," said Hitchcock, "but what does it reveal?"

Jack ran his fingers down the face of the note, as if he could absorb the answer from the ink or trace a solution in the broad distinctive loops of the cursive letters. Handwritten.

"Look," he said. "Why does a kidnapper state the ransom demands by clipping letters from a newspaper, or circling words in an article?"

"Because he does not wish to be traced by other communication methods, or tied to the crime by his handwriting," Hitchcock answered. "If he has any professional standards at all."

"So why did he write three notes that leave no connection to the writer?" Jack pointed them out. "The chocolate note, the newspaper article, and our own note torn into a new message?" Jack's hand rested on the handwritten note. "But he left another in his own handwriting?"

"Perhaps he had someone else write the note?"

"But why would someone write it for him?" Jack said. "Even his accomplice wouldn't want to be traced, would she?"

"Perhaps she doesn't know any better," Hitchcock said.

"They both seemed like a pros at the mission."

"Regardless," said Hitchcock, "we have a kidnapper and several notes about the kidnapping. They must all be connected."

Jack looked down at the collection of things on the table. He let his mind drift back to finding each one. *How are they connected? How?* That circling thought in his head finally landed.

"Connected!" he cried. "Of course. You were right."

"Without question," Hitchcock said. He folded his hands at his belly. "About what?"

Jack fetched the paper clip from the trash can and held it before Hitchcock's face. "That this was a most important clue!"

He picked up the bills from Ransohoff's, the hotel, and the television store. He clipped them to the handwritten note, back in its blue envelope. "This was how I found the handwritten note in Aunt Edith's handbag."

Hitchcock stared at the little bundle of papers but said nothing.

"Don't you see?" Jack said as he pulled each piece of paper from the clip and laid it on the table. "Bill. Bill. Bill. My aunt kept all her bills together."

"So?"

"The reason this first ransom note is handwritten and was hidden in Aunt Edith's purse is because it's not a ransom note at all!"

"Then what is it?"

Jack read the note aloud: "We'll agree to two hundred thousand dollars. Bring it to the noon service at Mission Dolores on Monday. And let's not play games, or I'll be forced to end this job immediately. She'll be dead and you'll be blamed. Yours . . . S.'"

"Don't you see?" Jack said. "It's just another bill—for

goods delivered—or . . . or . . . services rendered. Aunt Edith pawned her rings to pay it. But never got the chance. It's not a ransom note at all. It's a bill!"

"I see," said Hitchcock, "but a bill for what?"

CHAPTER 19

SABOTEUR

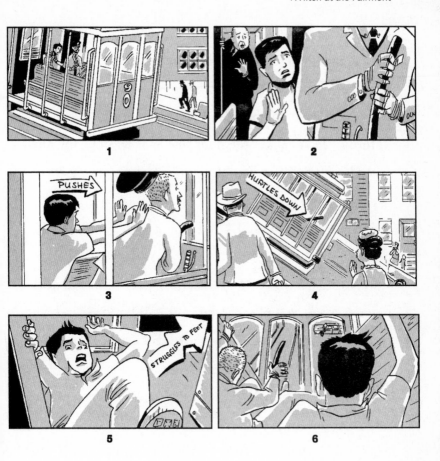

A CLATTER FROM THE MAIN ROOM interrupted anything Jack might have said. Jack jumped up and dashed through the bedroom door, Hitchcock on his heels. The door to the suite was open. The silver mail tray, upside down on the floor, rotated metallically on its rim, faster and faster until it clanked to a stop. From the hallway a bell signaled the arrival of the elevator.

"Go!" Hitchcock said.

Jack darted to the elevator. A white ski mask lay before it. Jack caught the door just as it was closing and forced it open. Shen was alone in the elevator.

"Going down," she said.

"Shen," Jack asked, "did you see who called the elevator?"

"No," Shen said. "No one was there when the door opened. Were you playing with the call button?"

Jack didn't answer. He turned to Hitchcock. "Whoever it was must have taken the stairs."

"I'll follow him," said Hitchcock. "My legs are longer! You go down to the lobby with Shen and see who comes out of the stairwell. But don't approach him. I'll not have you endangered."

"Check," said Jack. He stepped into the elevator. "Lobby."

Shen hesitated. Then closed the door and began the descent.

Jack still clasped the ransom note—no, the bill—in his hand. He shoved it into his pocket and stared at the brass arrow above the door that indicated the floor.

"Can't you make it go any faster?" he asked.

"Someone on three called. We need to slow down to stop."

"No! Don't! I need to get to the lobby, Shen. It's important."

Shen stood with her back against the wall, her right arm extended to operate the lift, her left arm angling across her stomach and chest, like she was reciting the Pledge of Allegiance with the wrong hand. Her thumb hooked over the second button on her jacket. A brass button. Jack's eyes followed the trail of buttons as it led down her lumpy jacket, under her arm, and reemerged near the bottom hem. Brass. Brass. Brass. But the last button of the jacket was different. Not brass. Sort of a white. Ivory maybe.

So Jack knew.

"You did it," he said.

"Please move to the back of the car," Shen said as they stopped on the third floor.

Jack lunged toward her as she moved to open the door. He grabbed her right arm.

"You kidnapped my aunt. I know it was you. You left

behind your button. I'd almost forgotten." He wasn't sure where the button was. He must have left it somewhere.

"Button?" said Shen. The arm she had crooked across her jacket moved to cover the buttons.

"You lost your brass button and sewed this white one on instead." Jack pulled at her arm. As he jerked it away, something fell from her jacket and crashed to the floor. Glass sprayed everywhere. The silver frame from Jack's suite lay at their feet.

Shen shoved open the elevator door and pushed Jack violently backward through it. He might have been able to keep his footing, but he tripped over the family waiting there. They fell in a heap.

"Out of service," Shen said. The elevator door rattled shut. When Jack got back to his feet, Shen was already headed to the lobby.

"I'm sorry," said Jack, stepping over the family and shaking splinters of glass from his pants cuffs. He pushed through the door to the stairwell and nearly ran into Hitchcock as he rounded the landing from the stairs above.

"Jack?" he said.

"It was Shen," Jack said, already running down the

stairs. "She was the one in the room. She stole the picture of my mother in the silver frame. And she was there the night of the kidnapping too. She left a brass button."

"Button?" Hitchcock said.

"I don't know what happened to it," said Jack, "but the night my aunt disappeared there was a brass button on the floor."

Hitchcock rounded the last flight of stairs just behind Jack. They bolted out into the lobby. Another operator was taking position in Shen's elevator. Jack guessed Shen had feigned some sort of emergency so she could escape. Jack didn't want to lose her. He sprinted across the lobby, and into the terrible grip of Mr. Sinclair, the head bellman.

"In a hurry again, boy?" he asked. He squeezed and pushed Jack's arm so hard that Jack had to bow a little to take the pressure off. "What is it this time? Another emergency, no doubt."

"Yes," said Jack. "Where's Shen? I need to see Shen."

"Then you would have done better to take the elevator than the stairs," Sinclair said. "She is the operator—"

"I haven't got time for this," Jack said. "It's important." A wash of numbness spread from where the bellman gripped his arm, tighter still.

"Tsk. Somehow I doubt that. You're lying again. I'd stake my reputation on it."

"With such a worthless ante, I doubt any bookie would take the bet," said Hitchcock, finally catching up. "Let the boy go."

The bellman's mustache curled into a sneer. "Someday you'll be sorry for acting so high-and-mighty."

"Today is not that day," Hitchcock said, and he took Jack's hand.

They circled round and round, but there was no sign of Shen in the lobby.

Opal was just propping open the door to Blum's. Jack headed over toward her.

"Hey, sugar," Opal said. "Where's your poet friend?"

"Ummm . . . ," Jack said.

"I'm afraid he met with an unfortunate accident," said Hitchcock. "Fell off a ladder during a poetry recital. Right onto his bongos."

"Was he hurt?" asked Opal.

"We won't be seeing him again, I fear," said the director.

"Oh." If Opal's pillowy form had left any place for her shoulders to slump, they would have.

"Opal," said Jack. "Opal have you seen Shen?"

"Sure, sugar. She was just here. Made some change from the till for the cable car and scooted out the California Street entrance."

"Thanks, Opal," Jack said, headed that way himself.

"Anything wrong?" Opal called. But Jack and the director had already left the building.

Outside, the cable car was just pulling away from its stop. On the backseat Shen picked the last shards of glass from the silver frame. Her eyes met Jack's as the cable car started its smooth descent down the street. She looked sad.

Jack and the director hastened after the cable car, calling for it to stop. At first they kept pace with the car, but when it rounded over the intersection with Powell Street, the grade became very steep. The car kept a steady pace down the hill, but the severe slope tugged at Jack, threatening to topple him with each step he took. He was forced to slow down or be dragged off his heels and skid to a bloody halt somewhere downhill. The cable car pulled away into traffic.

Hitchcock looked up and down the street. "Never a cab in this town when you need one."

But another cable car pulled up behind them, empty save for the conductor and the man at the controls. Any other potential passengers had hopped on the previous car—the one Shen was on. Jack jogged up to the car, grabbed the cool brass pole, and jumped up onto the wrought iron steps. Hitchcock followed. The vibration of the wheels on the steel rails traveled up Jack's body, from feet to teeth. The sound of whatever mysterious mechanism ground its slow gears in the slot in the road between the two rails clanked and rattled. Jack slid across the wooden benches and up to the man at the front of the car.

"You the driver?" he asked the man.

"The gripman, actually," the man answered.

"Can you catch up to that car down the hill?" asked Jack. "It's very important."

"Not really, son. See, when I pull this lever back, the cable car grabs a steel rope that is constantly circling in the slot. So when we are moving, all the cars travel at the same speed."

"What if you let go of the cable?" Jack asked.

"We'd go faster—" the gripman began.

But he didn't finish. At that moment Jack threw his

weight against the man and pushed the lever forward.

"Jack! No!" called Hitchcock. Too late.

The car jerked forward. The gripman fell to the side, Jack was brought to his knees, and the cable car fairly flew down the hill. Jack tried to get up, but as the car barreled down the hill, the ride became a series of jolts and bumps that made standing impossible.

Bystanders on the sidewalk were screaming now. The car shook and shimmied and jumped up and down on the tracks as it careened through the next intersection. The wind raked and tangled Jack's hair. Car horns blared. The gripman cursed, and finally stood. When he pulled back the grip lever, there was a grinding sound and it jumped from his hands. He pulled some other levers. The car squealed again and jolted forward. They were flying toward the car in front of them. People on that car were panicking now, jumping off.

They were going to collide.

CHAPTER 20

DOWNHILL

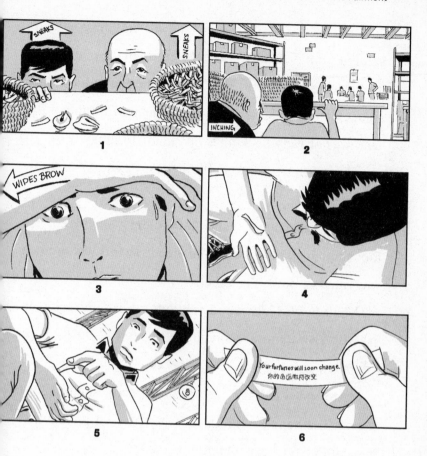

THE GRIPMAN ON JACK'S CAR heaved back on the emergency brake lever with all his might. This time it held. The car lurched again, then came to a stop just before hitting the car in front. Only a few feet separated the two.

"Everyone okay?" the gripman asked. The conductor saluted from the back, where he'd thrown the rear brakes. The gripman turned to Jack. "Kid, that better have been an accident, or you are in a whole heap of trouble." But Jack was already backing away, ready to jump.

The gripman blocked Hitchcock's exit. "You know this kid?"

"Yes," Hitchcock said. "My clumsy nephew." He looked at Jack and nodded his head toward where Shen was running down the street.

"This some Hollywood publicity stunt?" the gripman asked. "Yes. I know who you are."

"No stunt, I assure you. May we go?"

"Are you kidding?" the gripman said, squaring his stance. His hands curled into fists. "You do realize that this could have been a major accident?"

"Yet it wasn't," Hitchcock replied. "No one was hurt, thanks to you. And I am sure the boy didn't mean to bump you."

The gripman scratched his head. "Well . . . It's not like we don't know where to find you if there's a problem—famous guy like you." A sly squint brightened his eyes. "Tell you what. I might be persuaded to let you go if maybe I were to see a character named after me in your next movie."

"That could be arranged, I believe," Hitchcock said, extending his hand.

The gripman shook it. "Name's Popiano, but my friends call me Pop," he said.

Jack was already running after Shen as the gripman's words faded. Fortunately, her bright red uniform jacket stood out in the crowded streets of Chinatown.

Jack cut through knots of tourists, all gazing up at the red-and-green pagoda roofs that sloped out from the tops of modern brick buildings. These housed shops with porcelain figurines of dragons and cranes, or restaurants with leather-skinned ducks hanging in the windows, their necks wrapped tightly around thick metal hooks.

Shen turned left and right, left and right, weaving her way through the maze of streets that made up San Francisco's Chinatown. Jack wanted to catch her, but Hitchcock advised caution.

"I'm not sure a confrontation on the street is the best thing," he said, looking around. "There are sometimes certain . . . tensions in this city."

So they tracked Shen, careful not to lose sight of

her or be seen themselves. They passed shops with live fish splashing in metal buckets and cats skulking in the shadows, waiting for a chance to pounce. Vendors, displaying their wares for the day, brought out glass jars filled with roots and leaves. The smells were unfamiliar. Musky. Spicy. And occasionally the smell of something dead. Now Jack and Hitchcock were far from the sight-seeing spots. The customers milling about the shops were Chinese, buying items they actually used, not like the tourist trinkets for sale on Grant Avenue.

Jack was wary. He'd read about gangs in Chinatown—tongs, were they called?—that preyed on people who wandered down the wrong alley. And as shutters were cranked open and window shades snapped up, he heard people calling to one another in a language he didn't know—high and nasal and peppered with strange tones. Were they talking about him? Were they planning what to do with the young intruder and the old man with him? Jack saw tentacles of fog reaching out from the narrow side streets and heard the clatter of trashcan lids as the disappointed cats scrounged up a fallback meal. He shivered.

Then a Chinese woman arranging a little table of

teapots smiled warmly at him and tucked her long black hair over the gardenia behind her ear. It was the same smile and gesture he'd so often seen from his mother. Jack smiled back. The woman gave a wave and a wink, and Jack felt all his fear seep out through his feet. He wished his mother were there. She would have loved the adventure of it all.

"Shen's gone into that building," Hitchcock said.

They jogged up to the narrow storefront and shoed the door just before it closed. It was glass with gold letters:

XIAO LONG FORTUNE COOKIE COMPANY
EST. 1942

When they opened the door, the scent of caramelized sugar and vanilla nearly overwhelmed them. Jack's stomach growled. All around huge, colorful tins overflowed with small golden crescents and teetered one atop the other like the models of pagodas in the shops outside.

Several rows of high wooden worktables sat in a grid behind the fortune cookie mountains. At each table a stool, several pairs of chopsticks, and a small length of thin steel pipe idled with other tools Jack couldn't name. Here and there a disc of cookie lay abandoned, folded over on itself, or wrapped around a pipe, or merely left to harden flat. Each table had a low black metal bin filled with tiny slips of paper, some of which were also scattered about. Voices rose and fell beyond the tables. Jack and Hitchcock moved closer, careful to remain hidden behind the tables. Jack stood and leaned over the tabletop to get a better look.

A long table draped in red cloth stretched beneath high dark windows. Shen stood before it. Chinese men and women, some ancient, some middle-aged, sat behind it, shoulders sloped but spines erect. They looked harmless enough, but the young men who stood behind them most definitely did not. They were broad-shouldered, and many wore their shirtsleeves rolled up over biceps as round and hard as river rocks. Each one had a golden dragon embroidered on his shirt. Their faces were stern. There were no warm smiles like from the gardenia woman outside.

A briny sweat stippled Jack's forehead. As he quietly lifted his hand from the table to wipe it away, a slip of paper stuck to his palm. It was lettered in red

Chinese characters with an English translation. "Your fortunes will soon change," it read. And there were several more on the table that said the same thing. "Your fortunes will soon change." The black metal bin overflowed with more of the tiny slips. Over and over: "Your fortunes will soon change." "Your fortunes will soon change." Jack felt dizzy as these words carouseled in his brain.

He shook his head to break the spell, realizing the paper didn't say whether his fortunes would change for better or worse. His little silver charm slipped out between the buttons of his shirt. It struck the bin of fortunes and set it ringing.

Jack immediately ducked behind the table, but he barely had time to turn to Hitchcock before three dragon-shirted men surrounded them.

"Who are you?" the biggest one said.

Jack pushed his way between two of the men, but there was no way to squeeze through their compact, solid bodies. The biggest man threw Jack over his shoulder in a fireman's carry. Jack's cheek pressed against the man's muscled back. He felt the soft weave of his shirt and smelled again a strong scent of vanilla.

"Now see here," Hitchcock said. "There is no need for roughhousing." But the two other men took his arms and pushed him around the worktables to the center of the meeting.

The man lowered Jack into a seated position on the red-clothed table. The bright gold dragon embroidered on his shirt blocked Jack's view for a moment. But when the man stepped away, he was face-to-face with Shen.

Jack's hand arced out to paint Shen in a brushstroke of accusation. "Kidnapper!" he said.

"No," said Shen.

"Liar. I found your brass button on the floor the night my aunt disappeared. What have you done with her?"

"Nothing," said Shen, "yet."

"So you admit to having her."

"No, of course not. We don't have her yet," said Shen. "Yes, I was in the room that night, but your aunt was already gone."

"Then why were you there?" said Jack.

"For this." Shen held up the silver-framed picture. "I had it in my hands that night, but when I saw the message on the bed, I got scared and ran."

Jack jumped from the table, snatched the frame from

Shen, and cradled it to his chest. "Thief!" he said. "Thief, liar, and kidnapper!"

"I'm no kidnapper!" Shen yelled. "Your aunt is the kidnapper. Your aunt is the thief who stole people's lives."

"You stole my silver frame," Jack cried. "So don't say you aren't a thief."

"Frame?" Shen said. "Why would I want a cheap silver-plate frame. It's the picture of your aunt I needed."

"You kidnapped her!" Jack said again.

"If your aunt has been kidnapped, she deserved it. It is a case of the chickens coming home to roost."

CHAPTER 21

MR. AND MRS. SMITH

"ENOUGH." IT WAS ONE OF THE MIDDLE-AGED men at the table. He wore a suit and a beige porkpie hat. "Sharon, perhaps if you hear the boy out, we will learn something."

Hitchcock placed his hands on Jack's shoulders. "Perhaps that is advice we, too, might benefit from following. There is obviously more going on here than we think."

"And just what do you think is going on?" Shen asked.

"Well . . . ," Jack began, "my aunt disappeared Sunday night."

"We know," Shen snapped.

"Sharon, please," the man said.

Shen nodded to him. "Yes, Father."

"That night I found a brass button on the floor," Jack continued. "Just like the ones on Shen's jacket. Except she is missing one."

"And what do you think this means?" Shen's father asked.

"That she was there that night. In the room. That she kidnapped my aunt."

"And would your aunt have come along willingly? She is much bigger than Sharon," he said.

Jack looked at Shen. She was quite small. "Maybe she had a gun," he said. "Or help from her tong."

"Tong? Did you say 'tong'?" Shen asked. "What tong?"

Jack pointed at the men with the dragon shirts. A beat of silence followed. Then the men and women, young

and old, all began laughing at once. Even Shen smiled.
Jack had never seen her do that before.

"So this is my . . . tong?" Shen said.

"Well," Jack replied, "they all have the same shirt,
like a gang would." More laughter.

"And the name of my tong is . . . the Dragons?" said
Shen.

"Why not?" asked Jack, though he felt a bit foolish in
the face of the continuing sniggers.

"You are very backward," Shen said. "Tong! Hmph.
Did you read the sign on the door when you came in?"

Jack remembered. "Xiao Long Fortune Cookie
Company."

"Do you know what Xiao Long means?" Shen asked.

Jack shrugged.

Shen tapped the dragon on one of the men's shirts.
"'Little Dragon,'" she said. "These men work here.
They're bakers, not gangsters."

Flour did streak some of the men's shirts. And the
dragon sported a friendly, smiling cartoon face. It was
holding a fortune cookie.

"So what were you doing in his aunt's room?" Hitchcock
asked. "Why did you . . . borrow . . . that picture?"

Jim Averbeck

Shen's father stood. "I know you," he said to the director. "You are the one who tells on the television the true stories of the dark side of men."

"Well, yes," said Hitchcock, "though the tales are fiction."

"Fiction can sometimes speak truer than fact," the man said. "Your stories are true." This was exactly how Jack felt. He wished he had been able to think of how to say it before. But now he knew.

"So," Shen's father continued, "I have a tale for you. A true tale, but one for which an ending has not yet been written. Perhaps you two can help us find it." He placed his palms on the table and let his weight lean into it. The other men looked to him from either side. The laughter had died, and a somber tone wrapped like a shawl around the room. "Have you ever heard the word 'Shanghai'?" he asked.

"It's a city in China," Jack said.

"And another name for kidnapping," added Hitchcock darkly.

"But did you know the second meaning originated here in our city?" Shen's father said. "In the decades of the Gold Rush, sailors jumping ship to search for their fortune left ship after ship without a crew. Their captains began paying for men—willing or not, conscious or not—to fill the ranks. Men who ran boardinghouses for sailors found a way to increase their profits and open more beds for the next wave of shore leave. These men, these 'crimps,' as they were called, used various methods to render their victims unconscious—a blackjack to the head as the poor seaman slept, a few drops of laudanum in the beer, a cigar (on the house) laced with opium. The unlucky sailor was thrust through the trapdoor behind the bar, or the window facing the pier, or the front door on a dark night, and into the Whitehall boats that ferried them to the waiting ships. By the time the sailor woke up, he was on his way to Shanghai, or some other Far East port, his first month's wages paid to the man who'd turned him over to the captain. Soon it wasn't just sailors who found themselves in this position, but any able-bodied man not affluent enough to avoid it. There are even stories of corpses being sold to the ship captains, with rats sewn into their clothes to make them twitch enough to look alive."

"What's all this got to do with my Aunt Edith?" Jack asked. "The Gold Rush was way before she was born."

Jim Averbeck

"The last official shanghai happened in 1915," Shen's father continued. "The Gold Rush was over, and decent people demanded a crackdown on the practice. Laws were passed." He paused. "No one wanted to be a victim."

At the word "victim" there were small nods of the head and deeply drawn breaths around the room. Shen touched her father's hand. He smiled at her and went on. "But partnerships had been established, contacts made, a pipeline opened. And there was still a demand for slaves of one type or another. There were places where the city fathers turned a blind eye. Places whose population they thought undesirable, and whose land they felt was too valuable for those who lived there."

"Like Chinatown," Shen broke in. "Close to where Edith Crowley, the daughter of Paddy Crowley, one of the most notorious crimps, converted his boardinghouse into an orphanage. She found there a new supply of labor to sell in the form of children no one would miss."

"My aunt?" said Jack.

Shen shrugged. "Maybe. We think. We know she is Edith Smith. The question is, was she once Edith Crowley? My father was one of those in the 'care' of this woman. As were several other gentlemen seated at this table. Eventually the Feds shut her down and she went into hiding. But not before many children were enslaved here or overseas."

Shen's father sighed. "How we won our freedom would make for many long tales. But know this: We survivors have formed a league sworn to answer the wrongs done to us, and to prevent them from happening to others. We have been tracking members of the kidnapping ring for twenty years."

"So you kidnapped my aunt?" said Jack, softer now.

"No," the old man said. "When the fish hunts the cat, it is no longer a fish. We do not wish to become like our quarry. Times have changed. We have found men in the police force we trust. Men we work with. Now we and our operatives gather information, here and across the ocean. We find ways to see that justice is done. But we don't go to the police until we are sure we have the right person." He sat down. Suddenly he looked like the oldest man there.

"It's why we need that photograph," Shen said. "My father saw your aunt when we were having lunch at Blum's. He thought he recognized her. But thirty years is a long time. He remembers the matron as a slender young woman."

Jack clutched the frame to his chest. He knew his aunt was harsh, but he'd never imagined she was as evil as all that. And what if he gave Shen the photo? What would become of his aunt then? Even if they found her, she'd be taken away—again. And Jack would have no one—again.

But if the photo was the proof they needed, he didn't have to give it to them. It was his after all.

"It was decades ago," Jack said. "Even if my aunt is the woman you're looking for, who does it help if you put her in jail?"

There was an exchange in Chinese between Shen and the old-timers at the table, a brief debate that Jack couldn't understand. Finally the old man said, in English, "This boy is young, but he has seen very much. Tell him, Sharon. He should know so he can choose, even if the burden will make his sleep unsound."

Shen turned to Jack. "It may not be a decades-old story. As I said, many children were shipped overseas. Our vow for justice stretches across the ocean, and many of those victims are now our operatives. Overseas we have seen signs that the pipeline is opening again. Some weeks ago a ship, the *Aventure Malgache,* left port from Madagascar. The ship and its captain were among the worst of the traffickers connected to the orphanage. Last night the ship anchored in the waters out past the Farallons."

"Their old pickup point," her father said, pain in his eyes.

"On this side of the Pacific we have seen some of Edith Crowley's crew putting new locks on old warehouses. And shadowy figures pushed into cars, taken from place to place. And plates of food pushed through the space beneath bolted doors."

"So you think she's in business again," Jack said. He thought of the "bill" they had found. He might have reason to believe this too.

"So you see," Shen concluded, "this is important. Now. Today."

Jack looked at the picture of his aunt. She was young in the photo. Thin. She was smiling. But it was a smile with a cruel twist. She may have gotten bigger, but it seemed her heart hadn't grown with her. She was mean at any size. But could she really be someone who sold kids into slavery? Besides, she was family, even if only by law. And she was the only wall that stood between Jack and a state orphanage.

But was she also a trapdoor, leading one-way to slavery for her victims?

"Please, Jack," Shen said. "We need the photo."

Jack slid his aunt's wedding photo out of the frame, as he had every evening since she had put it there. He handed it to Shen. "You don't really need the picture," Jack said.

"We do," said Shen.

"No," said Jack, "I mean, my aunt once told me she ran an orphanage. And the photo is less important than her maiden name. It's written on the back." He turned the photograph over. Glued there was the wedding invitation he had seen many times:

*You are cordially invited
to the wedding celebration
of Miss Edith Crowley
to Mister Timothy Smith.
St. Paulus Lutheran Church
San Francisco
at one o'clock
March twentieth
Nineteen hundred and thirty-eight*

"It's her," one of the men behind Shen said in accented English.

"Yes, of course," replied Shen. "My father always thought she was the one who ran the orphanage. And now we have proof." Jack felt his stomach somersault, knowing that giving over the photo meant he was alone again, after all his efforts.

But the man wasn't looking at the wedding invitation.

He was looking at the picture still in the silver frame.

Jack's drawing of his mother.

The man pointed.

He said something in Chinese.

Then again, "It's her."

Shen gently took the silver frame from Jack and showed it to the man. Then she spoke to him in Chinese.

She turned back to Jack and held out the picture.

"He says that's the woman held captive. The woman we believe they're sending to the *Aventure Malgache*."

CHAPTER 22

FAMILY PLOT

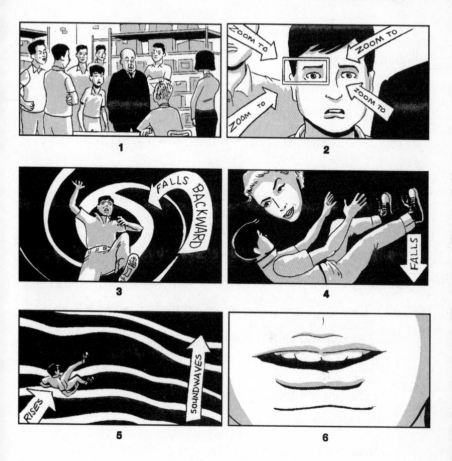

THE WORDS ECHOED DOWN the bottomless pit inside Jack. But now he was dragged with the words, falling into himself. It was as if everything outside his own body dimmed and warped and stretched before him. He sank into blackness. He reached out, but Shen, holding the picture of his mother, receded above him, dragging all the light with her. The world was dizzying, disturbing, twisted.

But an answer boomed from the pit as he fell. An insistent drumbeat echoed from below, pounding Jack with wave after wave, slowing his fall. Time had stopped. All was perfectly still for an instant. Jack floated, weightless, disconnected. Then the pounding renewed, stronger, as it bounced off the walls, until Jack was being born aloft. Time began to flow again. As the sound pushed Jack upward, it sharpened and clarified into a word. A word that reverberated around Jack until he surfaced and said it out loud.

"Alive."

Jack found himself surrounded again—by the bakers of the Xiao Long Fortune Cookie Company, the older Chinese men and women, Shen, and Hitchcock.

And then the word became a question.

"Alive?" Jack said. He took the picture of his mother. "This woman, my mother, is alive?"

The young man who had spoken nodded. "She was. Weeks ago."

"Tell me! Tell me everything!" Jack said.

The young man looked to Shen, who stepped toward

Jack and gently ran her fingers along one side of the drawing.

"This is your mother?" Shen asked.

"Yes."

"Who you believe to be dead?" Shen asked.

"No!" Jack cried, trying to cut her off before she said the last word. He didn't want it to drown out the echo still ringing in his heart. But he was too late. Now that dreaded word rooted and grew in his head.

"I don't know," Jack said. The silver frame was cold in his hand. Bottom-of-the-ocean cold. "She drove off a cliff—on purpose. There was a note."

"But was . . . ," Hitchcock began. He knelt on one knee and looked Jack in the eye. "But was there a body? And who identified it?"

"There was no body," Jack said. He spoke more quickly now. "They never found her. The car was an old convertible. They figure she washed out to sea." Then his shoulders slumped. "But look, there was a crowd of witnesses. They saw my mother drive the car off the cliff. That's what they told the police."

"Witnesses can be made-to-order," Hitchcock said. "We'll agree they saw someone drive off the cliff, but was it your mother? It did happen in Los Angeles, after all. Home of Hollywood, land of make-believe. Why, give me a stuntman and the proper equipment, and I can give you ten ways to stage the scenario you just described, all with witnesses, and all a complete deception."

Jack wasn't sure. The word in his heart and the word in his head were doing battle. His experience was that adults leave. One by one. They don't come back.

Shen was skeptical too. She turned to the man who had pointed to the drawing, and conversed again in Chinese. It got quite heated at one point, until Shen finished, in English, "Well, if you can't be sure, you should be more careful about what you say. It's his *mother*."

"When did he see her?" Jack asked. "Where?"

"He *thinks* he saw her in several of the warehouses and rooms the traffickers use. Never in one place long enough for him to gather sufficient evidence to alert the authorities," Shen answered.

Dead. That word that Shen had spoken still bounced around his head, trying to overwhelm the thought in his heart. But other things were now bouncing around his head as well. Missing bodies. Made-to-order witnesses. And a ransom note that was really a bill.

A bill for a service rendered.

Jack felt an insistent clamor of hope well up inside him. Hitchcock had said they needed to find an overlooked clue. But they hadn't overlooked it at all. They had only misread it.

"Moving her around," Jack asked. "Was there a small, well-dressed man, or a tall, beefy woman with horn-rim glasses?"

Shen translated. When the man finished answering, she turned to Jack.

"Both," she said. "How did you know?"

Jack's heart drummed a racket in his chest. The pieces fit. Things made sense. "Because all the time we thought we were solving my aunt's kidnapping, we were really solving my mother's suicide."

Shen gave him a blank look.

Jack turned to Hitchcock. "You see, don't you?"

"A little, perhaps," Hitchcock replied.

"Look," Jack said. He took out the handwritten note that was still in his pocket. His hands trembled until Hitchcock reached out to steady them.

"Calmly," Hitchcock said.

Jack took a breath. "Before we ran after Shen, you asked what this bill was for. Look again."

We'll agree to $200,000.

Bring it to the noon service at Mission Dolores on Monday.

And let's not play games, or I'll be forced to end this job immediately.

She'll be dead and you'll be blamed.

Yours,

S.

"See the last line?" Jack said. "'She'll be dead and you'll be blamed.' But if it is a bill, then it was for Aunt Edith to read, not us. If that last line was a threat to Aunt Edith, it would read '*You'll* be dead.' Not 'She'll be dead.'"

"If it is a bill," said Hitchcock, "a theory which, I believe, you have based on a paper clip, then you think the 'she' in that line is this woman seen at these warehouses."

"My mom," Jack said. "Look, we know Aunt Edith is a kidnapper, and it seems she's starting up business again. She kidnapped my mom, and then was kidnapped herself."

"Then who has your aunt?" asked Hitchcock.

Jack thought. "Whoever wrote the other notes," he answered. "We never received a ransom demand from The Suave Man. His note was handwritten. A bill. But we received other ransom notes. We've been chasing the wrong kidnapper. But look, here's the important thing. The *bill* reads 'She'll be dead.' 'She.' Like the woman they saw captive. 'She'll' meaning 'she will.' Will! Future. She could still be alive. And she could be my mother."

Hitchcock paced a small circle. "But, Jack, you may be seeing only what you want. He's not certain it's your mother."

"Does it matter?" Shen said.

Jack rounded on her. "What do you mean? Of course it does. It matters a lot, see."

"What I mean is, this woman, she is an innocent. A victim of Edith Crowley who may be sent into slavery any moment. She needs our help. It is our duty to find her."

"Oh," Jack said. "Right. I mean, you're right. It is our duty."

"But how?" Hitchcock said. "Her trail is weeks cold."

"One trail is still warm," said Shen's father. "Jack knows."

Jack did know, but part of him was reluctant to say. "My aunt," he said. He'd always had reason to dislike her, but now he loathed her. She was the one person he never wished to see again, and the one person he had to find. "If we find my Aunt Edith, we find the woman. If my aunt got the bill, then she was the one to request the service. And believe me, she'd know every step of the plan so she would get her money's worth. To save my mother's life—"

"We may need to rescue the woman who killed her," Hitchcock finished.

The room was silent. All were lost in their own thoughts. Jack wondered what the next step should be.

"In the cinema," Hitchcock finally said, "motivation of the character must be resolved, revealed, and clarified for the audience to understand the plot. So we must ask, if Jack's aunt did have his mother kidnapped, why? If the note is indeed a bill, then the expense was high. What did she or will she get in return?"

"Nothing," said Jack. "My mom was an actress. She wasn't a star yet, so we weren't rich. My aunt got nothing." Jack shrugged. "All she got from my mother was a full orphan. All she got was me."

"Your aunt has sold orphans in the past," Shen said.

"Then why isn't Jack also in the hands of the man who took his mother?" asked Hitchcock. "And pardon me for being indelicate, but would the return on an orphan and his mother really be worth more than two hundred thousand dollars?"

"No," said Shen, "I suppose not."

"Was there a will?" Hitchcock asked.

Jack remembered that day when Aunt Edith came to the funeral home and stole him away. "She had some legal papers when she picked me up. But even if there was a will, my mother had nothing. Just me."

"Perhaps the papers say differently," Hitchcock said. "Where are they?"

"Her room is the only place I can think of," Jack said. "And we've already looked pretty well in there."

"But we didn't know what we were looking for," Hitchcock said. "I think our next step is to search again. We must find those papers."

"Or search for the man who is holding the blond woman," Shen said.

"Well, whatever we do, we need to do it fast," Jack said, "or my mother may die a second time."

CHAPTER 23

RICH AND STRANGE

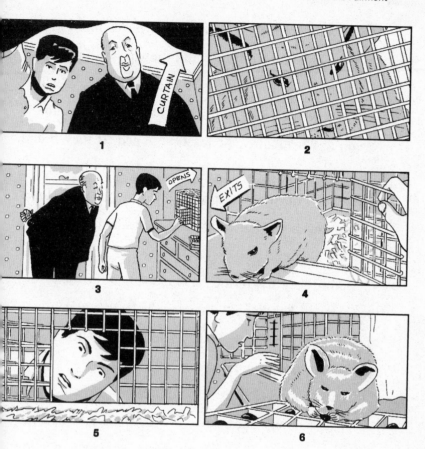

SHEN'S FATHER DROVE HITCHCOCK, Shen, and Jack back to the Fairmont Hotel.

"After all, we are allies now," Shen said. "We all want the same thing. To bring your aunt to justice and to save the woman, whoever she is."

My mother, Jack thought. What he couldn't figure out was why Aunt Edith would kidnap her. Surely not just to get Jack as a servant to fetch her chocolates and clean her messes. Jack knew he'd made the right choice, revealing her identity. At least he hoped. If they found his aunt, she would be put away, whether the captive woman was his mother or not. If he was one step closer to becoming a ward of the state, or one step farther away, Jack wasn't sure.

Before they'd left, they'd decided that the men from the factory—her "tong," Shen laughed—would continue to search for The Suave Man, while Jack, Hitchcock, and Shen pursued Aunt Edith.

"Sharon will be our eyes in this matter," her father said.

"That's good," Jack said. "Maybe she can find something we couldn't. We think my aunt is somewhere in the hotel. But that would be a lot of rooms to search."

"Plus the back of the house," said Shen.

"The what?"

"The back of the house. The Fairmont is much larger than the places the guests see. There are stairways and levels below, where only the staff go. There's the Engineering Department, the seamstress office.

Shipping. Receiving. The carpenters have a shop. Room service kitchens. A darkroom for the hotel photographer. There are whole rooms devoted to dishes and silverware. And much more. Your aunt could be anywhere."

At the hotel Shen returned to her elevator, thanking the operator who had covered for her.

"I was lucky no one important noticed my absence," she said, "but I better keep to my post and learn what I can from here. You'd be surprised what people reveal in an elevator."

Jack and Hitchcock retreated to Aunt Edith's room. Muffin was reaching through the bars of his cage toward the chocolates Jack had put there, but stopped to watch them with eyes like polished lead shot. His whiskers bristled in a disapproving frown as his head swiveled back and forth to follow their movements.

"Anything important to my aunt would be in here. It's the one room she wouldn't even let the maids into. I'll go through the dresser. Can you can start with the closet?"

Jack rifled through the dresser drawers, searching each article of clothing, pulling out the drawer itself and checking underneath and behind it. Hitchcock examined the closet, then under the bed, beneath the mattress, and in the nightstand drawers. Muffin harangued them with chattering squeaks and squawks whenever they came close to his cage.

"Nothing," Hitchcock said when he'd finished.

"Same here, but I have one more drawer to do," said Jack.

"Then I suggest you proceed."

"Only . . . well . . . look . . ." Jack hesitated. A red heat feathered his ears and cheeks. "It's her underwear drawer."

He stared at Hitchcock.

Hitchcock stared back.

Then at his own shoe, which had a spot on it.

He began to buff the tip of his shoe on the back of his pant leg. His gaze again fell on Jack, who was still staring at him.

"I'm only eleven," Jack said.

Hitchcock stopped buffing and stood firmly on two feet. "Yes. I suppose that must be taken into account." He grasped the remaining drawer's handle. "Well, into the abyss," he said.

"Hmmm . . . Ha . . . ," he said.

"Well, look," he mumbled.

Then he shouted "Good Lord!" and eased something from the drawer.

"What, what is it? Did you find the papers?" Hitchcock's back blocked Jack's view. But Hitchcock held something large up in front of him. His fingers hooked two embroidered elastic straps, one on each side.

"No," Hitchcock answered, "but something equally . . . ummm . . . noteworthy."

"A clue?" asked Jack.

"Not to any mystery you need investigate at your tender age," Hitchcock said. When Jack tried to maneuver around him, Hitchcock stuffed the article into the bottom of the drawer, saying, "Please, I shouldn't like to be accused of contributing to the delinquency of a minor." He pulled out the drawer, checking bottom and sides, and set it on the floor. He investigated its slot in the dresser, thumping all four sides and the rear.

"Nothing at all here. Not anywhere in the room. Could she have put her important papers in the hotel safe?" Hitchcock asked.

"I don't think so. The hotel staff would have access. Aunt Edith doesn't trust people."

"Then whom does she trust?" asked Hitchcock.

Jack closed his eyes and scratched behind both ears. His eyes popped open, and his gaze swept over to the occupant of the cage on the dresser. Hitchcock followed his stare.

"Weasels aren't typically known for their trustworthiness," he said.

"It's a chinchilla," said Jack.

"Perhaps it is also a guardian," Hitchcock replied.

Muffin cast Jack a wary look. The cage smelled of cedar, with an undertone of something musky and feral.

"Don't worry, Muffin. We just want to take a little look at your cage." He unlatched and opened the door, then took a step back.

Muffin poked his head out the door. He slinked out of the cage and over to the earthquake anniversary chocolates. He began to nibble at one, wiping his face with his paws to get every little bit.

Jack slid the cage away from Muffin, who *chutted* but didn't interrupt his enjoyment of the chocolate. Jack removed the water and food from the cage and checked underneath it. He felt through the cedar chips that lined the interior. They crackled and crunched as his hands ran along the perimeter of the cage.

"There's some kind of metal plate here," he said. "I can't quite get the edge of it." He snapped open his pocketknife, then plunged his hands back under the cedar shavings. "Got it!"

He hitched the plate up, and the shavings tumbled to the back of the cage. The plate had concealed a file, with a manila envelope and a few other papers. "Yes!" he said, and handed it all to Hitchcock.

Hitchcock sat down to examine the papers. Jack heard the papers shuffling, and Hitchcock's throaty "hmmm"s and "oh"s as he carefully looked at each one.

Jack's own attention wandered over to the cage where he'd found the papers. There was something odd about the cedar chips. Some of them weren't chips at all. Jack picked up a handful, and found he was doing his own examination of papers. But these weren't long sheets full of legal words and signed by concerned parties. These papers were little shreds that had been concealed under the cedar chips. Little shreds of blue lined paper, with cursive letters and words in the scratchy penmanship Jack knew belonged to Schultzie. But the shreds were far too small to put back together. He'd never know what they'd said. Jack tightened his fist around the paper scraps, compressing them into a little ball. He wished Aunt Edith were here now, so he could shove them down her lying throat. It took six deep, steady breaths before he could unball his fist.

When he did, Hitchcock spoke. "My dear Jack Fair, did you know that you are what is referred to as filthy rich?"

"What?"

"I've only looked at this for a few moments, but I believe there is quite a large trust out there in your name, with rather more than a few assets. Including, I might add, a stake in one very prominent hotel in San Francisco, located on the corner of California and Mason Streets."

Jack plopped onto the bed next to Hitchcock. "I own this hotel?"

"Part of it. The Fairmont. Its name came from your family name, and the fact that it sits on a high hill, overlooking San Francisco Bay," Hitchcock said as he thumbed through the papers again. "There is quite a bit of interesting information here."

Jack took the file. First he looked inside the manila envelope. Written on the outside, in his mother's handwriting, was "Important Papers." There were two wills, and a paper titled "Transfer of Legal Guardianship" clipped to a handwritten note from Mom. There were a few other documents. Jack didn't understand most of it, though it surprised him how thin the packet was. Shouldn't such world-shaking documents be inches thick? One paper especially caught his eye. He ran his finger over the marriage license, tracing his father's signature—Jonathan Fair. He'd never seen it before. It seemed to Jack that the way his father made his *J*s wasn't too far off from the way Jack himself did.

There were other papers in the file besides his mother's. There was a yellowing magazine article from a year ago entitled "The Missing Heir of Bonanza Jim Fair." There were copies of birth certificates, including that of Jack's father. The oldest certificate was for James Fair Jr., whose birth date was listed as November 18, 1861. Hitchcock gently held up this certificate. It appeared to be quite old.

"James Fair Jr. would have been . . ."—the director ticked off the fingers of his free hand with his thumb— "your great-grandfather."

Jack took the certificate. In the space listing the child's mother, someone had written Miss Charlotte Vance. Nothing was written in the space beside "Father's Name."

A photo slipped out from the stack of papers. It was wallet-size and yellowing. It showed a man in a Marine Corps dress uniform. A man with dark eyes and black hair.

Jack took the sketchbook from his pocket and turned to the image he had drawn the previous night, and compared. The man in the photo had jug ears, and the chin was a bit less prominent. But the eyes . . . the eyes were exactly the same. And they were Jack's.

For a long time Jack just stared.

Hitchcock coughed and pulled a paper from the file. "This letter is most illuminating," he said.

Jack read the letter.

Dear Mrs. Smith,

Thank you for your letter of March 8, 1956, informing us that you are the legal guardian of one Jack Fair and establishing his legal position as heir to the newly discovered Comstock trust. As you can imagine, the discovery of the "lost heir letter" among the cache of papers found at the Fairmont Hotel by the Earthquake Celebration Historical Committee has caused quite a lot of interest. No fewer than thirty people have come forward claiming to be the missing descendant of James Fair Jr., all with birth certificates and other legal records.

We are, of course, investigating all claims with the intent of authenticating the identity of the true heir. We look forward to receiving from you the required birth records as well as anything else you may be able to provide to establish the legitimacy of your claim.

Specifically, the legal papers establishing the trust bore a wax seal, as was more common in those days, bearing a numeric code. The trust stipulates that provision of these numbers is required as the "final proof" of the identity of the heir. We are informing all claimants of the seal's existence, in the hope that one will be able to provide the "final proof" and thus settle this matter expeditiously.

Yours,

Abelard Everett Poppelwaite

Poppelwaite, Jones, and Whitaker

Attorneys at Law

"And you think I am the heir?" Jack asked. He was afraid to stand up. The floor was moving in waves, the hotel swaying. He'd never keep to his feet.

"So it would seem," the director said.

"Or it could just be another scheme by Aunt Edith," Jack said. "She was always asking me about numbers and codes, but I didn't know what she meant. Hey! Do you suppose whoever kidnapped my aunt is one of these 'claimants'?"

The pair sat side by side, each regarding the other, as if by locking eyes they could unlock the answer to this question.

"The true ransom note did say 'the numbers better be right,'" Hitchcock said.

"And this letter asks for a numeric code," Jack finished. "Whoever kidnapped Aunt Edith knew about this. They think Aunt Edith really has this code."

"In which case you may well be the real heir," said Hitchcock.

Jack jumped at a crashing sound. Muffin, who was staggering around the top of the dresser, had bumped into his food bowl and sent it plunging to the floor. Muffin pitched off the edge of the dresser and into the underwear drawer, where he curled up and emitted soft little sighing sounds.

"What's the matter with the weasel?" Hitchcock asked.

"Chinchilla," Jack said. "I don't know." He poked Muffin with his finger and gave him a gentle shake. Muffin did not respond at all.

"That's strange. I can't wake him."

Hitchcock stood beside Jack. He gave the drawer a sharp kick. Then another. Muffin rocked with the motion of the drawer but otherwise didn't respond.

"The rodent's been drugged," Hitchcock said.

"But why would someone drug a chinchilla?" Jack asked.

Hitchcock picked up the half-eaten chocolate from the dresser and held it out in answer. "Perhaps it was a case of mistaken identity."

CHAPTER 24

SUSPICION

"AUNT EDITH'S CHOCOLATES WERE DRUGGED?" Jack said. "So that's how they got her out of here without her making a fuss."

"Though it doesn't explain how they moved her," Hitchcock said, "it does narrow our lists of suspects."

Jack nodded. "Because only someone who had access to the chocolates—"

"Could have drugged them," Hitchcock finished. "Now who falls into that category?"

"Just me," Jack said, "and Opal, I guess."

"Then she is at the top of the list of people to suspect," said Hitchcock.

"No," said Jack. Opal was the sweetest person he had met since coming to this city. She could never do something to hurt Jack. "Besides, she was with me at the time Aunt Edith was kidnapped."

"Then she is at the top of the list of people to consult," Hitchcock said.

Opal was standing on a step stool reaching for something on a shelf when they got to Blum's. She teetered back and forth like a pink beach ball on a trained seal's nose.

"Hey, Opal," Jack said.

"Be right down, sugar," she answered. She brought down a stack of boxes and peered around them at Jack. But before she spoke, she caught sight of Hitchcock's belly. "Oh!" she said, her voice swooping up at the end.

She quickly set the boxes behind her. "You're all better." She looked at her reflection in the chrome of the malt mixer and fluffed up her hair. But when she turned back, she saw Hitchcock. "Oh," she said again, flat this time. "I thought you were someone else."

Jack got right to the point. "Opal, who made up all those anniversary chocolate boxes?"

"Ugh!" she said. She pointed to the stack of boxes behind her. "This here is the last lot, and I don't want to think about them. It's a ton of work for just little old me. I've been sweating like a hen at the Fox County fair."

"You can't be doing it all yourself," Jack said. He hoped she wasn't.

"I'm manufacturing," Opal said. "Charlie the bellhop is distribution. Why all the questions?"

Jack filled her in on all they knew about the kidnapping of his aunt and the drugged chocolates.

"You don't suppose Charlie drugged them?" Jack asked.

"I don't see how," Opal said. She took one of the empty boxes and wrapped it in the gold paper used for the anniversary boxes. Then she took an oval seal that read "Blum's" and moistened its back with a damp sponge. She pressed this on the box where the folds of gold paper came together. "Once this dries, there's no way to open the box without tearing the seal. Was your seal torn?"

"No," Jack said.

Hitchcock turned the box over in his hands. He shook it. He pulled at the folds in the paper. "Perhaps they steamed the seal off."

"That would melt the chocolates, hon. Ruin 'em," Opal said. "These aren't those waxy rocks you can get over at See's. These are delicate."

"Look, if you didn't and he couldn't, then who drugged the chocolates?" Jack said, frustrated.

"Who else had access to them?" Hitchcock asked.

"No one," Opal said, and Jack's hopes dropped like a brick in a rain barrel. "Except for the examples."

"The examples?" Jack asked.

"That's right," Opal said. "Mr. Sinclair demanded to inspect the first ten boxes. I didn't seal those, of course." She clapped a hand to her mouth. "You don't think he— Well, it must have been him."

"Did you watch him inspect them?"

"Sugar, with Ruby and Pearl gone on their

honeymoons, I've been run off my feet around here. Inspecting his inspection wasn't on my agenda. Oh!" Her eyebrows popped. "If he drugged a guest, he's sure to get fired."

"At the very least," said Hitchcock.

"Well, I want in on that," Opal said. She reached into the glass case and pulled out three chocolates. She slid one to Jack and the other to the director. "These here are Catch-a-Crook Caramels."

She held hers up, and Jack touched his to it. After a moment Hitchcock did too.

"To the sharpest kind of justice," Opal said. "Now. How do we catch him?"

This was the topic of discussion when Jack and Hitchcock returned to his suite. Various plans were proposed and rejected. Once, Hitchcock smiled and started to speak, then shook his head. "No. Wouldn't work," he said.

"What wouldn't work?" Jack asked.

Hitchcock paced in front of the window, explaining.

"I once read a story where a police detective tricks a man into confessing murder by hiring an actress to play the ghost of the murdered woman. He sets the mood, makes the light fall on the actress just right, so she looks like the victim. He even gets a dog to play the part of the old woman's pet. Finally the murderer cracks and admits to the crime. But you see why it can't work."

"Why not?"

"We presume your aunt isn't dead."

"Oh. Right," Jack said, disappointed. Each proposal was a line running parallel to his mother. They brought him no closer to her. Then he brightened. "But who said she has to be! What would Sinclair think if he thought he saw my aunt in the lobby? I mean, he wouldn't think she was a ghost. But what would he think?"

"Hm . . . Yes, I see. That she'd escaped," Hitchcock said. "Of course."

"And then he'd go check, wouldn't he? I mean, if he wasn't sure if it was her but it seemed like it might be? He'd go to where he was keeping her to check."

"Yes, yes," said Hitchcock, "I see what you mean."

Jack retrieved the pad for storyboards. He drew out rectangles as he had seen the director do. "I'm sure we can come up with a way," he said. He bent down and picked up the sleeping Muffin. "See? We've already filled the role of the pet."

"We'll need some help, though," Hitchcock said. "This will be a complicated scene if it is to be convincing. Sinclair must see what we want him to see, but not with his full attention. We'll need to provide distractions. People in the crowd to make sure he goes where we want him and so forth. Extras, if you will."

Jack looked up from the pad. "Subsurface Shakespeare," he said.

"I beg your pardon?"

"Subsurface Shakespeare was my mother's old acting troupe in LA. I'm sure they'd do anything they could to help. And they are great actors." Jack let out a sigh. "But they're in the middle of a production. *Wild West Hamlet*. They couldn't leave that to come up here."

Hitchcock picked up the phone. "Do you have their number? Perhaps I can convince them."

While Hitchcock spoke quietly on the phone, Jack closed his eyes. He envisioned the lobby, then drew out the storyboards for their upcoming deception. The susurration of pencil gliding on paper was like music: the strings of long arcing curves, the brass of strong straight lines, the percussive beats of crosshatching, and the reedy softness of shading—a symphony for finding his mother.

Hitchcock hung up.

"I spoke with a gentleman named George. Once I'd convinced him who I was, he seemed quite eager to help. He said they'd 'make mad the guilty and appall the free, confound the ignorant, and amaze indeed,'" Hitchcock said.

"Does that mean they'll come?" Jack asked.

"I believe so. But he could provide no actress of your aunt's . . . dimensions, shall we say. We must find an actress to play the pivotal part. And on such short notice."

"You must know lots of actresses," Jack said.

"None without agents. In other words, none who will work for free," said Hitchcock, "and in any case it is considered bad form to audition your actresses in a hotel."

"What would she need to be like?" Jack asked.

"Well, she wouldn't need to speak, certainly," Hitchcock said, still pacing in front of the window, squinting as the streetlights blinked on outside. "We could cast her in shadow, or just give glimpses of her. So she really just needs to be able to gesture and follow direction. And, of course, she'll need to be the right size and shape for the costume—a duplicate of the clothing your aunt wore when she went missing."

The director's silhouette filled the window as he paced in front of it.

"Does the actress need to be a she?" Jack asked.

"No, I suppose not," Hitchcock answered.

Jack made a square with his hands and held it at arm's length. He peered through it at the rotund shadow Hitchcock cast.

"Then I think we have our man," Jack said. "We just need his costume."

CHAPTER 25

ALWAYS TELL YOUR WIFE

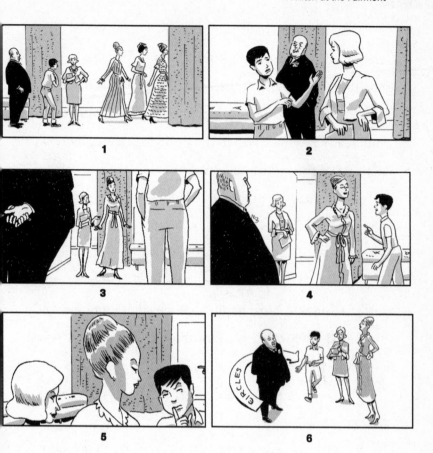

RANSOHOFF'S WOMEN'S SPECIALTY SHOP occupied a multistory building on Post Street, just off Union Square. A flock of pigeons tapped a Morse code of hunger along the sidewalk with their beaks, searching for seeds and scraps to eat. A fight broke out when one uncovered a dead mouse that had gotten stuck in the sewer grate, each bird's head piston-ing back and forth as it ran to hop into the fray. Soon the dead rodent and its discoverer disappeared beneath a frenzy of gray wings, pink talons, and beady red eyes. When the birds separated, there was nothing of the mouse to be seen.

More graceful, more dignified, yet just as insistent on getting what they wanted, a flock of women surrounded a salesman inside the department store, vying for his attention and voicing their individual demands all at once. To Jack's surprise the man cordially and patiently answered each request. Ransohoff's catered to a select clientele who expected nothing less.

"Are you quite sure this is where she got it?" Hitchcock asked.

"This was the store the bill came from," Jack said.

"Ah, Mr. Hitchcock. It is Mr. Hitchcock, isn't it? What an honor to have you in our store," the salesman greeted them.

"Thank you," said Hitchcock. "My godson and I would like to do some shopping and thought your charming store looked like just the place."

"You do realize, sir, that this is a ladies' garment store?"

"That's just it, you see," said Hitchcock. "The boy would like to buy a dressing gown for his aunt. Naturally we thought to come here. You see, we'd like to avoid the commotion my presence might cause, and you have a reputation for superior service."

"Yes, of course, sir. We maintain several private parlors for our more noteworthy clients. I'm sure one of them would suit your needs." He flipped the switch of a small intercom on the counter and bowed forward to speak into it. "Mrs. Brown, two gentlemen for the Gardenia Room."

A voice came through in answer. The intercom made it high and chirpy, like a staccato teakettle. "Shall I come down to escort them up?"

Hitchcock gave a little shake of the head.

"That won't be necessary, Mrs. Brown. They'll meet you at the top of the stairs." He indicated the way with a wave of his hand. "If I can be of any more assistance, please let me know. Otherwise, our Mrs. Brown will take care of you."

"Our" Mrs. Brown wore gray—a stylish women's suit with a tailored skirt and a jacket with turned-up cuffs over a cream silk blouse. In her heels she was the height of fashion at under five feet.

"Right this way," she said. It wasn't the intercom that had rendered her voice so high and chirpy after all. It came naturally to Mrs. Brown. She guided them through the hallway, which let off on either side to parlors where women sat watching models posing in stylish dresses and shoes. Mrs. Brown came to a room where she held back a velvet curtain.

"The boy would like to buy a white dressing gown for his aunt," Hitchcock said.

Mrs. Brown smiled and indicated that they should take a seat on the sofa that stood against the wall. "I'll be back in a moment with a few selections," she said, ducking back through the curtain.

The room was painted the palest shade of blue, like a robin's egg dusted with pearl. In the center of the room was an ornate table with a crystal bowl of white gardenias. Hitchcock got up and sniffed the gardenias, then selected one to slip into the buttonhole of his lapel.

Mrs. Brown returned. "It will be just a moment," she said. She seemed about to say more to the director, but stopped herself.

"Yes?" Hitchcock prompted.

"Well, sir, I was just wondering . . . Are you that

man from the television? Alfred Hitchcock?"

"Why, yes, madam, I am."

"Oh, I just love your show. I watch it whenever I can, though my husband always tells me I shouldn't pay attention to any of the silly things on it. He says I should stick to cooking and cleaning and selling dresses." She paused. "You must know a lot about murder and the like."

"Only as much as any good American citizen would do."

"Oh, Mr. Hitchcock," she said, blushing.

"I excelled on the shooting, bludgeoning, and strangulation portions of my naturalization exam."

"Oh, honestly," she said, laughing. Then she fell quiet and struck a very charming pose, with her finger to her chin. "You know, I read a story once about a woman who did in her husband by whacking him over the head with a frozen leg of lamb. Then she cooked it up and fed it to the police when they came to investigate, so they could never find the murder weapon."

"Yes. 'Lamb to the Slaughter' by Roald Dahl," said Hitchcock. "I am familiar with it. We plan to film it for my show."

"How marvelous." She hesitated a bit. Then, "It's just that, I wonder if a frozen lasagna would work as well?"

"I suppose—"

"Because my husband likes Italian, you see."

"My dear woman," Hitchcock said, "I am sure any frozen entree would work, provided it were of sufficient weight and could be gripped and swung."

"Oh, good." Mrs. Brown clasped her hands together with a sharp clap.

"And also provided the wielder of such a weapon had sufficient nerve and was prepared to spend her life behind bars, as she would no doubt be caught."

Mrs. Brown's smile faded. "Perhaps I should see what is keeping the models."

In a short while a parade of young women came in one by one, each wearing a white dressing gown that trailed on the floor behind her.

"No, no! They're none of them right!" Jack said after the sixth one.

"The little gentleman certainly seems to know what he wants," said Mrs. Brown.

"Jeez. Look—this one had sort of a ruffly collar and a square neckline."

"I liked the second one," Hitchcock said.

"No, that's not it," Jack said. "It wouldn't suit you—I mean my aunt."

"Oh! I think I know the one you want," said Mrs. Brown. "A very popular design. Let me check." She went out and returned briefly with a file full of papers and another model.

"That's the one," said Jack.

"Fine." She looked at her file. "We just received a shipment. What size were you looking for?"

Jack dragged Hitchcock to his feet. He circled around Hitchcock with his arms spread out, surrounding the director's shoulders, then waist, then hips, enclosing him in parentheses. "About this size," he said.

"Oh, I'm so sorry. We don't stock ladies' plus sizes—or extra plus. We'll have to special-order it."

"But we need it by this afternoon," Jack said.

"Well . . ." She consulted her file again. "We do have one rather large one, but I'm afraid it was special-ordered by another customer. A Sarah Thompson."

"That's my aunt," Jack lied. "See. I knew she'd like that one. It would be okay, wouldn't it, if I bought it for her?"

"Well, I suppose we could allow that. We'll just need to call your aunt to confirm."

"But that would ruin the surprise. Oh, please," Jack said.

Mrs. Brown chewed her lower lip.

"Hmmm . . . all right. Just be sure to give it to her before Friday, when she's due to come pick it up. It would be so awkward if she showed up and we hadn't got the gown."

"Oh, thank you," Jack said. "Auntie Sarah will just love it."

Outside the store the pigeons had moved on to better hunting grounds.

"The real Sarah will be terribly disappointed," Hitchcock said.

"Not if everything works out," Jack said, hoisting the red-and-gold box from Ransohoff's onto his shoulder. "We can return this on Thursday, with a day to spare. Just don't take off the tags."

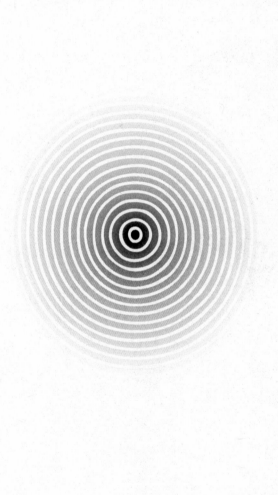

CHAPTER 26

STAGE FRIGHT

THE SUBSURFACE SHAKESPEARE troupe arrived at the hotel early Wednesday morning. They had driven all night, and most were still in their costumes from the previous evening's performance. Shen and Opal, who'd been expecting them, escorted them immediately up to Jack.

Jack opened the door to Hitchcock's suite. In swept a man sporting dusty leather chaps and a Stetson. "A bed, a bed, my kingdom for a bed!" he called.

It was George Barrister, lead actor and sometimes director of the troupe. Opal stood next to him, ducking a little as he threw his arms wide in a gesture of imploration. A group of other actors followed, all friends of Jack's mother—family, almost. Maybe a full orphan was less alone than Jack thought.

But it was the last person to enter who most surprised him.

"Schultzie!"

"Hello, Jack," Schultzie said. The floor beneath Jack's feet suddenly seemed more solid, more secure, as if the fulcrum of Schultzie's presence had made it pivot from a dangerous incline to perfectly horizontal.

"We needed a substitute stage manager," George said. "Our own has a diner to run and a wife who is expecting. Now, about that bed—"

"Sorry, Mr. Barrister. No time for a nap," Jack said. "We have rehearsing to do to make this work. And remember, everything depends on this going exactly as planned."

"Coffee, then," called George. "My kingdom for a

cup! An actor with caffeine is made of sterner stuff!"

"I'll go get a pot from the store," Opal said. She flattened the sides of her skirt against her moon-round hips. "On the house. And maybe a little something to eat. A big strong man like you needs to keep up his strength."

"George seems rather dramatic," Hitchcock whispered to Jack.

"Uh-huh . . . more than usual," Jack said. "I think he's auditioning for you."

"Tell him he already has the part."

Jack pulled Schultzie to the side, as the actors settled in.

"I'm glad to see you," Jack said.

"Like Mr. Barrister said," Schultzie replied, "they needed a stage manager." There was something odd and reserved in his voice.

"I didn't get any of your letters," Jack said.

"Jeez," Schultzie said, "I wrote to you every week."

"I just found them last night. In shreds."

"Shreds? I told you how Dad said we'd love for you to move in with us, but he doubted your aunt would allow it. She claimed she had legal custody of you."

"Aunt Edith tore up your letters," Jack said. He would throttle her if they ever found her.

Schultzie's reserve immediately broke. "I knew something was wrong. I wasn't sure what to do until last night," he said. "Dad and I were at *Wild West Hamlet* when the call came for Mr. Barrister. Did you know they stopped the show so he could take the call?"

"Really?"

"There weren't too many people there anyway. Mr. Barrister called us backstage and explained things. I told my dad I had to come. He made Mr. Barrister promise that I wouldn't do anything dangerous." He shoved his hands into his pockets. "I guess that's why I'm stage manager."

Jack put his arm around his friend's shoulders, even though he had to stand on his toes to do it. "Look, I'm just glad you're here," he said.

"Me too," said Schultzie. His heart was big as ever.

Soon Opal returned with trays of coffee, tea, and two boxes of Blum's special Coffee Crunch Cake. She carried two particularly large pieces over to George.

"'Sweets to the sweet,'" she said, handing him one.

George accepted the cake, but his eyes never left Opal's. "*Hamlet,* act five, scene one," he said.

"That's right, sweetie," said Opal. "My daddy ran

Southern Fried Shakespeare for donkey's years. Let's just hope it's happier circumstances now than in the play." She gently touched George's buckskin sleeve.

George took her puffy hand in his. "'Oh, that I were a glove upon that hand,'" he said.

Opal blushed. "Oh! That is a happier circumstance," she said, and bit into her cake.

When the actors were fed, Jack pulled out the storyboards he had drawn. He searched for somewhere to spread them out.

Hitchcock pushed aside the remaining papers on his desk. "Put them here," he said.

Each sketch was a rectangular frame depicting the hotel's lobby. In the lower-right corner was a time. The first one was at three p.m.

Jack looked at Hitchcock. He'd practiced what to say with the director. Hitchcock smiled reassuringly and nodded. Jack spoke. "These sketches show how each of you must move, making sure Mr. Sinclair, the head bellman, sees enough but not too much. The times must be followed as closely as possible, though of course some improvisation will be required."

George stood. "Ah. The play's the thing wherein

we'll break the bellman's evil scheme." He took the storyboards and assigned the actors their parts.

Meanwhile Hitchcock proceeded to Aunt Edith's suite with Jack and Maxine, who had a bit part in every play but was especially good with makeup. There Hitchcock donned the dressing gown from Ransohoff's.

"Will I pass as your aunt?"

Jack looked Hitchcock up and down. "Your hair," he said.

"Oh, no!" Hitchcock said. He covered his head as if protecting the thin coating of hair left on it. "But my dear boy, there's not much to be done. I fear I don't have enough hair to be a convincing aunt."

"No," Jack conceded, "but Aunt Edith does—by the boxful." Soon he offered the director several wigs in fancy boxes.

"Blond is always to be preferred, Jack," Hitchcock said, snugging the wig onto his head.

"Hmph!" said Maxine, a redhead. "Come on. Let's get started on the makeup." She herded Hitchcock toward the bathroom, its countertop filled with Aunt Edith's beauty supplies.

Jack gave her a picture of Aunt Edith from the

dressing table. "Are you sure you can do it?" he asked.

Maxine looked from the photograph to Hitchcock. "Piece of cake," she said. "He's halfway there already."

"One more thing." Jack went to his aunt's dresser and pulled on the embroidered elastic strap sticking out of a middle drawer. "Ah. There it is. We'll need you to look a little more . . . What did you call it? Noteworthy." He held out the brassiere. "I'll need you to fill this."

"Alas," Hitchcock said, pressing his hands to his chest, "I'm afraid I cannot."

Jack tossed it to Hitchcock, who caught it. "Please, Mr. Hitchcock. You're almost perfect."

As Hitchcock struggled into the behemoth brassiere beneath the dressing gown, Jack picked up the phone. "Hello. Room service," he said.

"You're hungry at a time like this?" Hitchcock asked.

"Shhh," Jack said, then spoke into the phone. "Yes. This is Edith Smith's suite. Could you send up a couple of grapefruits? Whole." Jack looked over at Hitchcock, who had managed to don the gargantuan undergarment. "Better make that cantaloupes," he said.

When Schultzie gave the half-hour call, Hitchcock was still in the bathroom with Maxine.

"Is he ready?" Schultzie called.

"You can't rush art," Maxine said.

"This has to run like clockwork," Schultzie replied. "Some of the actors have already gone down. We didn't want them all to get off the elevator in a gang. So when 'places' is called, this thing is happening whether he's ready or not."

"You sure you weren't a stage manager in another life?" Maxine asked.

"Clockwork," Schultzie said again, and went to the other suite.

Jack fidgeted for a while, wishing he had given himself more to do. But he knew it was best to rely on his friends. They were professionals. His job was to see that Hitchcock was where he needed to be when the deception began, and to play his own part in it. Jack decided to pop over to the other suite and see how the actors there were doing.

He was in the middle of the hallway when the door to Hitchcock's suite swung open. Three actors emerged, followed by Schultzie. "Break a leg," Schultzie called as the actors trooped toward the elevator. He turned to Jack. "I was just coming to give you the fifteen-minute call. . . . He ready yet?"

Jack shrugged. "Who's left in there?"

"Just George and Marie. They'll go down when I give the five-minute call, but they won't be able to see if Mr. Hitchcock is there when I call 'places.' They'll start whether he's there or not." Schultzie pointed to his watch.

"I know. Clockwork," Jack said. "I'll go see if he's ready."

Before Jack reached his room, the elevator arrived with a ding to take the three actors down. The door slid open, and Shen, seeing him, began to gesticulate, waving her hand and pointing to his room. Jack didn't have time to work out what she meant before the passenger in the elevator pushed her way out from behind Shen. Alice Trapp emerged, clipboard first. And she had a policeman with her.

Clockwork, Jack thought. *But a bureaucrat has just been thrown into the gears.*

CHAPTER 27

THE CALL OF YOUTH

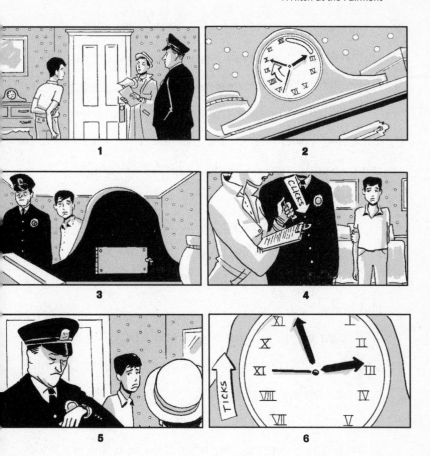

ALICE TRAPP TROTTED DOWN THE HALL, already making notes on her clipboard.

"Now isn't really a good time," Jack said.

"We have to keep your best interest in mind," Alice Trapp replied, pushing into his room. "This is Deputy

Whatley from the San Francisco Sheriff's Office."

"Police?" Spiders of fear crept up Jack's neck as he remembered the kidnapper's demand for no police.

"I'm afraid I need to make positive contact with your aunt, and verify her identity, or the deputy will have to remove you from the home," said Alice Trapp.

"But—"

"And if she isn't here at the moment, we'll also need to remove you from the home."

Jack glanced at the clock on the side table. Hitchcock had better be ready.

"Aunt Edith, that social worker is here," Jack called. Then he said to the deputy, "My aunt is in the bathroom."

"She seems to spend a lot of time in there," Alice Trapp said. The deputy said nothing but made a circuit of the living room, peering behind the curtains and under the tables. Did he expect to find a hidden assassin? A dead body?

The clock on the table showed nearly three. Jack had to dispose of Alice Trapp and shuttle Hitchcock into place right away. Soon the curtain would go up on the scene, and the star still primped in his dressing room!

"Can you come back a little later? My aunt is doing her beauty routine, and it can take a while."

Alice Trapp consulted her clipboard. "We'll wait."

Jack had never noticed the ticking of the clock on the table before, but now it thundered in his ears like the bass drum of a slave ship beating out time. Each tick rowed his plans closer to failure and his hopes of finding his mother farther from reality.

"Perhaps you'd be more comfortable waiting in the lobby. We could come down and meet you when she's out," Jack said.

Alice Trapp clicked open her pen. "I don't think so. There are some legal papers that need to be signed, among other things," she said, and bowed her head to her clipboard to make a few marks. The deputy was examining the couch cushions.

The quiet *snick* of a door opening and then closing sounded in the room.

The afternoon sun blazed through the curtains to cast a green haze on the door to Aunt Edith's bedroom. There stood Hitchcock, the very reflection of Aunt Edith in the white ruffled dressing gown, holding a tray with her handbag, a manila file, and a gold-wrapped box.

"Why, Jack, dear," he said, his voice two octaves higher than usual, "why didn't you say we had company?"

Jack could not speak. Maxine was destined for fame, if her current work was any indication. Jack thought people, like snowflakes, were never alike, but any difference between Hitchcock and his aunt was imperceptible. Seeing his "aunt," a shade of fear whipped through Jack.

"This is Deputy Whatley," Jack said when he'd found his voice, "and Miss Trapp you'll remember from yesterday."

Hitchcock made as if to put the tray on the table. Jack removed the clock to make room, and tapped its face as he passed in front of Hitchcock, who gave an almost undetectable nod.

Hitchcock held out his hand to the deputy, palm down. When the deputy moved to shake it, Hitchcock pulled back so that the deputy had only his fingers. Then he navigated their clasped hands to the deputy's lips. What could the deputy do? He kissed one of the giant rings Hitchcock was wearing.

"Charmed," Hitchcock said. "And, Alice! How nice to see you again."

The deputy dropped Hitchcock's hand. "You the boy's aunt?" he asked.

"Guilty." Hitchcock giggled. "Has he done something wrong?"

"We'll need to see some ID," Alice Trapp said.

"Of course." Hitchcock reached into the handbag and produced Aunt Edith's passport. The deputy picked at the loose corner of the photo affixed to it. He stared at the image, then at Hitchcock.

"You've lost a little weight," he said.

"Well, thank you, you charming man," Hitchcock replied. "I've been trying so hard. A girl's got to watch her figure, or no one else will!" He handed the deputy the file from the tray. "And here are the papers establishing me as the boy's guardian."

Deputy Whatley scanned the papers. He gave them to Alice Trapp. "I'm satisfied," he said.

Alice looked through the papers and identification as well, then handed them back to Hitchcock. "It looks like everything is in order," she admitted. There was a knock at the door.

"Five-minute call," Schultzie shouted.

"Five minutes to what?" asked Alice Trapp. "Who is that?"

"Just the maid, dear. She'll want to clean the room

in five minutes. Well. So nice to have seen you again," Hitchcock said, and graciously indicated that Miss Trapp should precede him to the door.

But the social worker planted herself on the couch and dragged the deputy after her. She withdrew six or seven pages from her clipboard and clipped them on top. "We just need to fill out a little paperwork to document our visit."

Jack caught Hitchcock's eye. He said nothing, but his head inclined toward the clock. Hitchcock smiled calmly.

"Paperwork. Of course," Hitchcock said. "But first a little refreshment. The management was so kind as to send these up to celebrate the earthquake anniversary."

He offered the gold foil box.

"Chocolate?" he said.

CHAPTER 28

THE SKIN GAME

"PLACES," SCHULTZIE CALLED. "Hurry up! You two should already be down there."

Shen held the elevator, waiting for them to arrive.

"I'm sorry," she said. "I couldn't keep that woman away. The policeman seemed suspicious when I tried."

"It's all right," Jack said. "We . . . managed them. Let's just get downstairs, quick." The deception had likely already started. It had been carefully blocked out in the storyboards, and the actors were well rehearsed. Jack closed his eyes. "See as the camera sees," Hitchcock had told him. Even now George and Marie would be harassing Mr. Sinclair.

See as the camera sees.

Jack did.

"Yes, madam. I believe Ernie's would meet your dinner requirements quite well," Mr. Sinclair would say. The woman corralled him by the front door some time ago, after he'd quelled a disturbance there caused by a different woman with a lasso and a man with a fake human skull.

"I just need to be sure we can get a good steak there," the woman says. "My husband made all his money in cattle, so he's quite the expert. I wouldn't want to go to a place that thinks dressing up cheap cuts with a little parsley is acceptable."

"No, madam, of course not. Ernie's has several steak offerings that use only the finest-quality beef." She's

been prattling on for quite some time now, while her husband in the Stetson keeps chiming in with, "My kingdom
for a steak."

"I mean, any cut may be just fine for average people,
but as I said, my husband is quite demanding about his
steak, as he well has a right to be. When you look at my
husband, you're looking at over sixty percent of the meat
in this country."

"Yes, madam."

"And next year he'll be expanding into poultry."

Just then a commotion starts across the lobby. The
bellman sees Jack running out of Blum's. Jack nearly
knocks over a baby carriage and is headed for the marble
column closest to the elevator. He is running so awk-
wardly because he is holding something large, a jumbo
box of assorted chocolates.

"Chocolates," Sinclair mumbles. "But who's going
to eat them?"

"Chocolates?" the woman says. "No, chickens.
Chickens! Next year he'll be getting into chickens."

"Yes, madam," the bellman says, though his eyes
never leave Jack as the boy crosses the lobby and dis-
appears behind a column. When the bellman moves in

Jack's direction, the woman catches him by the arm and walks him over toward Blum's.

"Of course, poultry will never replace beef on the American table, but chickens have been grossly under-exploited in this country," she says. "You could say there's a lot of scratch to be had from chickens."

The bellman gestures the doorman over. "Please hail a taxi for the lady and the gentleman. They'll be dining tonight at Ernie's."

"Well, I'm not exactly sure we've made that decision yet," the woman says. "Do they have a good steak at Ernie's?" she asks the doorman.

The bellman turns toward where he last saw Jack, but Opal calls him as she pushes open the sweet-shop door. "Why, Mr. Sinclair," she says, "have you seen Jack Fair? He just bought a box of chocolates, and he left without his change."

"Chocolates? For whom?" the bellman asks.

"Beats me," Opal replies. "His aunt, I'd guess. At least, he got the biggest box of the kind she likes—without the coconut creams."

"Well, find out for certain next time," the bellman snaps.

"Listen, Bub, I thought I already made it clear that you are not my boss. Why don't you just ask Jack? Isn't that him over there?" Opal points to a column across the lobby.

The bellman quicksteps toward Jack, noticing that the torchère next to the column casts the shadow of an unseen person. The shadow faces Jack, evidently a woman, her hair in disarray. The bellman watches as a be-ringed hand reaches from behind the column and picks chocolates from the box Jack is holding. Then the shadow pops them one, two, three into its mouth.

The bellman picks up his pace, but a man in a gingham shirt and a buckskin vest steps in front of him. Who let all these dratted cowboys in? *the bellman might wonder.*

"Excuse me," the cowboy says, but when the bellman moves to the left, so does the man.

"Sorry." Both move right.

"Pardon." Left.

"Well, dang. If I knew this was goin' to be a dance, I'da brung my fiddle," says the man.

Sinclair pushes the man aside and runs toward the column, but a woman in a calico dress sets her suitcase right in front of him. He trips and falls.

"I'm so sorry," the woman says. "Of course, this really isn't a good place to be running."

The bellman gets up and steps over her bag. "Out of my way, you stupid woman."

"That ain't no way to speak to a lady," she says, pushing up her sleeves and raising her fists.

A man in a white Stetson hat now steps between them. Two other Stetsons come up beside him. The men herd Mr. Sinclair in a direction so he can't quite see behind the column.

Sinclair sidesteps the men. There's a clear path to the column.

But Jack is gone. Two half-eaten chocolates rest in the black sand of the ashtray there. Their gooey white centers are mixed with what looks like lipstick. Bright pink lipstick.

Over near the elevator Mr. Sinclair spots Jack walking with a woman in a white dressing gown, but the bellman loses them behind a group of men and women wearing cowboy boots.

"Excuse me," he says when he gets there, but the crowd doesn't part until the elevator door slides shut. Through the last few inches of closing door, he sees a *large woman in a white dressing gown. She's holding up an animal and giving it little kisses.*

"Oh, Poopsie. Mumsy was so afraid," she says

"Going up," Shen says. "Step to the rear, madam."

CHAPTER 29

THE 39 STEPS

"OH, POOPSIE. MUMSY WAS SO AFRAID," Hitchcock said.

"Going up," Shen said. "Step to the rear, madam."

The elevator door snapped shut on the exasperated face of the bellman.

"That was close," Jack said.

Shen dropped Hitchcock and Jack off on the second floor. She continued to the fifth floor, in case the bellman was watching the elevator's indicator.

Jack beckoned Hitchcock down the second floor hallway. The staircase near Shen's elevator was open and visible as it wound down to the lobby. So the pair trotted to the south staircase, which was easier to sneak down unnoticed. It came out near the bell desk. Once they'd descended the stairs, Jack spied around the corner. Hitchcock joined him, still in the dressing gown and blond wig. The end of a pink leash dangled from his handbag.

The Shakespeareans were to keep track of the bellman, keep him away from the south staircase, and report on his movements to Jack. But the bellman stood at his station. He held up a ring of keys. These he slipped into his pocket. Then he walked briskly down the hall away from the main lobby, past the shops that lined the California Street side of the hotel.

"Let's go," Jack said, and cat-pawed into the lobby.

"Quietly," Hitchcock whispered.

The bellman turned left, into the hall that ran parallel to the main entrance, but at the back of the hotel.

The rear entrances of the bars and restaurants that dominated the center of the main lobby were on his left. The Venetian Ballroom was on his right. He passed the framed pictures of Tony Bennett and Ella Fitzgerald by the entrance that announced their upcoming dates. Just past these he came to a door panel that was painted the same charcoal gray as the wall. He touched a button, and the panel slid away. It wasn't exactly a secret entrance, but it was certainly unobtrusive. The bellman descended the stairs inside.

Hitchcock and Jack ducked in before the panel slid shut. All the elegance of the grand hotel vanished. They were on a sort of landing. The lower wall was painted a sloppy dark blue and was a stained white above. The narrow stairway descended to the left. Ahead was a freight elevator. A half dozen buckets and mops were shoved against the wall opposite it.

Jack pointed to the elevator. "Maybe that's how they moved Aunt Edith," he whispered.

Hitchcock nodded. "How would they get her there from the room, though?"

"Maybe they rolled her," said Jack.

Hitchcock looked puzzled. "Like a bowling ball?"

"No! On a luggage cart!" Jack said.

"Oh."

They followed Sinclair down the stairs, which were fine marble incompatible with the shabbiness around them. The pair nearly lost the bellman several times as they followed him through a labyrinth of sagging plaster ceilings and cracked, peeling paint, down more stairs, through more hallways. The back of the house was a city unto itself. They walked on the balls of their feet to keep their shoes from squeaking. Stacked along the walls were all sorts of things the hotel might need—chairs, old furniture, banquet tables. An antique washstand stood alone in one corner.

They steered around another corner and found themselves in a large room. Rollaway beds, made up with white linens, stood on end like tombstones, row after row, six wide and at least twenty deep. Standing directly in an aisle between two rows, Jack could see all the way to the far wall of the room. But if he weren't centered in an aisle, the beds appeared to be a solid wall of white from his perspective, behind which the bellman had disappeared.

Jack carefully picked his way from row to row,

afraid each time he stepped into an aisle that he would be exposed and be seen by Mr. Sinclair. Once or twice he caught a glimpse of the bellman, and quickly jumped behind a bed, pressing himself into the bleachy smell of the mattress.

The sound of keys being dropped, and then a mild curse, came from the far end of the room. A door swung open and hit a wall. Jack risked exposure and dashed down the aisle past the last five rows. Three doors pierced the moldy plaster wall at the end of the room. One was slightly ajar.

Hitchcock ambled up behind Jack, slightly winded.

"It's too risky to peek in," he whispered. "We'll have to wait."

"But we may never get that door open again," Jack said. The door was opened into the next room just enough that he could see the strike plate with the rectangular hole in which the spindle of the door latch would catch. Jack smiled and opened the box of chocolates he still carried. He selected several of the caramels—his favorite, and just right for what he had in mind.

"What—," Hitchcock began, but Jack put his finger to his lips.

He jammed one of the caramels into the rectangular space on the strike plate. The caramel disappeared into the hole, and Jack pressed it farther in until it smashed into the doorjamb. Then he added another and another, until the hole was filled with them.

The doorknob rattled. Jack had just enough time to slide behind a rollaway before the bellman emerged, a sneer tattooed on his face. He closed the door and pocketed the keys. He looked into an old mirror leaning against the wall, combing his hair over his Formica-smooth dome. He turned his head this way and that, then kissed his fingers and touched them to the mirror. "Perfect," he said. Jack and Hitchcock slid around their respective beds as the bellman headed back toward the lobby, doing a little skip step as he disappeared around a corner.

Jack returned to the jammed door and reached for the knob. Had the caramels done the trick? He turned the handle.

Click. The door opened.

"We're in," Jack said.

Hitchcock tapped the little sign affixed to the door as they passed through.

"Lost bags," Jack read. "Hmph. I might have known."

Old luggage filled the dusty room. Bags of various types and sizes stretched along an entire wall, from floor to ceiling. Three large trunks crouched in the center of the room.

Otherwise the room was empty.

"She's not here," Jack said, and sank down to sit beside one of the trunks. He leaned his head up against it and closed his eyes. "I really thought we'd find her."

"She must be here," Hitchcock answered. "Why else would the bellman come here with such urgency?"

"Then where is she?" Jack asked.

Hitchcock paced a circle around the room, scratching his head beneath the blond wig. His eyes fell on the three large trunks. Jack followed his gaze.

"They're not big enough," Jack said.

"Even all three together?" Hitchcock asked.

"But even you said there wasn't time to . . . make her fit."

"They have had several days since then."

Jack gasped, jumped away from the trunk, and backed up against the wall of bags. Hitchcock opened the center trunk.

"Good heavens!" he said.

"Is it Aunt Edith?" Jack asked.

"Not unless she was Miss January 1944," Hitchcock replied, holding up a magazine called *Pinup Girl*. He removed the open padlocks from the other trunks and threw back their lids. "Same thing," he said. "A few old magazines to remind the troops what they were fighting for."

"Pinup magazines!" Jack said. "The bellman came down here to look at pinup magazines?"

"Of course I didn't," an oily voice said from the direction of the door.

The bellman entered the room and slid home the chain lock on the inside of the door.

CHAPTER 30

BLACKMAIL

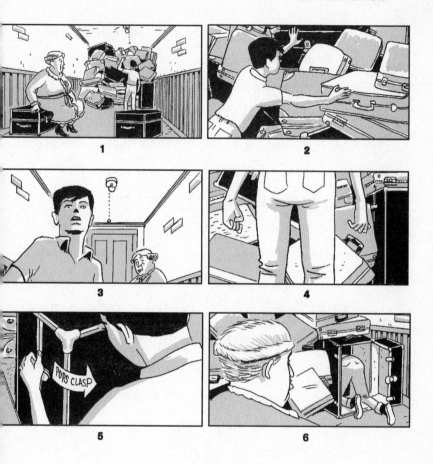

SINCLAIR FACED JACK. "Did you think I didn't see you in the mirror?"

"Where's my aunt?" Jack said.

"Why, she's right there beside you," the bellman said, pointing at Hitchcock. His mustache covered his mouth like a mud flap, but Jack could sense the smirk there.

The bellman drew a knife from his pocket. He tilted his head and tapped the point of the knife on his chin, considering. "But, no. That isn't really her, is it?" He closed one eye and used the knife to trace Hitchcock's outline in the air before him. "A reasonable facsimile, though, I'll give you that." He went back to tapping, point to chin. Tap. Tap. Tap. "Too bad for her she's a loose end."

"I want to see my aunt," Jack said.

"Well, we all have wants, don't we, boy?" the bellman said. "Wants are wanterful things. Get it? WANTerful? Ha! You can do a lot of things with wants. Sometimes wants can be exchanged. I have something you want. And you have something I want."

"That's blackmail," said Hitchcock.

"That's quid pro quo," said the bellman. He made a little arc in the air with the knife point. "And the knife makes my quid more valuable than your quo."

"What do you want from me?" asked Jack.

"Just seven little numbers," the bellman replied.

Jack nervously tugged at the chain beneath his collar. "So you know about the lost heir trust," he said.

"Know about it?" the bellman replied. "I found it. That money should be mine. I was sent down to help the ladies from the Earthquake Celebration Historical Committee. A job, I might add, that should not fall to the head bellman. But there I was. I found the paper and was just reading it, when one of those committee females shrieked in my ear. She'd been reading over my shoulder. I got a glance at those seven little numbers, but before I could memorize them, I was surrounded by a gaggle of lady historians, honking like wild geese."

"And now you want the numbers," said Jack.

"My life would be so much easier if I had them," said the bellman. "And yours would be so much longer." Tap. Tap. Tap.

"Don't you think it is going to look kind of fishy if the first person to find the will also claims to be the heir?" Jack said.

"Ah, but I didn't find it. Not officially. Those honking geese took all the credit."

"But you have no papers or documentation," said Jack.

"Of course I do," said Sinclair. "All faked. That's easy enough to do. In fact, I thought you and your aunt were working the same con at first. Imagine my surprise to find that after spending time with your aunt, I am now convinced you're the real McCoy."

"Where is she?" Jack said again.

"Seven."

Tap.

"Little."

Tap.

"Numbers."

Tap.

Jack hung his head. "Okay." He took a deep breath. "Nine, one, three, four, three, six, six," he said.

The tapping stopped.

"You really should not have done that," the bell-man said. He slithered around the trunks, advancing on Jack and Hitchcock. "Is it possible after all these weeks together that you think I am stupid? I said I didn't memorize the numbers, but I do remember that right up front was a two." He sighed. "I suppose your fate was inevitable. It wouldn't do to have both of us possessing the right ID papers and the numeric code."

"If you hurt him, you'll never get the numbers," Hitchcock said.

"Then I'll start with you. Then his other aunt," the bellman said. "I'll get what I want. What I deserve."

"I daresay you will," said Hitchcock. He launched himself toward the bellman. For all his bulk he moved swiftly. And he held a keen advantage over the bellman, being taller by a head and heavier by a hundredweight. But the dressing gown, as one might expect, proved his downfall. He stepped on the hem and tripped, just as the bellman brought down the knife. It plunged with a squelching noise into Hitchcock's chest. A sickening stain appeared on the white dressing gown, spreading from the knife hilt. Hitchcock's fall wrenched the weapon from the bellman's hands.

"Mr. Hitchcock!" Jack screamed. The director couldn't be dead. Not after all they had been through. It couldn't end like this. Jack felt sickness curling like a snake in his stomach. Then he wished he hadn't screamed, for he'd caught the attention of the bellman, who turned toward him. Fear ran electric claws up his back. The bellman was between Jack and the door. But he was also between Jack and a large empty trunk. Jack didn't think twice. He flew toward Sinclair. He threw all his weight against him.

"He stuck with me!" yelled Jack. "He stuck with me, and you took him away!"

Had the bellman been firmly planted, Jack's full-body thrust might have done no good. But Sinclair had been turning, and a large belly in a white gown was right behind him—at knee level. The bellman fell backward over Hitchcock and tumbled right into the open trunk.

Not entirely, of course. His hands and feet splayed over the side of the trunk. Jack circled to the back of it and pushed the lid closed. He leapt hard onto it. With a yelp the bellman turtled his hands and feet inside. Jack tried to latch the trunk, but the bellman kept pushing the lid up. He was bigger than Jack. With each push the lid was raised a little higher. Each time the lid went down, Jack tried to slam home the latch, but before he could, the bellman would push again. Jack feared he would fly off the trunk and the bellman would get out.

Jack pushed down one more time, and suddenly it was as if he were the heavyweight world champion. The lid shut with a firm, decisive *thunk*. Jack reached for the latch, but found a ring-covered hand was already there, slamming the latch into place and adding a padlock from one of the other trunks.

"That should hold him," Hitchcock said, bouncing up and down a bit as he sat on the trunk.

"Mr. Hitchcock!" Jack said. "You're alive!" He looked at the stain on the dressing gown. "But how . . ."

Hitchcock pulled the knife from his chest and removed something from beneath the gown. "I've never been partial to cantaloupe," Hitchcock said, "but I assure you, from now on it shall rank as my favorite of fruits."

Jack grabbed the cantaloupe from Hitchcock and kissed it, then threw it aside and launched himself toward the director. He wrapped his arms around the ruffle-covered neck and hugged him tightly. Hitchcock's arms embraced him just as tightly. They sat there for a moment, neither one saying a word.

A knock from the trunk reminded them they had some issues to attend to.

"Think he can breathe?" Jack asked.

In answer the director pushed against the trunk lid to find a springy section. "I don't suppose anything crucial is pressed up against here, do you?" he asked. He stabbed the knife into the trunk and cut a little hole. A squeal came from inside.

Jack pressed his lips against the air hole. "Where is my aunt?" he said.

There was no response. Hitchcock thumped the trunk with the hilt of the knife. Threats of more air holes did no good. The bellman wasn't talking.

"He'll be of no more help," Hitchcock said. "But she must be here somewhere. Why else would he come down here?"

Jack stood. "Aunt Edith!" he called.

A muffled banging came from the stack of luggage. Jack pressed his palms against it. "These bags aren't against the wall," he said. "There's a space behind them. But how did he stack them up so quickly? He was only in here a few minutes."

"There must be a way to get behind them without unstacking them," Hitchcock said.

A large case stood upright in the lower right corner of the "wall." Unlike the others, this bag wasn't lying on its side. The broad top of the case faced out toward the room. Jack popped the clasp. It swung open like a door. The back of the case had been cut out. The edges of the hole were jagged.

"It leads to the space behind the bags," Jack said. "C'mon."

"I don't believe I will fit through the hole," Hitchcock said. "Go on. I'll follow when I've made a large enough entrance." He dragged one of the empty trunks to the wall. Using it as a step ladder, he took down bags from the top of the stack.

Jack crawled through the secret entrance. The space behind was dark and narrow. Jack was reminded of some of the crevices he'd squeezed through on his caving trips. Against the wall, opposite the suitcase entrance, was a camping lantern and a pack of matches. Jack lit the lantern. He held it at arm's length to see the far side of the "luggage cave."

There, on a sagging luggage cart, her hands tied to it, Aunt Edith squatted, kicking a suitcase at the bottom of the pile. She was gagged, but her eyes reflected the lantern light like the polished points of two obsidian knives.

CHAPTER 31

I CONFESS

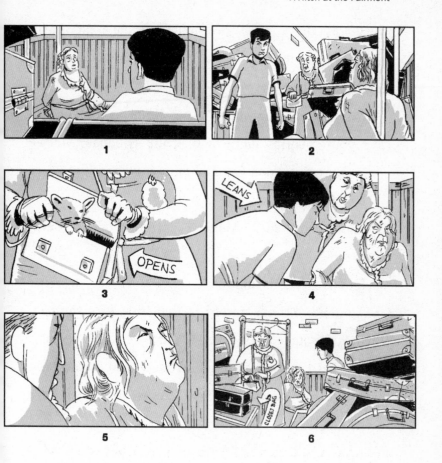

"SHE'S HERE," JACK CALLED. His aunt was disheveled and dirty, and Jack thought she deserved to feel twice as bad as she looked. The gag was a filthy old towel, tied in back. It was repulsive. She was repulsive. But Jack felt sad for her too. Even though she claimed to be a "survivor," the past few days must have been an ordeal. Jack loosened the gag and worked it past the wattle of flesh under her chin.

"My sweet young boy," Aunt Edith said. "Here to save your favorite auntie. Oh, thank goodness you've come. Now be a good boy and untie my hands."

Jack stepped back.

"Come now, Jack. Auntie is in no mood for jokes. Untie me!"

Jack crossed his arms.

Aunt Edith's lips pursed in that little way she had. Her nose twitched. "Jack," she said. "Dear. You don't know what I've been through. Abducted and held prisoner here by that brutal man. I must have been here weeks and weeks. Just sitting on this hard cart, wondering what would come of me. And barely any food. Why, I've practically wasted away to nothing. And the worst of all, not knowing what my fate would be. Oh, Jack, it's been dreadful."

"Then you must know how my mother feels," Jack said. His sympathy evaporated, leaving an angry residue.

"Your mother? I'm sorry, Jack, but I don't understand. Of course, we were all so sorry about what happened to her, but I am sure her . . . departure . . . was quick and painless. Nothing compared to what I've had to endure." Those little obsidian eyes darted left and right.

Jack remained silent.

A section of the bag wall tumbled away, and Hitchcock stepped into the space.

"My aunt," Jack said by way of introduction.

"My word!" Hitchcock said, taking in her great girth, of which he and two cantaloupes were merely a fraction.

"My dress," said Aunt Edith. "What is that woman doing in my dress?"

"We're working to find my mother," said Jack.

"Your mother is dead."

"She better not be," said Jack, the last of his pity vanishing. "Not if you value your life." He turned to Hitchcock. "What's the sentence for murder and kidnapping?"

"That would constitute a capital offense," Hitchcock said. "Though, they no longer hang people in California." Was that relief on Aunt Edith's face? "I believe the gas chamber is the modern, preferred method. One is located just across the bay, in San Quentin."

"You kidnapped my mother," Jack said. "You were

going to sell her into slavery. But you didn't pay the man you hired to kidnap her. Now that man is threatening my mother's life."

"I'm the one who was kidnapped," said Aunt Edith.

"Yes. A kidnapper who was kidnapped herself," said Jack.

"That's what we refer to as ironic," said Hitchcock.

"We saved you," said Jack. "Now it is time for you to pay us back. Where is my mother?"

Aunt Edith's voice iced over. "You seem to have figured out a great deal in the weeks I've been held hostage," she said.

"You've been gone less than three days," Jack said.

"Well, have you figured out how to prove any of this? I'm not doing anything to help you. I'm sure I don't know what you are talking about. Kidnapped your mother indeed! What evidence do you have? And who will believe an orphan boy who's living on the streets?"

"I'm not living on the streets," Jack said.

"Not yet," Aunt Edith replied.

"Are you threatening to throw me out of the hotel?" Jack asked.

"I have no legal obligation to take care of you," Aunt

Edith said. "That note from your mother just stated her intention. It doesn't bind me in any way."

"All right," Jack said. "Let me get the owner of the hotel, and you can tell him to throw me out." Jack turned his back on Aunt Edith and made as if to walk out over the tumbled luggage. But before he did, he turned back around and bowed slightly with his hands clasped in front of him. "Yes, madam. How may I be of assistance?"

Aunt Edith stared at Jack, her face pinched up, her nose twitching as she thought. "You know . . . ," she said.

"That I am part owner of the hotel?" Jack said. "Yes, we know. We found the papers in Muffin's cage."

Aunt Edith's nose started again. Twitch. Twitch. "The papers don't prove a thing," she said. "To claim your inheritance you need a numeric code. Without it you've got nothing."

Points of fear peppered Jack's stomach. She was right. Without the numbers his claim to the hotel amounted to nothing. And without a home he became just another orphan boy on the streets or in state care. Who would believe anything he said?

"What makes you think we don't have the numbers?" Jack asked.

"You don't think I've searched everything you own? Everything your mother owned?" Aunt Edith said. "During the funeral I examined every paltry item in your and your mother's apartment, then shipped it up here and searched it again. I looked at every scribble on every slip of paper, but none of them was the required number. Mostly just phone numbers of that ridiculous acting club your mother belonged to. If I'd found the numbers, I might have been able to convince that dreadful bellman to let me go and partner up. He had planned to play the heir himself. He just needed the seven little numbers, as he kept reminding me. If I had them, you wouldn't be needed at all."

"You're evil," Jack said.

"I'm a survivor," Aunt Edith replied. "You have got nothing—I repeat, nothing—on me."

Hitchcock stepped forward. "My dear woman," he said, "I beg to differ. We do have something. Something very compelling, in fact."

"Oh, really. And what is that?"

"A hostage," Hitchcock replied.

He brandished the handbag. The pink leash snaked out from it. He undid the bag's snap and yanked on the leash. Muffin's little head popped up. He blinked his eyes and opened his mouth wide, showing his sharp little teeth and pink tongue. "We have your weasel," Hitchcock said.

"Weasel! I'll have you know that Muffin is a pure-bred Alpine chinchilla."

"Then he'll be all the more attractive to the furriers on Maiden Lane," Jack said.

"I understand Alpine chinchilla earmuffs are all the rage," Hitchcock added.

"You wouldn't dare!" said Aunt Edith. She pulled against the ties that held her.

"We would not only dare. We would do," said Hitchcock. "When weighing the life of a weasel against that of a mother, the rodent comes up sadly underweight."

Aunt Edith had done nothing yet to admit her crime. Her head swiveled left and right, as if she could find some other option closed up in the luggage sets around her.

"Very well," Hitchcock said. He dropped Muffin back into the handbag and closed it with a snap.

"Wait," Aunt Edith said. "Stefano, the man I hired to kidnap your mother, has a boat at Fisherman's Wharf. I don't know the slip number. Untie me, and I'll take you there."

CHAPTER 32

BON VOYAGE

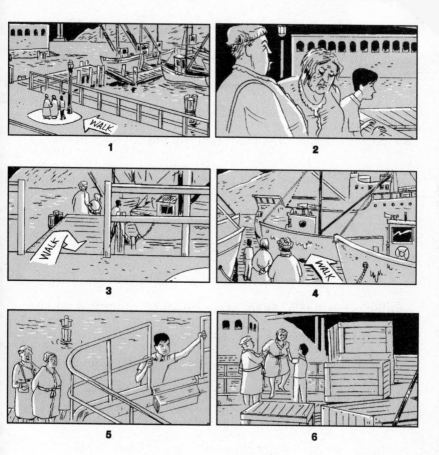

THE CLACK, CLACK OF LINES KNOCKING against masts
swelled and faded in time with the waves at Fisherman's
Wharf. A foghorn moaned. A gull cried as it flew
overhead and disappeared into the fog bank that crept up
the center of the bay.

's the trawler with the red stripe," Aunt Edith said, po— ing to a large shrimp boat in a slip at the far end of the dock.

The boat looked abandoned, as indeed did the entire marina. Many of the boats had slipped out into the bay to await the Festival of Progress fireworks show that would start in a little while to celebrate the earthquake anniversary. Those left behind had furled sails or were battened down and dark.

Jack, Hitchcock, and Aunt Edith padded silently down the dock. There were no lights illuminating the boat. The name painted just below the bow gunwale was barely legible. It might have been *Bon Voyage*. The red stripe along its hull was chipped, and barnacles formed crusty pockets below the waterline. A high main mast thrust up straight behind the pilothouse. Three long booms crowded up to the mast. These were arms, hinged at the bottom to the mast, that were lowered to extend far over the sides or back of the boat, to trail nets. Or they could have been if they were neatly maintained like the others at the wharf, instead of a tangle of rigging and ropes. The whole place stank of dead fish and decomposing kelp. *Abandoned boats don't last long on their own,* thought Jack as he climbed onto it. Hitchcock hoisted up the skirt of his dressing gown and hopped easily aboard. The two of them helped Aunt Edith lumber on.

Old nets littered the stern. There was clearly no one on deck. The pilothouse was dark, empty. A quick inspection belowdecks showed it, too, was uninhabited.

Jack glared at his aunt. "There's no one here!" he said. "Was this some kind of trick?"

Aunt Edith smiled and shrugged.

Jack calmly lifted the handbag from Hitchcock's wrist and held it out over the water. They could all hear Muffin scratching inside it.

"I'll do it," Jack said.

Aunt Edith made a move toward Jack, but Hitchcock held her back.

"Two against one isn't fair," she said. The handbag swung back and forth, hooked by Jack's slim finger. "The *Aventure Malgache* should have arrived by now and will wait just outside the Golden Gate. Captain Grummaker is an old acquaintance of mine. Stefano was to use this boat to bring your mother to him during the height of the fireworks, when any witnesses would be distracted and the coast guard would be busy with all the drunken pleasure-boaters. From there she would be brought to her new life."

"Slavery, you mean!" Jack said. "If she's been hurt . . ."

"She'll be fine. Even if Stefano threatened to, he wouldn't kill her. They don't pay for dead slaves, you know. Not anymore."

She settled her bulk onto a crate of gear to wait. Jack pulled Hitchcock aside.

"What if she's wrong?" Jack asked. "What if they don't come?"

"She seems rather confident," Hitchcock replied.

Jack threaded the silver charm out of his shirt and began worrying it, rolling it between his fingers and into his palm.

"But Aunt Edith's been locked up for days," he said. "And we never gave this Stefano his money. What if he makes good on his threat. What if he kills her?"

Hitchcock squeezed Jack's shoulder silently.

The minutes ticked by, measured by the clattering of the lines and the shush of the breaking waves. The fog advanced, thicker, heavier, creeping under cuffs and collars and dampening spirits.

Each time the *clack, clack* swelled again, Jack gripped the silver charm and looked toward the gangway. Was it footsteps this time?

"She will be here," Hitchcock said.

Jack wasn't so sure. The world around him disappeared in a wash of gray, as if to foreshadow his fate.

"I'll be alone," he said. "If we don't save my mother, I'll have no one."

"So it may seem," the director said. He tossed the trailing sleeves of his gown over his arms, then stretched his hands out. "But perhaps your vision is too narrow." He formed a frame with his fingers so they both could gaze through it. A gray, formless square was all there was to see. "In real life no frame bounds our possibilities. No director limits what we are shown. Do you know what I see?"

Jack shook his head.

"I see a troupe of actors using their talents to help a friend. Now you try."

Jack squeezed the silver charm tightly in his fist. The fog swirled in the frame of the director's hands. "I see Opal."

"And what is she doing?"

"Feeding me." Jack smiled. "A Cheer-Up Chocolate Chew."

"Who else?"

"Schultzie," Jack said. "He's writing me a letter, inviting me to stay with him and his dad." He shot an angry look at Aunt Edith. "And he's hand-delivering it."

"And do you know what else I see?" Hitchcock continued. "A director of films who has grown to respect the talent and bravery of a certain young man, and would never let him come to harm." He gazed again through the frame of his hands. "So, a final lesson. In the cinema we see with our eyes." His hands flew apart, breaking the frame, and arced around to envelope Jack's fist. "In life we see with our hearts."

They sat for a moment in unbroken silence. Then the clacking began again. Hitchcock let his hands fall. Jack opened his fist, the bones of his hand creaky like when he clenched a pencil too long.

In the dim marina lights he rubbed at the impression the charm had left on the pad of flesh between his wrist and thumb. He thought to trace the letters he had so often seen on the charm, IPSE DIS. But the impression was, of course, a mirror image.

210 3291

"Huh!" Jack said, pulling Hitchcock aside. "I see something else."

He held his hand up to Hitchcock.

"Look. Seven little numbers."

CHAPTER 33

NORTH BY NORTHWEST

THE CLACKING LINGERED LONG after the most recent swell had passed. Footsteps. Footsteps rattled down the gangway toward the dock. Jack and Hitchcock ducked behind the shrimp nets and gear, dragging Aunt Edith after them. A bright blue light flared overhead, and a boom echoed along the bay. The earthquake anniversary show had begun. Fireworks threw halos of light through the fog scrim that had settled over the marina. Shadowy figures on the gangway materialized and winked out with each burst of light. One shadow was small, not much bigger than a child, but moved with the assurance of a man. The other was large and oxlike. The light bounced off her horn-rim glasses. With greedy eyes Aunt Edith watched them approach, but Hitchcock put his finger to his lips, then gestured to the handbag and ran his thumb across his neck. A third figure stumbled between the other two, a tall, slim woman. All three disappeared when the first volley of fireworks drifted as ash to the water.

Another boom, and a white light threw The Suave Man, Stefano, into closer view. The woman who was his ox of an accomplice trundled behind. In the fading light the slim woman between held her head high. She was dirty. Her face was turned away, but there was no mistaking her hair—golden and elegantly twisted on top of her head, despite the wisps that stuck out like dandelion puffs.

"Mom," Jack whispered. His heart kettle-drummed

in his chest. He had to close his eyes and count to ten to keep himself from gasping in noisy draughts of air.

He opened his eyes again, willing them to adjust and pierce the opaque night. A strobe of low flashes shot through the lines and masts of surrounding boats.

His mother was there.

She was alive.

All chill vanished. Jack's flesh wanted to leap from his bones like butter from a hot griddle. His voice wanted to call his mother with a report to rival the pyrotechnics above him.

But Hitchcock stopped him. The director had spied something else in the flashing lights. He pointed to The Ox and then raised a hand with the thumb and index finger extended. Just like at the mission, The Ox had a gun.

Stefano hopped on board. He turned on the light in the pilothouse. The Ox ambled along the dock. She held Mom's bound wrists, while casting off the lines. She stepped heavily onto the boat as it pulled out of the slip, jerking Jack's mother after her. The boat rocked, and Jack's mother stumbled against The Ox, whose eyes squinted savagely behind her horn-rims. She pushed Mom brutally to the deck.

Jack, who for nearly a month had let so many feelings fall silently into that bottomless pit inside, howled in anger and fear. "No!"

And a great number of things happened at once.

The Ox aimed her gun toward the pile of nets.

Hitchcock grabbed a long gaff hook, such as is used to haul in fish.

Stefano threw the throttle to full. The boat lurched forward.

Jack fell.

The handbag bounced across the deck, pink leash trailing behind. Aunt Edith, who hadn't lost her ability to exploit weakness in an instant, snatched it up.

"Two against two. Now the odds are even," she cried. "Stefano. Come quick. You have unwanted passengers."

The Ox drew a bead on the nets, but Hitchcock was far too quick for her. He swung the hook with all his might. The Ox squealed. The hook landed square on the back of her gun hand. A shot rang out as the gun struck the rail, the sound lost in the noise of the fireworks. The gun slid along the gunwale and tumbled overboard.

But Hitchcock wasn't the only one who could improvise a weapon. The Ox grabbed a harpoon gun and aimed it at Hitchcock. It had a longer range than his hook. Jack's mother tried to interfere, but The Ox was simply too big. She shoved Jack's mother roughly toward the pilothouse and The Suave Man.

"Mom!" Jack called.

"Jack?" his mother said. "Jack!"

Jack and Hitchcock moved to get her, but Stefano was too quick.

He tugged her bound wrists and forced her into the pilothouse. "Take care of the boy," he told The Ox, "but don't hurt the two old women. One of them owes me two hundred thousand dollars." He pushed Jack's mother belowdeck.

"Jack, run!" she called before the hatch slammed shut. The Suave Man threw the hasp and padlocked the hatch. Dropping the key into his pocket, he returned to the wheel.

Jack did run, but toward his mother. The Ox raised the harpoon gun. Jack froze. He looked around. There was nothing for him to hide behind. The Ox took careful aim at Jack's heart.

"No escape this time," she said. The boat bobbed and dipped through the waves. But she stood firm, a fulcrum of stillness. The world seesawed around her. "Nowhere to go."

She squeezed the trigger.

And shot wide when a shrimp net dropped over her. Jack felt the breeze on his face as the harpoon shot past him and broke through the pilothouse window. It lodged between the spokes of the wheel, locking it in place. Stefano tried to move the wheel but couldn't. There was no way to steer.

Hitchcock swung another shrimp net over his head, this one intended for Aunt Edith. She screamed, but she wasn't looking at Hitchcock. She pointed. One of the red towers of the Golden Gate Bridge reared up in the fog directly ahead.

The Suave Man cut the engine, but too late. There was a terrible grinding sound as the boat ran into the concrete fender, the oval-shaped wall that thrust up from the water a few feet from the tower's concrete base, encircling and protecting it. Splinters from the shabby deck stabbed into Jack's palms as he broke his fall.

Such was the force of the collision that the trawler heeled over, its mast, booms, and rigging dragging along the fender until they collapsed over the top of it, like a drunken sailor throwing his arm over a buddy's shoulder. Now the hull was suspended by the tangled wreck of the mast. Waves lifted the boat and slammed it down against the concrete.

"Blast," Hitchcock said. He landed on the deck, his net on top of him.

Aunt Edith went down too, painfully, because she threw up her hands to keep the handbag from slamming too hard.

Stefano was the first one back on his feet. He leapt over Jack and climbed the mast to the concrete wall.

Jack raced to the hatch.

"Mom!"

The splinters throbbed in his hands. Gooseflesh stippled his arms. He pulled at the padlock. It wouldn't open. He pried at the hasp with his pocketknife, but the knife broke. The boat was constructed for work in the rough northern Pacific Ocean. The hatch would not budge.

Jack pressed his forehead against the hatch. "Mom!"

"Jack!" Mom called from the other side.

"Mom! We'll get you out of there. Just hang on." Jack felt a giggle burst up from inside. Would every emotion he'd buried in the past month come bubbling up all at once? His breath was coming in crumbs. He couldn't get enough air.

"Jack," his mother said, "listen to me. Calm down, honey."

Jack gulped some air, then let it out slowly. One. Two. Three deep breaths.

"Jack," his mother said, "I want you to get off this boat now."

"What? Not a chance."

"Jack, there is water coming in down here. The boat is sinking. Get off."

Dismay spread through Jack like ink in water, then froze into hardened resolve.

"I won't let you die again." He pulled and twisted the padlock, driving the splinters in his palms even deeper. He pounded on the door.

"Jack." His mother's voice was firm. "Do as you're told!" Then her voice softened. "I love you."

"No! No!"

Then the director was there, pushing the gaff hook into the loop of the padlock. He and Jack threw all their weight against it. The hook bent. The lock remained.

"Jack. Go!" his mother called from beyond the door.

Hitchcock's eyes were wide. "I don't see what else to do," Hitchcock said.

Jack looked up at the concrete island. Somewhere up there was Stefano, and in his pocket the key.

"Keep trying," Jack said. "I'll get the key."

CHAPTER 34

ROPE

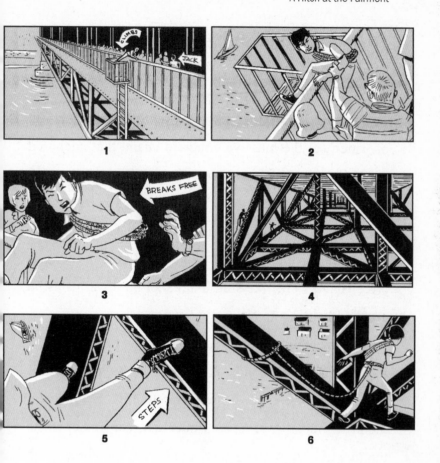

JACK SNAGGED A COILED LENGTH OF ROPE from the deck. He slung it over his shoulder and scrambled up the rigging and booms. Each time the waves slammed the boat against the concrete fender, they threatened to shake Jack loose. As Jack reached the high point where

375

the mast wrapped over the fender and descended the other side, the boat lurched and rolled. Soon the trawler would break free and sink.

On the other side of the fender, separated by a few feet of water, sat the massive concrete island that anchored the bridge's tall steel tower. The rigging jumped up and down with the waves. Worse, it was being pulled back over the fender by the weight of the sinking boat. Jack leapt for the rusty red rungs embedded in the concrete island's clifflike side. Pain shot up his arms as he grabbed hold.

Jack climbed. The grit and rust of the rungs left reddish stains on his hands. At the top he hopped the rail surrounding the edge of the concrete cliff. Behind him the boat's metallic arms continued to groan and creak as the tide tried to pull the boat away from the fender. The twang of lines snapping punctuated the clamor.

Dark shapes rose before Jack and soared over his head—the great steel walls of the bridge's south tower, a series of huge rectangular monoliths, coming together in sharp corners, held by a regular pattern of rivets as big as Jack's fist. He groped his way forward, wishing he'd grabbed a flashlight. Inching around the massive columns that thrust up from the concrete, he wasn't sure he'd see Stefano even if he tripped over him.

Kaboom! The island lit up from a flashing white brilliance that lingered in the sky. The fireworks exploded high above the fog, casting an eerie illumination, like a slow-motion thunderstorm. A black rectangle of doorway pierced the base of the huge steel tower, a stark contrast to the brightly lit scene around him. But as the light faded, the darkness seemed to leap out and envelope Jack.

Another charge exploded, blue. Jack sprang through the open door before the light faded. He was inside the tower. Sounds of labored breathing and shoe leather against metal echoed in the darkness above him. Another burst lit the skies. Enough light crept through the doorway for Jack to make out ladders stretching up the sides of the huge vertical tunnels. The ladders climbed through section after section via perfectly round holes in the horizontal cross plates, then disappeared into darkness.

Jack hauled himself up. The bridge towers were tall, easily two hundred feet to the roadway—the height of a twenty-story building. He'd climbed that much on the caving trips with Schultzie, but it was no piece of cake.

The rope chafed and scratched Jack's neck. As he climbed, his sweat made the scratches sting. Each time he gripped a rung, the splinters in his palms shot hot rapiers up his arms.

A cough from above spurred him to an increased pace. Hand over hand, rung by rung he made the ascent. He had no idea if he could catch Stefano, but he had to try.

Halfway up, the darkness reigned complete, and the thick steel walls muffled the sound of the fireworks. Unlike some deep caves he'd visited, the bridge was far from silent. It vibrated with a regular pulse. Was it from the cars on the deck above, or from Jack's own beating heart? The hollow center of the tower amplified the *drip, drip* of water and the scrape of steel against a thousand rivets. Still Jack climbed.

"Garrr!" Stefano roared above him, not too far. Metal grated against metal, and soft flesh thumped against unyielding steel. He must have come to the access door at the deck. He was trying to open it.

Boom! Another firework went off. Its light glowed above Jack. Stefano had managed to open the door. Jack could see him. But he could also see Jack.

Jack scrambled up the few remaining rungs. Stefano

slammed the door, but Jack shoved his rope between it and the jamb. Stefano pushed against the door, but he wasn't much bigger than Jack. More, Jack had the advantage of youth and overwhelming need. He threw his weight against the door. It opened. Stefano stumbled into a crowd. They were on the pedestrian walk on the east side of the bridge, where people pressed against the bridge railing and watched the show.

Stefano tried to wedge his way through the crowd, but it was too dense. There was no escape by that route. He climbed over the railing. The steel truss that supported the road deck ran along the side of the railing. The top of it formed a ledge that stuck out from the railing about twelve inches. Various pipes and cables ran on top of it, and a sort of track, like for one set of train wheels. To the right was the railing, to the left, a drop into the bay. The ledge was lower than the road, so that as Stefano picked his way along it, his head was below the top of the railing.

Jack followed him. Only a few people on the bridge weren't looking at the sky. A woman screamed, "Oh, dear! Somebody stop that boy." A man grabbed him. But Jack twisted and slipped out of reach.

The delay allowed Stefano to get ahead. He inched along, carefully in the dark, toward the southern end of the bridge, where he could climb off and disappear into the night.

"Hey, you!" someone shouted. "Get back up here!"

A pair of policemen, probably assigned to crowd control, were pointing at Stefano and pushing through the crowd along the rail.

"Make a hole!"

Between them and Stefano a maintenance gondola hung over the side of the bridge, a cagelike scaffold that moved along the track Jack had noticed. Stefano hopped onto it. He broke the tiny lock that secured a trapdoor and scrambled down to the lower level.

Still Jack followed.

Stefano climbed out from the gondola's lower level and onto a steel stairway that was part of the bridge. It led down to the honeycomb of steel that formed the underpinnings of the road.

Jack grabbed a beam, ready to swing after him. The cold steel of the beam cooled the pain in Jack's hands. He felt the solidity of this bridge that stood, mighty and unmoving, while the ocean tides tore constantly at its feet. The whole span flashed in the next strobe of light. Stefano had made it to the lowest level of the truss. Now he eased his way carefully, slowly, along the slick top of the steel beam.

Jack closed his eyes for a moment and imagined the bridge's strength flowing into his body. He envisioned the structure as if he were going to draw it. Two parallel lines formed a graceful, horizontal arc in the darkness behind his eyes—the top and bottom of the bridge truss. Dozens of diagonal braces, like ladders with X-shaped rungs, zigzagged between these parallel lines. Wherever a diagonal touched the parallel lines, solid vertical posts sprang up or down from one parallel to the other. In his mind Jack saw the path Stefano took. The man walked on the beam, holding the diagonals, up to a point. But when an up-sloping diagonal soared out of reach above his head, he was forced to let go and inch along like a tightrope walker, navigate around the vertical post, and continue slowly until the next down-sloping diagonal again came within reach.

Jack saw a better way. In his mind a golden path followed up and down with the diagonals. It wasn't as direct, but he could monkey up and down the X-shaped cross bracing much more quickly than The Suave Man could creep along, trying to keep his balance. Jack need never let go of the diagonals. It would be like mounting and descending a ladder.

He opened his eyes. He wrapped the rope around his waist and tied the other end to the truss. With his mind map firmly in place, Jack moved confidently toward the suave little man, unwinding the rope over his head as he went.

Stefano crept along, sliding his feet inch by inch on the fog-slicked bridge.

Jack climbed up and down the diagonals. As he did, he wove through every third or fourth X-shaped rung like a needle through cloth. His rope stitched its way behind him, adding to his confidence, until a misfired rocket exploded close to the bridge. The crowd above hooted and shrieked, a jumble of terror and delight.

Jack slipped.

The brace he'd been descending rushed up to punch him in the gut, thrusting air from his lungs and certainty from his legs. He grabbed for it as he slid, but missed. He tumbled off the side, spinning like a dropped spool of thread.

Jack caught the rope. He dangled beneath the bridge,

desperately trying to catch his breath. Far below, tiny reflected sunbursts in red, yellow, and blue capped the waves. The boat with his mother dragged like chalk on a slate, leaving bits of itself as it grated along the concrete wall.

Jack hoisted himself up onto the bridge and continued quickly on. He overtook Stefano as the man negotiated one of the vertical posts.

"Give me the key," Jack said.

"I think not," said the man. A staccato of explosions ripped the air. "Things didn't go as planned, but with no witnesses this will be just another boating accident."

"Don't look down," said Jack.

Stefano did. He gave a weepy little shriek, closed his eyes, and clung to the vertical post. He pressed his cheek to it. His breath came in short gulps. With a low gurgly growl he opened his eyes and glared at Jack. He took a small step away from the post.

"I know you and your aunt are squeamish about a bit of murder, but you'll find some things are necessary if you stay in the kidnapping business long enough." His face shifted from red to blue to green as the fireworks lit the foggy night.

"Business?" Jack said. "I'm not in her business."

"You brought my payment to the mission," Stefano said. Another small step.

"I thought it was a ransom," Jack said. "I wanted to save my mother."

The flare and pulse of light built to a crescendo and faded in the fog above.

The Suave Man stopped. "That woman in the hold is your mother?" Step.

"Yes."

Stefano looked confused. "A boy shouldn't be without his mother," he said.

"Give me the key."

"My mother died when I was a little boy. Barely known, always missed," The Suave Man said. One hand held tight to the bridge post. He reached out for the next rising diagonal. "Who knows what I might have been had she survived. Still—Miss Marion raised me as her own. Taught me everything she knew, except for shooting. She is a crack shot, while I could never take to guns."

"The woman back there? But she's still on the boat."

"I'm not worried," said Stefano. "She's a crack

swimmer, too." Stefano resumed his inching progress along the bridge.

"But she's caught. In a net," Jack said.

"A net?"

"It's sinking. The boat," Jack said. "Give me the key. Give me the key, and I'll get them both off the boat."

Stefano hesitated, midstep. His eyes met Jack's. "Promise," he said. "Promise to get Miss Marion off first."

"Yes."

Stefano took one hand from the post and reached deep into his pocket. The fireworks started again. Stars and thunder fractured the night, startling him. He slipped. He reached out, seized the collar of Jack's shirt. Buttons popped. The chain around Jack's neck caught and held Stefano for just a moment before it burst. But it was long enough for Jack to catch Stefano's sleeve with one hand, the broken chain with the other.

Stefano's weight pulled Jack forward. He slid down the diagonal, until his waist wedged in the V shape where the brace met the vertical post.

The dog tags cut the palm of Jack's left fist. The other end of the slender chain wrapped round The Suave Man's hand. Jack's right hand twisted the nubbly fabric of Stefano's sleeve. Jack heaved both Stefano's arms toward him. The chain broke entirely, and Stefano dangled beneath Jack, holding by one hand.

The man was slipping. The coarse tweed of the sleeve slid from Jack's grasp, replaced by the smooth hot skin of Stefano's wrist.

"The key!" Jack called. But The Suave Man looked helplessly up at him, dread rimming his eyes.

Jack looked at his father's dog tags and the coffin charm in his left hand. IPSE DIS. A worthy man. Stefano's slick, sweaty wrist shifted in his right hand.

Jack had to get the key.

He opened his left hand and let the dog tags and charm drop. They reflected the fireworks, green and gold and blue, before they disappeared in the fog below.

Jack clutched The Suave Man's wrist now with both hands.

But it wasn't enough. Gravity was stronger than Jack. Jack's hands slid over the man's wrist, slick with sea spray, fog, and sweat. Jack's grip widened as Stefano's fist was pulled between his hands. The man's hand opened to curl his fingers around Jack's.

Jack gripped tighter. Sharp points of pain stippled

his left hand. The fireworks grand finale lit the sky. With each burst of noise and light, Stefano's hand inched down Jack's. The sky blazed with a final salvo of every possible color. The tighter Jack clutched, the less hand he held, until Stefano's fingertips slicked past his own.

The Suave Man fell, disappearing into the fog—his face a mask of red terror in the fireworks' light, his scream lost in the percussive cacophony of their explosions.

"No!" Jack cried. His hands were clasped together, like a prayer was left where The Suave Man's hand had been seconds ago.

He brought his hands to his heart, and opened them.

In them was a brass key, its teeth edged in blood.

CHAPTER 35

LIFEBOAT

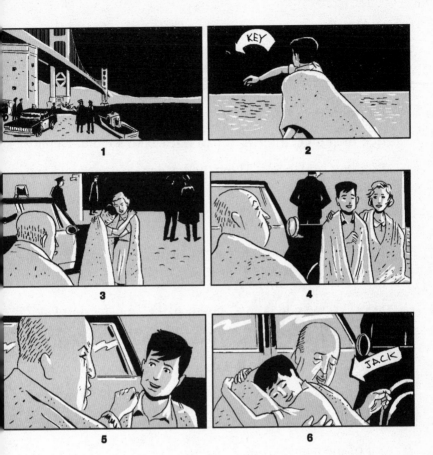

"I GUESS WE WON'T NEED THIS ANYMORE," Jack said. He tossed the key far out into the bay.

"I guess not," his mother said. She pulled Jack toward her and hugged him tightly. The scratchy wool blanket the police had provided slipped from his shoulders, but here in his mother's embrace, he was plenty warm enough.

They stood atop the seawall at Fort Point, across the water from the bridge tower. A police boat had ferried them over after Jack had released his mom. Deputy Whatley and Alice Trapp had been on the boat, and George, Opal, and Shen had been waiting with the police cars at Fort Point.

Now the deputy helped Mr. Hitchcock scramble up the wall.

"This would be a good place for a stairway," Hitchcock said. He carried Aunt Edith's handbag, but his wig was gone, his makeup washed away. He was in shorts and shirtsleeves beneath the tattered remains of the dressing gown. An embroidered elastic strap stuck out of the handbag.

"I guess we won't be able to return the gown," Jack said.

"Aunt Sarah will be greatly disappointed," Hitchcock replied.

"Aunt Sarah?" Jack's mom said.

The brutish ox woman was led away in handcuffs. Aunt Edith followed her, Deputy Whatley holding her arm. "But I tell you I never gave you a drugged choco-late. That's preposterous!" she said.

"Yes, ma'am," the deputy said.

Alice Trapp tapped her pen on her clipboard. With a final, unfriendly glance at Jack's mother, she scratched a final check mark, turned on her heel, and left.

Aunt Edith stopped abruptly when she was escorted past Hitchcock. "Where's my Poopsie?" she said.

Hitchcock opened the handbag and pulled on the leash. "You mean the weasel?" he asked.

"Weasel!" said Aunt Edith. "I'll have you know that's a purebred—"

"Shanghai wharf rat," Deputy Whatley finished.

"I beg your pardon!"

"That's a Shanghai wharf rat," the deputy continued. "We just arrested a man in Chinatown for selling them as 'Alpine chinchillas.' Who'd believe a thing like that?"

Aunt Edith looked at Muffin. Her nose twitched, but her eyes got watery. "Mummy loves him anyway," she said, and held out her arms, shackles rattling.

But Muffin must have sensed where Aunt Edith was headed, and he'd had enough of cages. With a twist and a chirp, he leapt from Hitchcock's grasp and disappeared down a sewer grate, dragging his pink leather leash behind him.

Deputy Whatley led Aunt Edith away.

Mom's eyes followed them. "You say she hired Stefano to kidnap me, and then she was kidnapped and held hostage herself, by someone else?"

"Yes," Jack said. "By a bellman at our hotel."

Mom's eyes returned to Jack. "Then I feel more pity toward her than anger. But only a little bit more. And all this was because your father was some kind of heir to a fortune?"

Jack nodded. "He was. And I am. She kidnapped you to get me. But the trust required that a numeric code be provided. She couldn't find it, so she couldn't pay off Stefano. Then the bellman thought she had the code and kidnapped her to get it."

She pulled Jack close. "Oh, Jack. Kidnappers, thieves, and murderers! How did you manage?"

"I had expert help," Jack said.

"A dubious expertise," Hitchcock said, "yet I am glad it helped."

Jack wrapped his arms around a surprised Hitchcock. "Mr. Hitchcock, I don't think I can ever thank you enough."

Hitchcock dropped gracefully to his knee. "We'll work something out, my dear boy," he said. "Perhaps for starters you could lend me your mother. I believe I have a part on my show for which she'd be perfect."

Jack hugged the director again.

"And call me Hitch. After all we've been through, that seems more proper."

Hitch pulled away from the tight embrace and put his hand on Jack's heart. "Your father's tags," he said.

They no longer hung from Jack's neck. Jack marveled that he hadn't noticed their missing weight since he'd let them fall. "I lost them on the bridge," he said.

"But my dear boy," Hitch replied, "then you've lost a fortune."

Jack looked at his mother, thinking how he, himself, was already rich. He closed his eyes and envisioned the silver charm, letting it rotate in his mind.

Then he opened his eyes, turned to Hitch, and winked.

"IPSE DIS," he said.

AUTHOR'S NOTE

THERE WERE TWO ALFRED HITCHCOCKS.

The first Alfred Hitchcock was a real person. He was a husband, father, and film director who created some of the most thrilling and frightening movies ever brought to the screen. He was born in 1899, not long after the cinema itself, and he and the industry grew up together, each deeply affecting the other's development.

The second Hitchcock was a fictional character—a jovially macabre uncle always ready to poke fun at the first Hitchcock's efforts. This public character was invented by the director himself, with the aid of his publicity staff and writers—most notably James Allardice, who created the introduction spots for the *Alfred Hitchcock Presents* television show and wrote many of the director's public speeches.

Like Alfred Hitchcock, *A Hitch at the Fairmont* is a blend of fact and fiction. The character of the director in the book is a product of my own research into the real Hitchcock and my musings on the delightful personality he used to entertain the public. He's the person I would have liked to have run into if I were living at the Fairmont Hotel in 1956—especially if there were a mystery to solve. And while the things he, Jack, and the rest of my fictional cast experience are made up, the events have a basis in reality.

In many Hitchcock films the main characters are unwillingly bound together, sometimes physically with handcuffs (as in *The 39 Steps* or *Saboteur*) or sometimes metaphorically by things like familial ties *(Shadow of a Doubt)* or hasty bargains *(Strangers on a Train)*. In my book I chose the nonphysical route, shackling Hitchcock and Jack together with a fictional device: the police won't help because they believe Hitchcock is pulling a publicity stunt. The truth is that Hitchcock really was known as a practical joker. For example, he once had a dinner party where all the food had been dyed blue, just to see what his guests' reactions would be. And, though it didn't happen in Los Angeles, just like in this book he did once have a draft horse delivered to an actor's dressing room. My fictional director runs from the confrontation with the police because he is afraid of them. The real Alfred Hitchcock said many times in public that he feared the police and recounted the story of being locked up as a child as part of a lesson on behavior concocted by his father and a policeman friend.

If my own fascination with Alfred Hitchcock and his films was one motivation for writing this book, so was my desire to learn more of the history of my adopted hometown, San Francisco. The city of my imagination doesn't veer far from the real one in which I live. After all, cities are made of more than just buildings and streets. They are made of stories that get richer, deeper, and perhaps truer as the years pass. Here are some of the historical facts about San Francisco that shaped the story in my book.

Although there are no networks of avenging Shanghai survivors, nor any orphanages that supplied kidnappers with a source of unwilling slaves, shanghaiing was a part of San Francisco history. It was practiced during the Gold Rush days all along the West Coast of America. Ships arrived with goods and immigrants as a result of the rush, but soon found themselves with no crew, as sailors jumped ship to strike out for the California hills in search of gold and silver. A brisk business in kidnapping able-bodied men and pressing them into forced service aboard ships thrived. Crimps (unscrupulous men paid by the body to find men for a ship) would render their victims unconscious and forge their signature on the ship's rolls. It was illegal for any sailor who had signed on to leave the ship before the voyage was finished. The crimp would collect the victim's first few months' wages from the captain of the ship. One story even told of a crimp who, desperate for more bodies, sewed rats into the clothing of a dead man to fool the captain into believing the corpse was alive so he could collect his fee. The last official shanghai took place in 1915. A number of laws, culminating in the Seamen's Act of that year, gave more rights to sailors and effectively ended the practice of shanghaiing. But human trafficking and forced labor exist in parts of the world to this day.

My research for this book provided me with many interesting opportunities, and one of the best was the rare privilege I had to tour the Fairmont Hotel, from the ten-thousand-dollars-a-night penthouse (where a door slammed right after my guide told me the suite was haunted) to the very room Alfred Hitchcock stayed in to the "back of the house" (the area used by the staff). While I have changed some aspects of the physical layout of the hotel, many—like the rollaway beds standing like tombstones, and the "secret" passage used by the staff—appear just as they are in real life. The "back of the house" is a maze of tiny hallways, twisting stairways, and cavernous rooms stuffed with everything needed to keep the current hotel running, as well as forgotten remnants from the hotel's past. There are whole rooms devoted to dirty dishes (and others to clean ones). There are boilers and high-voltage electrical works, linen rooms, seamstress tables, racks of uniforms, carpentry shops—the list goes on. It would be easy to stash someone down there, with confidence that they would not be found.

Though the hotel was built with the Fair family's wealth from the silver mines of Nevada's Comstock Lode, there was no lost heir of the family fortune. (And in any case the legal knots associated with any claim on the Fairmont Hotel would have been tangled indeed, as ownership of the hotel had passed from the Fair family by 1956, when our story takes place.) But the Fairmont Hotel did play a large role in San Francisco history. It was nearly complete in April 1906, when the great San Francisco earthquake struck, followed by days of raging fires. The hotel had been built using a steel substructure and the relatively new technology of reinforced concrete, which uses embedded steel bars to provide extra strength. So the building proved capable of surviving the quake. Unfortunately, all the interior fixtures were destroyed in the fire that followed. Nevertheless, the owners continued construction, and when the Fairmont Hotel opened on the one-year anniversary of the quake, it was heralded as a sign that the city had been reborn. The hotel continues to be a vibrant part of San Francisco culture. It has played host to presidents, royalty, foreign dignitaries, and even Hollywood directors. And the members of staff are as friendly as can be. There is not, nor has there ever been, a kidnapper among them.

Most of the story ideas for Hitchcock's films came from novels or stories he'd purchased, then reworked and reenvisioned with his brilliant, inventive collaborators, including his wife, Alma, and a crowd of screenwriters. I had fun in this book imagining that Alfred Hitchcock's adventure with Jack inspired elements of the films he made after 1956. This is, of course, fiction. But within that fiction is a smattering of facts. For example, in 1961 there really was an enormous flock of birds that descended on a seaside town near Santa Cruz, California, and Hitchcock would certainly have known about it, since he had a home nearby. Undoubtedly he did his own blend of fact and fiction when he created his classic film *The Birds* from that true incident and from a story by Daphne du Maurier. And while the plot of *Vertigo* came from a French novel, *D'entre les morts*, and not from Jack remaking Hitchcock in the image of his aunt, the director *was* known to dress up as a woman for publicity stunts and possibly even for a secret cameo (in *North by Northwest*).

Vertigo is considered Alfred Hitchcock's masterpiece and was recently named the greatest film of all time by the British Film Institute. It is also the intersection of my fascination with Hitchcock and with San Francisco history. During the time period in which *A Hitch at the Fairmont* takes place, the director would have been preparing to film *Vertigo*, and in my imagination, he himself came to San Francisco to review his choice of filming locations.

The cinema as it exists today would not be the same without Alfred Hitchcock. He invented or popularized many of the techniques of filming and storytelling still in use. Indeed, so prevalent are his methods that his name has become an adjective, "Hitchcockian," used to describe a certain manner of film. Hitchcockian films are stories of innocent, average people falsely accused of crimes or thrust into dangerous circumstances. There is often a cool female heroine who, no damsel in distress, uses her courage and wits to aid, or thwart, the hero. She is usually blond. The plot is set into motion by a MacGuffin, some goal or object the hero must obtain, though its identity is not integral to the story. Hitchcockian movies employ interesting camera angles and techniques to heighten the tension in the story. And always at the heart of a Hitchcockian film is a human story about human emotions.

I THINK I'VE SEEN THAT ONE:

An Abbreviated Filmography of Alfred Hitchcock

The chapter titles in this book are taken from famous and not-so-famous Hitchcock films. Here is a list of those films and a little bit about each one.

Warning: There may be spoilers ahead, particularly if you want to look for Alfred Hitchcock's cameo appearances in the films themselves without any help.

Chapter 1. Young and Innocent (1937)

Summary: Robert Tisdall, falsely accused of murder when the belt from his raincoat is found at a murder scene, convinces Erica Burgoyne to help him find his missing raincoat and the true murderer.

Most Thrilling Moment: Erica drives her car into an abandoned mine to escape pursuit. The floor collapses in a cave-in, swallowing the car, and nearly the heroine.

Innovative Technique: A long shot from high overhead in the hotel zooms in to the murderer's eye twitch.

Cameo: Hitchcock is outside the courtroom with a camera.

Chapter 2. Spellbound (1945)

Summary: When Dr. Anthony Edwardes takes over a mental hospital, Dr. Constance Petersen becomes suspicious. She soon discovers that the man is an imposter who believes he killed the real Edwardes and took his place. Using psychoanalysis and dream interpretation, she helps him prove his innocence.

Famous Scene: Hitchcock employed surrealist artist Salvador Dalí to design the dream sequence, a sharp-imaged scene full of symbolism.

Cameo: Hitchcock comes out of the elevator at the Empire State Hotel carrying a violin case.

Chapter 3. The Lodger (1927)

Summary: When a mysterious man residing at a boardinghouse begins creeping out at night, his landlord thinks he may be the Avenger, a killer stalking the streets of London.

Famous Scene: In this silent film Hitchcock wanted to show the nervous pacing of the lodger. To do it he built a glass floor and filmed the character walking from below. He superimposed this shot above the heads of the landlords (and their swinging chandelier) as they listen from the room beneath his.

Cameo: Hitchcock appears as the man at a desk in the newsroom with a telephone, and again in front of the mob that has chased the lodger.

Chapter 4. The Lady Vanishes (1938)

Summary: Iris Henderson befriends an elderly English woman on a train traveling in Europe. When Iris wakes up from a nap, she discovers the woman has disappeared, and everyone on the train denies they ever saw her.

The MacGuffin: A secret message encoded in a tune.

Cameo: Hitchcock appears near the end of the film in Victoria Station walking between the train and some luggage, smoking a cigarette.

Chapter 5. Torn Curtain (1966)

Summary: During the Cold War American scientist Michael Armstrong defects to East Germany to spy for the West.

Famous Scene: Armstrong must kill his Communist handler, Gromek, and do it silently so as not to alert Gromek's companion. Unlike most movie murders, it is difficult, it was filmed with no musical score, and it takes more than three minutes to achieve (with the aid of a knife, hands, a shovel, and a gas oven).

Cameo: Hitchcock is holding a baby in the hotel lobby early in the film.

Chapter 6. The Trouble with Harry (1955)

Summary: A dark comedy in which the trouble with Harry is that he is dead but won't stay buried. Several of the citizens of Highwater, Vermont, believe they were the one who killed him, and so they bury and then disinter him multiple times.

Did You Know? This was Shirley MacLaine's first film.

Cameo: Hitch walks past the limousine of a wealthy man who wants to buy Sam's painting.

Chapter 7. The White Shadow (1924)

Summary: A story of twin sisters, one good, one evil.

Did You Know? Hitchcock was an assistant director. This film was considered lost for decades, until the first thirty minutes of it was discovered in the New Zealand Film Archive in 2011. Half the film is still missing.

Chapter 8. Vertigo (1958)

Summary: Ex-policeman "Scottie" Ferguson is asked by an old college pal, Gavin Elster, to follow his wife, Madeleine, whom Elster fears is going mad. Scottie falls in love and, after Madeleine kills herself, finds a woman who looks like her, and makes her over in Madeleine's image.

Innovative Technique: The "vertigo effect" is achieved by a "dolly out–zoom in," meaning the camera is physically pulled (dollied) away from the subject while the lens zooms in. It creates a visually jarring effect to mirror the psychological turmoil of the characters. The technique was developed by cameraman Irmin Roberts for *Vertigo* and has been used in countless films since, including *Jaws*, *E.T.*, *Battlestar Galactica*, and *GoodFellas*.

Cameo: Hitchcock walks by the shipyard office of Gavin Elster carrying a trumpet or bugle case.

Chapter 9. To Catch a Thief (1955)

Summary: Retired jewel thief John Robie must prove that he is not the cat burglar currently stealing from wealthy tourists on the French Riviera.

Famous Scene: Francie Stevens, the character played by Grace Kelly, speeds along a windy road in a sports car. Years later, as the real-life Princess Grace of Monaco, Grace Kelly would die in a car accident on a similar road not far from where the scene was shot.

Cameo: Hitchcock sits on a bus next to John Robie.

Chapter 10. The Ring (1927)

Summary: The ring in my story is a piece of Aunt Edith's jewelry, but the movie title refers to a boxing ring. In the movie two boxers fall in love with the same woman.

Did You Know? This was the first film on which Hitchcock worked with Alma Reville, his future wife.

Cameo: None.

Chapter 11. Rebecca (1940)

Summary: A shy, colorless young woman marries a wealthy widower and moves to his palatial home, Manderley, where she is terrorized by his first wife's maid.

Famous Scene: The evil housekeeper, Mrs. Danvers, is enveloped by flames as Manderley burns.

Cameo: Hitchcock walks behind the character Jack Favell (played by George Sanders) as Jack speaks with a policeman.

Chapter 12. Secret Agent (1936)

Summary: During World War One a novelist and spy is sent to Switzerland to kill a German agent.

Did You Know? This movie was based on the *Ashenden* stories by Somerset Maugham, a real British novelist who was also a spy.

Cameo: None.

Chapter 13. The Wrong Man (1956)

Summary: A musician is wrongly accused of robbing an insurance company.

Did You Know? The movie is based on the true story of Manny Balestrero.

Cameo: Not really a cameo, but he appears at the beginning of the film to introduce it.

Chapter 14. The Man Who Knew Too Much (1934, 1956)

Summary: Hitchcock actually filmed two versions of this movie. In both films a couple traveling abroad learns of a plot to assassinate a foreign dignitary. Their child is kidnapped to keep them silent.

Famous Scene: In both films the assassination takes place during a crash of cymbals at a concert at the Royal Albert Hall.

Cameo: In the 1956 version Hitchcock watches tumblers at the market in Marrakesh. In the 1934 version he may be the man crossing the street as a bus passes by.

Chapter 15. Woman to Woman (1923)

Summary: A British officer in World War One falls in love with a French dancer and promises to marry her, but a battlefield injury causes amnesia, and he marries another woman instead.

Did You Know? Alfred Hitchcock was an assistant director and helped write the screenplay. This lost film is one of the British Film Institute's "75 Most Wanted."

Chapter 16. The Birds (1963)

Summary: Birds go crazy and attack the inhabitants of a seaside town in California.

Famous Scene: Melanie Daniels is trapped in a phone booth as seagulls smash into it from all sides.

Cameo: Hitchcock leaves the pet store with two dogs as Melanie Daniels enters it.

Chapter 17. Rear Window (1954)

Summary: L. B. Jeffries is a photographer trapped in his apartment with a broken leg. He thinks he witnesses a murder in the apartment across the way.

Did You Know? The American Film Institute ranks *Rear Window* as the third-best mystery film of all time. Four of the top ten films are by Alfred Hitchcock. The others are *Vertigo* (#1), *North by Northwest* (#7), and *Dial M for Murder* (#9).

Cameo: Hitchcock winds the clock in the apartment of the musician across the courtyard.

Chapter 18. Shadow of a Doubt (1943)

Summary: A young woman, bored with her small-town life, eagerly enjoys her beloved uncle Charlie's visit, until she begins to suspect he may be a murderer.

Famous Scene: When the train carrying Uncle Charlie pulls into the station, smoke from its stack blots out the sun, symbolizing the evil it carries on board.

Cameo: Hitchcock is on the train, playing cards.

Chapter 19. Saboteur (1942)

Summary: During World War Two, Barry Kane is falsely accused of starting a fire at the aircraft factory where he works. He enlists the aid of blond and reluctant Patricia Martin to prove his innocence.

Famous Scene: The true saboteur dangles from the top of the Statue of Liberty as Barry Kane tries to save him.

Cameo: Hitchcock stands in front of Cut Rate Drugs in New York as the saboteur's car arrives.

Chapter 20. Downhill (1927)

Summary: After boarding-school student Roddy Berwick takes the blame for a school friend's misdeeds, his life falls apart.

Innovative Technique: For this black-and-white film, Hitchcock had prints of the scenes where Roddy is ill tinted a sickly green to reflect his physical state.

Cameo: None.

Chapter 21. Mr. and Mrs. Smith (1941)

Summary: Mr. and Mrs. Smith are shocked to learn that, due to a legal technicality, they aren't married and can resume their lives as single adults.

Did You Know? Carole Lombard, a famous actress of her day, prevailed upon her friend Alfred Hitchcock to film this light comedy. Though it is a

Hitchcock film, it can't really be considered "Hitchcockian."

Cameo: Hitchcock passes in front of Mr. Smith's building.

Chapter 22. Family Plot (1976)

Summary: A psychic/con artist is paid to track down the missing heir to the Rainbird fortune, only to find that the heir is a kidnapper and jewel thief.

Did You Know? Although Hitchcock never names the location in the movie, this film was shot in San Francisco. Hitchcock stayed at the Fairmont Hotel during filming.

Cameo: Hitchcock's famous profile is seen in silhouette in a window at the Registry of Births and Deaths.

Chapter 23. Rich and Strange (1931)

Summary: A couple receives an inheritance and embarks on a round-the-world trip, suffering a breakup, a swindle, and a shipwreck along the way.

Did You Know? The title comes from Shakespeare's play *The Tempest*: "Full fathom five thy father lies; / Of his bones are coral made; / Those are pearls that were his eyes; / Nothing of him that doth fade / But doth suffer a sea-change / Into something rich and strange."

Cameo: None.

Chapter 24. Suspicion (1941)

Summary: Mousy newlywed Lina fears her irresponsible husband, Johnnie, may be trying to kill her.

Innovative Technique: Hitchcock calls attention to a potentially poisoned glass of milk by making it glow malevolently; he had placed a lighted bulb inside the glass.

Cameo: Hitchcock has two. He mails a letter, and he walks a horse on-screen at the hunt.

Chapter 25. Always Tell Your Wife (1923)

Summary: This lost short film (only one reel survives) is the remake of a film about a man who fakes a cold to meet a blackmailer.

Did You Know? When the original director left the film, assistant director Alfred Hitchcock and star Seymour Hicks took over.

Chapter 26. Stage Fright (1950)

Summary: When aspiring actress Eve Gill's friend claims to have been framed for murder, Eve investigates by posing as a maid for the woman her friend says really committed the crime.

Did You Know? Alfred Hitchcock's daughter, Patricia, had a part in this film as the hilariously named Chubby Bannister.

Cameo: Hitchcock passes Eve Gill on the street and looks back at her in apparent astonishment.

Chapter 27. The Call of Youth (1921)

Summary: This short romance film is now lost.

Did You Know? Hitchcock did not direct, but it was one of the first films with which he was connected. He designed the intertitles (cards that showed dialogue in early silent films).

Chapter 28. The Skin Game (1931)

Summary: Two wealthy families feud over a piece of rural English real estate. Based on a John Galsworthy play.

Did You Know? A "skin game" is a con or swindle.

Cameo: None.

Chapter 29. The 39 Steps (1935)

Summary: Richard Hannay meets a woman who claims she is a spy trying to prevent sensitive information from leaving England in the hands of a foreign enemy. When she is stabbed in his flat, Hannay is accused and on the run. This is the second film (after *The Lodger*) to use Hitchcock's common theme of an innocent man unjustly accused.

The MacGuffin: Plans for a new aircraft engine that are somehow being smuggled out of the country.

Cameo: Hitchcock walks past as Hannay and the spy board a bus after a riot at a music hall.

Chapter 30. Blackmail (1929)

Summary: Alice White is attacked by a man in his apartment, and she kills him with a knife. Fearful, she covers up her presence at the scene of the crime, and is subsequently blackmailed by someone who saw her there.

Innovative Technique: This film was originally intended to be silent, but with the arrival of "talkies" Hitchcock was given the go-ahead to use sound. He did so memorably. In the scene where Alice's family sits down to eat, a neighbor's gossip blurs into gibberish, except for the repeated use of the word "knife," highlighting the guilt Alice feels for stabbing a man to death.

Cameo: As he tries to read a paper on the subway, Hitchcock is pestered by a small boy.

Chapter 31. I Confess (1953)

Summary: Father Michael, a Catholic priest, hears the confession of a murderer, but because of the seal of the confessional (which prohibits priests from discussing what they have heard during confession), Father Michael is unable to use his knowledge to defend himself when he is accused of the murder.

Did You Know? Although the film is black and white, Montgomery Clift, the actor who played Father Michael, insisted on wearing contact lenses so his eyes would be the same color as his character's.

Cameo: Hitchcock crosses the top of a staircase just after the opening credits.

Chapter 32. Bon Voyage (1944)

Summary: A Royal Air Force pilot goes down in German territory in World War Two.

Did You Know? This was one of two short propaganda films Hitchcock made during World War Two.

Cameo: None.

Chapter 33. North by Northwest (1959)

Summary: New York business executive Roger Thornhill is mistaken for a government spy and falsely accused of murdering a man at the United Nations. He travels across America to find the real culprits.

Famous Scene: Thornhill is pursued by a murderous pilot in a crop dusting plane in the middle of cornfields south of Chicago.

Cameo: Hitchcock misses a bus right after the credits, the bus door slamming shut in his face.

Chapter 34. Rope (1948)

Summary: Two college chums murder a third just to prove they can do it. That evening they have a party with friends of the victim and serve the meal from the trunk where the body is stored.

Innovative Technique: Each eight-minute take in this movie (the length of time of a fresh reel of film) is one continuous shot with no edits. This meant the actors had to recite their lines perfectly or begin again from the start, and that stagehands had to move furniture and scenery as the actors moved around the room with the camera following.

Cameo: Hitchcock is seen walking on the street with a newspaper just after the credits, and possibly his famous outline is seen as a neon sign in an ad for Reduco out the apartment window.

Chapter 35. Lifeboat (1944)

Summary: During World War Two a group of American and British civilians are stuck in a lifeboat after their ship and a German U-boat trade torpedoes. The final passenger to climb aboard their lifeboat is a German sailor from the U-boat.

Did You Know? The movie was shot in a large studio water tank, and several of the cast suffered seasickness during the filming.

Cameo: Hitchcock appears as both the "before" and "after" image in a newspaper ad for a weight-loss drug called Reduco.